STRANGE AND UNUSUAL

STRANGE AND UNUSUAL

GOTH DROW UNLEASHED™ BOOK ONE

MARTHA CARR

MICHAEL ANDERLE

Cover by Mihaela Voicu
http://www.mihaelavoicu.com/
A Michael Anderle Production

LMBPN Publishing
PMB 196, 2540 South Maryland Pkwy
Las Vegas, NV 89109

First US Edition, February, 2021
(Previously published as a part of the megabook Once *Upon A Midnight Drow)*
eBook ISBN: 978-1-64971-573-9
Print ISBN: 978-1-64971-574-6

THE STRANGE AND UNUSUAL TEAM

Thanks to the Beta Readers

John Ashmore, Kelly O'Donnell, Mary Morris, Larry Omans, Rachel Beckford, Daniel Wiegert

Thanks to the JIT Readers

If I've missed anyone, please let us know!

Angel LaVey
Daniel Weigert
Deb Mader
Debi Sateren
Diane L. Smith
Jackey Hankard-Brodie
James Caplan
Jeff Eaton
Jeff Goode
John Ashmore
John Ashmore
Micky Cocker
Misty Roa
Paul Westman
Peter Manis
Veronica Stephan-Miller

Editor

The Skyhunter Editing Team

DEDICATIONS

From Martha

To everyone who still believes in magic
and all the possibilities that holds.
To all the readers who make this
entire ride so much fun.
And to my son, Louie and so many wonderful friends who
remind me all the time of what
really matters and how wonderful
life can be in any given moment.

From Michael

To Family, Friends and
Those Who Love
To Read.
May We All Enjoy Grace
To Live The Life We Are
Called.

CHAPTER ONE

It was time to do the impossible.

L'zar Verdys felt it coursing through him—the rightness of the moment, the tug pulling at his core to rise to the call and put into motion everything the soothsayer had predicted. For two hundred years, he'd waited for this night.

"Lights out in five." The night guard strolled down the walkway of cellblock Alpha, his boots clicking on the metal mesh.

L'zar's neighbor, Relaude, let out a low whistle. "Not gonna give us a pass for the new year, huh?"

The guard's rhythmic footsteps stopped at the cell on L'zar's right, and the metallic *ping* of the man's cattle prod for magicals echoed through the block, a light *tap-tap-tap* against the bars. "You don't get a pass for another fifty years, Relaude."

"Forty-nine."

The weapon cracked against the cell bars, emitting a sizzling flash of purple sparks when it struck the cell's magic-dampening wards. "We can double that if you want. Or you can keep your fat orc mouth shut."

Relaude let out a low, rumbling chuckle but didn't say another word.

L'zar Verdys stretched out on the thin mattress of his single bunk, slate-gray arms folded behind his head of white hair as the guard picked up his slow, rhythmic march down the cells lining Alpha block. It sounded like Richardson, and sure enough, there was Richardson's bulbous nose lit up in perfect profile as the man passed L'zar's cell. The guard didn't pause as he swept his gaze over the drow prisoner's tidy box of a room. He just lifted one eyebrow in contempt, then continued down the row.

It's the last thing these idiots expect. L'zar Verdys doesn't make a sound, and it's almost like he doesn't even exist. They'll notice when I'm gone, all right. And by the time they find out which direction I went, I'll already have everything in motion.

If the gateway between the borders of this world and the other couldn't stop L'zar from crossing over a dozen times as he sought to fulfill the soothsayer's prophecy, minor dampening wards and humans with low-tech tasers and fell darts didn't stand a chance.

Let them think I've got my head down for the rest of it.

L'zar sniffed, shifted his head against his folded arms so his pointed ears could breathe a little, and crossed one booted foot over the other.

Tonight, I'm getting out.

Richardson's echoing footsteps receded down the block. Silence settled over Alpha until the guard in the tower pulled a lever that looked like a breaker reset more than the light switch on a max-security prison. "Happy New Year, convicts. Way to break in the twenty-first century."

The lights cracked off with an echoing *boom*. Darkness blanketed Alpha block, punctured only by the red lights flaring to life above the guard tower.

Red for 'locked up tight.' What a stupid human misconception.

The block echoed with the coughs, grunts, snores, and farts of Chateau D'rahl's inmates as a stillness settled over them for the night in their single suites of concrete and metal frames and high-voltage dampening wards. L'zar waited patiently through all of it until the symphony of bodily functions came to a standstill, then he pushed up on his bed, glanced through the bars of his cell door at that dauntless red light, and stood.

"Hey, Verdys," Relaude gurgled from the next cell over. "Stayin' up to watch the ball drop?"

L'zar moved toward the steel toilet at the back of his cell.

"Man," Relaude kept on, "what I wouldn't give for some end-o'-the-year grog and a battle pit. Might be what I miss most about home." The orc's voice brought its usual muffled thickness through his sawed-off tusks, the ends of which protruded at broken angles from his thick lower jaw. L'zar saw those tusks in his mind's eye every time his neighbor spoke. "Hell, I'd even fight *you*."

L'zar snorted. "You'd lose." The drow worked around his prison-issue sweatpants to relieve himself. *Just another inmate hittin' the John before hittin' the sack.* The whole time, he was counting down to the perfect moment.

Relaude snorted. "You don't think I could kick your drow ass back to Ambar'ogúl?"

"Not if we were already in an 'Ogúl battle pit, greenskin."

Another low chuckle came from the next cell over. "That how you got popped and dragged into this hellhole? Tried to mind-fuck the CDO into lettin' you off clean by arguing semantics?"

"You know what 'semantics' means?" L'zar flushed the steel toilet and took two steps away from it along the back wall of his cell.

A *thump* rattled the cement wall, doubtless from Relaude's thick fist. "Hey, if you were as smart as you think you are, you wouldn't be locked up next to me, would ya?"

"Watch me," L'zar whispered.

An irritated growl permeated the opposite wall of the orc's cell. "Shut the hell up, Relaude. Trying to sleep."

"Aw, come on. You don't wanna count down to midnight with me, Troj?"

"Listen. If you don't shut your fat green face, when these doors open in the morning, I'll count down to your last breath."

Relaude chuckled, and the cot beneath the massive orc groaned when he flopped back onto the thin mattress. "Y2K. Gotta give it to these human chumps, am I right? Makin' such a big deal about the end of the world and all. They don't even know the half of it."

That might've been the only thing out of Relaude's mouth in weeks L'zar thought incisive, yet saying so to the orc was only an invitation for more attention.

Relaude scratched his hairy green armpit, a blade scraping a whetstone. "Dumb and tiny and weak," he groused.

"Shut up!" came Troj's exasperated voice. "I swear by all that's unholy…"

Positioned less than a foot from the back wall of his cell, L'zar waited for his pesky orc neighbor's laughter to fade. Alpha block settled into another round of half-enforced silence, and the drow closed his eyes to listen for his next signal.

The door to the guard tower clicked open and shut behind whichever one of them had drawn straws to re-up on their coffee for the night shift. L'zar's pointed ears twitched at the muffled *thump* of the other guard's boots propping up on the console. That was Jones, then, settling in for a night of reading whatever cheap book he'd grabbed off the library cart.

And L'zar stayed beside his toilet, facing the wall like he'd lost his mind.

The drow's fingers worked an intricate pattern in front of his thigh, undetectable by the swiveling cameras set high on

Alpha block's walls. The air shimmered around him, and his illusion spell formed at the back of the cell. Any guard who checked the cameras or stepped past while on patrol would see the drow's back as he stood beside the toilet. The real L'zar would be long gone before anyone realized his projected image hadn't moved in hours.

He placed his other hand on the concrete wall and muttered the words he'd been waiting twenty-five years in this dump to say. Just a whisper, but the spell phased his hand through the wall, and the rest of him followed. No alarms, no flashing lights, nothing.

L'zar had discovered Chateau D'rahl's budget could not pay for wards on all four walls of every cell.

Relaude was right. Dumb and puny and weak.

L'zar glanced both ways down the abandoned corridor stretching behind Alpha block's newer cells. No one was there. Not a single guard knew the original bones of this place. Smirking, L'zar closed his eyes and brought up the memory of the prison's layout. Almost fifty years ago, he had known he'd be making his way through these walls from the inside out instead of the other way around. Before the renovations.

He set off for the sealed staircase. Mundane construction, yet it could stop him as well as any warded wall, not to mention the ten-foot box he'd called home for a quarter-century. For a drow thief, impossible didn't exist. Not tonight.

Fifteen minutes later, L'zar crouched beneath the grove of bare cherry trees beyond the fence around Chateau D'rahl.

"Barbed wire." He snorted and shook his head. "Humans have so much to learn."

His fingers moved in twisting gestures, and a tailored, pinstriped suit took the place of his gray prison pants and white t-shirt. The long white hair pulled in a knot behind his head shortened and darkened, followed by the erasure of the dark gray, nearly purple pigment of his race's skin. He flexed much shorter fingers on pink-hued hands, his flesh now bright beneath the moonlight. No one would see the pointed ears of his race beneath the light-brown curls he'd adopted.

Destiny tugged at him like a hook through his chest. Beneath the bright lights spilling over so much stone and concrete and iron while dressed as a businessman in a trim suit from the 1920s, L'zar turned from Chateau D'rahl and followed the tingling trail of magic he could no longer ignore.

"Where is she?"

By human standards, the night was chilly, yet the drow thought nothing of the cold. He moved down the frontage road, away from Chateau D'rahl and toward the heart of Washington D.C. Even if he'd driven, it wouldn't have taken him as quickly as his own two feet through the industrial district hiding the high-security magical prison. He was a blur in the moonlight as he crossed the river into Capitol Hill and encountered the overwhelming New Year's glimmer of lights and traffic and bars.

He hurried along the sidewalk and fought to keep his eyes open as he followed the trail of magic.

Not her magic, no. Mine. And the magic of our—

L'zar wouldn't let himself finish the thought. He had to find the woman first, whoever she was—putting the magical cart in front of the flying horse wouldn't do him any favors.

Once he made it to 16th Street, the busy street echoed with the undertones of live bands blasting from every bar, of laughter rising from open car windows and restaurant doors. A bellhop in a bright-red suit with gold buttons nodded at L'zar as the 1920s businessman stepped in front of the hotel entrance. The man pushed a luggage trolley across the sidewalk toward a car waiting at the curb.

L'zar froze. A tingling feeling yanked him sideways. Slowly, he peered at the hotel's entrance and noticed the illuminated silver and white St. Regis Hotel sign's marquee. Below it, a half-dozen silver balloons buffeted about in the stiff breeze blowing down 16th Street.

I've seen those balloons before. This is it.

L'zar made his way through the revolving doors and stopped himself from phasing through the glass partitions. D.C.'s most elegant socialites filled the lobby and beyond. They had come to welcome Y2K with a bang. The thought made the drow smirk as he scanned dozens of faces. The soothsayer hadn't given him a name or an image or even a specific year. However, tonight felt different from all the other nights. Tonight, the call blazed like a siren.

The right place at the right time. Now I need the right...

A group of females in short, glittering dresses and beaded headbands passed by as they headed toward the event room off the bar. One woman offered him a coy smile, which the drow politely returned.

No, not her. Still...

The magic of prophecy in his veins pulled him after the women. L'zar waited as they made superficial conversation with two men standing just inside the ballroom doors. He waited until they entered the room, then went to follow. A man in a tuxedo stepped in front of him and cleared his throat "Your invitation, sir?"

The drow reached into the manufactured inside pocket of his jacket and whipped out a blank piece of cardstock. Without looking at the concierge, he snapped the fingers of his other hand, and his illusion spell did the rest.

After seeing whatever it was he wanted to see on the fake invitation, the man handed it back. "Enjoy your evening, sir."

L'zar snatched the card and made a show of tossing it into a silver trashcan by the doors. The fake invitation disappeared in a swirl of thin white smoke, and the drow moved into the ballroom like a panther on the hunt.

A four-string quartet played in the far corner, accompanying a man in a suit very much like L'zar's and singing a Louis Armstrong song. Silver tinsel hung from every surface, silver ornaments dangling from the ceiling. A massive banquet table lined the wall on his left, laden with caviar and finger sandwiches, cocktail shrimp, beef tartare, artisan cheese. After a quarter-century of gruel that didn't begin to meet state prison regulations—Chateau D'rahl wasn't state-regulated, of course—it took every bit of his will not to go to the table, shove people out of the way, and fill multiple plates.

A golden light caught his eye as it shimmered at the other end of the ballroom. The drow's body tingled from the pull buzzing through his veins. "Where are you?" he whispered, scanning the faces. "Show yourself…"

"Champagne?" A woman in a short cocktail dress passed in front of him with a tray of full, bubbling champagne flutes.

"Thank you." L'zar didn't look at her as he pulled a glass off the tray by its delicate stem and headed across the ballroom. Drinking was the last thing on his mind. This thread tying him to a woman he hadn't met yet was making him drunk enough.

"The elections turned out very much the way we expected…"

"…would be nice not to talk shop for one night, Senator, don't you think?"

"…when the Democratic Whip knocks on your door and asks for a favor…"

L'zar moved through the crowd, weaving between milling bodies and searching for that golden glow again. Part of him wanted to shed the illusion and gain the extra foot his drow form would have afforded, but this wasn't the place. Most people this side of the Border didn't know what a drow was.

Two men in suits and lit cigars—one of them pointing to

his monocle and chuckling—passed in front of the drow thief. L'zar huffed out a breath and flicked his finger. The monocle leapt from the man's eye and clattered to the ground. The man bent to retrieve it, and L'zar slipped through the opening in the crowd. With small, short bursts of magic, he moved the partygoers out of his way—a woman's beaded necklace pulling her sideways before snapping and spilling beads all over the marble floors; a stiff-backed caterer tripping over his own shoe; two cabinet members, judging by their snippets of conversation, both feeling a tug on the back of their suit jackets before turning around.

"Out of my way," L'zar muttered.

"I'm sorry?" A long-legged redhead in a dress of copper-colored fringe turned and flashed him a surprised smile.

"I said, hell of a day, huh?" The drow met her gaze, hoping he'd found her.

"And the day will be over in half an hour." She grinned. "I don't think we've met. I'm—"

The pull reignited in L'zar's chest, and he lurched away from the woman to follow it. *That's not her.* "Excuse me."

When he reached the other side of the ballroom, he searched the same place he'd seen a flash of golden light. He stopped, clenched his jaws, and turned to study the New Year's Eve party from a different angle. Still, he recognized no one. The woman he'd been trying to meet for centuries was nowhere to be seen, nowhere to be found.

A soft grunt conveyed L'zar's disappointment. Then, he lifted the champagne flute to his mouth and shook his head, hoping for destiny to tug again like a fishhook pulling through his cheek. "If that soothsayer's been playing me all this time..."

"You can't believe everything you hear these days, can you?" The woman's voice drew closer behind him, followed by a soft, subdued ring of laughter. "And if I were to have that conversation, Mr. Matthews, I'd like to see it written into my calendar first—"

A small weight bumped L'zar's back, and he tilted forward to keep his champagne from spilling.

"Oh, I am *so* sorry."

He turned, the pull buzzing in his chest.

She laughed again. "I didn't see you there."

L'zar Verdys stared at the woman patting the back of her neck, dark curls piled atop her head. She wore a simple black cocktail dress and functional pumps, a string of pearls and matching earrings. Her blue eyes shone up at him above her hesitant, apologetic smile.

I found her.

"You didn't…I didn't spill your drink, did I?"

The drow blinked and raised the champagne flute toward her in an un-sipped toast. "Not a drop."

"Oh, good." Her eyelashes fluttered, and a small flush of color rose to her cheeks. "Have…we met before?"

Only in a future foretold.

L'zar smiled. "I would remember if we did. My name's—"

"All right, Ms. Summerlin." A man wearing a ridiculous top hat interrupted them and dipped his head at the woman. "I'll have my secretary call your office and set something up. You look a little busy." He winked and turned away without acknowledging L'zar's presence.

"I look a little…?" She blinked and gave a startled giggle. "It's a *party*. And I'm…I'm sorry." When she looked up at L'zar again, her blush deepened. "You were about to tell me your name."

"Leon Verdys." L'zar offered his free hand, and he would have tossed the champagne flute behind him if that wasn't sure to make them both the center of attention. *That's the last thing we need.*

"Leon. You know, I'm very good with names, but I don't

remember yours. And you still seem so…" The woman licked her lips and shook her head, trying to clear it of the most robust sense of *déjà vu* she'd ever had. "Bianca Summerlin, Mr. Verdys. It's a pleasure to meet you."

The minute she slid her hand into his, the world might as well have stopped turning. A jolt of centuries-old certainty coursed through L'zar's entire being, and Bianca Summerlin gasped.

"Did you…" She stared at their clasped hands, then cleared her throat. "Did you feel that?"

"Feels like the end of the world." He didn't let go.

"I'm sorry?"

"Y2K and all that. Right?" The drow smiled with a human face that was not his, then gently released her hand.

"Something like that." She turned her head and studied him sidelong, then glanced at the champagne in his hand. "You're not drinking?"

"I was about to. Then you found me."

Bianca licked her lips, eyed him up and down, then lifted a hand toward the server coming by with another tray of champagne flutes. "I'll join you."

"I was hoping you would."

Bianca went to step toward the server. Before she could do so, L'zar reached out and deftly plucked a champagne flute from the tray as the server walked past. The man strode on, oblivious to the bubbly's weight having left his tray.

Bianca laughed when he handed her the drink. "Smooth."

He lifted his flute and toasted her. "To new beginnings."

"And hopefully not the end of the world." They clinked glasses, and before she raised hers to her lips, L'zar took a brazen step toward her.

"You know, I'd almost given up hope tonight."

"Oh?" Though she stared up at him without looking away, her breath hitched in her throat. "Hope for what?"

"That I'd find the perfect person to bring in the new year with."

Bianca laughed and lifted her champagne flute higher. "That's an excellent pickup line."

"Only if it's working." L'zar took his first sip without breaking her gaze. Beneath his illusion spell, he was still a good six inches taller than her.

She peered up at him over the rim of her glass. Another breathless laugh escaped her. "I can't believe I'm about to say this, Mr. Verdys—"

"Leon. Please."

"Leon. It might be working. Your line, that is. But don't let it go to your head."

"I would never."

"And I've had too much to drink." Grinning, caught in the web of destiny ensnaring them, Bianca sipped her champagne. She nearly spilled it down the front of her dress when the mic squealed and the ballroom announcer's voice cut through the end of the song.

"Dear friends, honored guests, and gracious benefactors, we are nearing the last minute of the century." A screen lit up over the doorway to the ballroom. "Please join us in counting down to the new year and the beginning of a new millennium!"

A cheer went up around the room, followed by laughter and a round of freshly poured champagne making its way through the crowd.

L'zar bent toward Bianca's ear and muttered, "You look nervous."

"Oh, I do, do I?" She offered a polite laugh, but the returning blush gave her away. She didn't lean away from his lips, which were nearly brushing her ear.

"I promise you don't need to be nervous. Not tonight."

She looked at him and blinked. "And what—"

"Ten! Nine! Eight!"

When L'zar winked, she looked away, only to down the entire glass of champagne in two gulps.

"Six! Five!"

"A night like this only happens once in a—"

"Century?" Bianca's smile returned, fueled by the same unquestionable pull that had brought the drow thief from the confines of Chateau D'rahl all the way to the St. Regis. "That's hardly an excuse to throw all caution to the wind, Mr. Ver...Leon."

L'zar leaned closer. "But *you* are."

"Three! Two!"

She was trapped in his gaze. "I..."

"One! Happy New Year!"

Amid the tinkle of cutlery chiming against crystal glass stems, the cheers and hoots, the laughter and uncorking of a dozen more champagne bottles, L'zar placed a hand on the small of Bianca Summerlin's back and bent to press his lips against hers.

What little willpower she'd held onto after three hours of drinking with Washington's political elite evaporated. The empty champagne flute slipped from her fingers and broke on the marble floor. No one noticed; for that matter, no one saw the tall man in the pinstriped suit and the blushing research economist, either, as they made their way somewhere far more private.

CHAPTER TWO

L'zar glanced at the clock on the bedside table: 3:27 a.m. Beside him in the king-sized bed with one-thousand-thread-count sheets, Bianca Summerlin lay motionless in sleep, her dark curls spilling in a tangled array on her pillow. The drow brushed a lock of hair away from her cheek, the sight of his human-colored skin against hers bringing him a momentary twinge of discomfort.

She sighed in her sleep, and he leaned and pressed a soft kiss against the corner of her mouth. "I found you for a reason, Bianca," he whispered. "I hope you remember that. And I'm sorry for how long you'll have to wait before you discover what that reason is. I'll be waiting too."

The corner of her mouth upturned in a dream-induced smile. The drow thief caressed her curls one final time, then slid from beneath the sheets and dressed. He was quick and silent, still full of energy despite having lain awake beside her for an hour until she drifted off into a heavy sleep.

He stopped at the minibar and mouthed a summons under his breath. A pale, shimmering light flared at his fingertips. When it faded, a copper-coated puzzle box covered in drow runes rested snugly in his palm. He placed it with an uncharacteristic tenderness beside Bianca's small black purse atop the minibar. He tapped the top of the box, and a wave of light spread from his fingertip around the trinket, then faded.

He nodded. "When it's time, you'll know what to do with this. Both of you will know."

With a parting glance at the beginning of his destiny lying in the hotel suite, L'zar placed a hand on the door and closed his eyes. Magically peeping through it, he spied no one about in the hallway, which was just as well. He muttered another spell and phased through the door, opting not to risk waking her by leaving the traditional way. Outside the suite, L'zar straightened the lapel of his illusionary suit and made for the elevator.

Now that he'd done his part, that tingling, pulsing tug on his being had gone. The drow moved through the streets of D.C. to a less frequented part of the city outside Capitol Heights. A cab might have given him a chance to relax and let someone else take the wheel for twenty minutes, but he wasn't finished.

And I can't let anyone see me until I'm ready to go back, even like this.

The abandoned warehouse on Nannie Helen Burroughs Avenue hadn't changed in twenty-six years. He hoped the inside hadn't changed, either.

When he reached the unmarked side door, L'zar's fingers moved in another complicated pattern until his spell illuminated the faint green glow of the security wards. "Just the way I left them." He chuckled and pressed his finger against the shimmering shape of a long, thin star with only four points. The wards flashed, then disappeared, and he pushed open the door.

Rusty hinges squealed, and a blue-skinned troll sitting at a long desk of computer monitors and keyboards whirled around. "Who the hell are you?"

"Oh, come on, Persh'al. Is that how you treat an old friend?"

"Look..." The troll chewed his bottom lip and raised both hands. "I don't know how the hell you got in, but whatever you think you're gonna find—"

L'zar snapped both hands' fingers, and his human glamour melted away. He gained another foot in height, his short brown hair lost all its color and dropped into the white knot tied loosely at the back of his neck. His pinstriped suit returned to a white t-shirt and a pair of thin gray pants with CDR printed down the left leg.

Persh'al leapt to his feet with a shout of surprise and slapped his hands together. "L'zar! You dirty thief."

The drow spread his arms and grinned. "That's what they tell me."

"Well, 'O'gúl Crown be damned." A bark of a laugh escaped the blue troll before Persh'al stalked across the warehouse's main room toward L'zar. "You're full of surprises, ain'tcha?"

"Comes with the territory."

The magicals clapped one another in a quick embrace before Persh'al stepped back and stared his old friend up and down. "What's with the getup?"

"I'm serving a hundred-year sentence, Persh'al. Chateau D'rahl ran out of ceremonial robes before they booked me."

"No!" The troll's golden eyes widened, and he clapped a hand to his head shaved bald on either side of the neon-orange mohawk sprouting from the center. "You broke out of high-security prison for O'gúleesh, and you decided to come here?"

"Well, it wasn't my first stop. But yeah."

Persh'al sniffed, looked the drow over one more time, then nodded and turned toward the three long desks spread out in rows in the center of the warehouse. "I wouldn't be my first stop, either. You sure nobody followed you?"

L'zar raised an eyebrow.

Persh'al snorted. "'Course, you're sure. Who am I kidding?"

They stopped at the first desk where lines of code blinked and scrolled in white, blue, and green across four different monitors. "I'm assuming you guys have been keeping an eye on things in here while I've been gone," L'zar said while glancing over the data feeds.

"Well, you'd be right." Persh'al nodded and folded his arms. "None of us wanted to see you chained and locked up, but we're not abandoning the ship just because you weren't here breathing down our necks."

"And here I thought the whole operation would fall apart without me."

Persh'al blinked and stared at his friend before huffing out a laugh. "I see prison hasn't humbled you a bit."

"I was born with an indestructible immunity against humility."

"If that's what you wanna call it."

"So, tell me what's happening with the rez at Border 4." The drow nodded at the center monitor and folded his arms.

"Everything's running smooth as ever, man. Fifteen came through in the last two weeks. Half a dozen orcs wanting to start some supply train. Four more trolls. Represent." Persh'al bumped his chest with his fist. "Only two Nightstalkers this time, which is a lot better for everyone if you ask me. They keep to themselves. And three goblins, but they don't count."

L'zar snorted. "They never do. Until they do."

"Yeah, well, we're watching everyone closely. As far as I know, none of the human organizations have noticed a thing, and they won't."

"You sound sure of that."

"Hey." The troll turned toward L'zar and spread his arms. "I see everything from right here in this executive freakin' desk chair, okay? Genuine Italian leather and everything. The humans on this side are never gonna crack this code, and they're never gonna know we've got our hands in these proverbial cookie jars."

The drow gave his friend a tired smile. "Never say never."

"Relax. My boys got it covered. Hey, they're still your boys too, don't forget. And they're gonna light the death flame torch when they hear you're back."

L'zar peered down at his blue-skinned friend and cocked his head. "No. This is all temporary, got it? I don't want any of the guys to know anything until I'm long gone." He turned and headed toward the torn, sunken couch against the far wall.

"Long gone?" Persh'al snatched up his fourth energy drink in the last five hours, took a pull, and lurched after his friend. "Where you goin' after this?"

L'zar slumped onto the couch, shifting around to get a broken spring out from under him. He propped his legs up along the cushions, crossing one ankle over the other. "Right where I belong."

"You think they're gonna let you back across the Border? Do they brainwash the inmates at Chateau D'rahl before they seal them up behind the wards that you, uh, somehow just broke out of?"

"Don't be an idiot."

"An idiot? Me?" The troll approached the couch and drained the rest of his energy drink. "Okay, I might not have a drow's superior intellect, but any dimwit with half a brain knows they'll cut you in half the minute you step foot in Ambar'ogúl."

"I'm not going back," L'zar muttered. He folded his arms behind his head and leaned back against the couch's armrest. "You know as well as I do I don't belong there any more than the humans."

Persh'al snorted. "That's stretching the truth a lot farther than it can go, I think."

"Think what you want." The drow took a deep breath of dust and rusted metal and the slightly burned odor of plastic casings in Persh'al's powered-up rigs. "Smells like you need some cleaner fans in your towers, by the way."

The troll glanced toward the desks and the custom computers he and his men had built from scratch. He scratched the back of his head, ruffling the spikes of his orange mohawk. "Hey, how long you been away? Did they have computers in the Chateau or something?"

"Limited access, but yeah."

"Nice." The troll nodded and pursed his lips. "Yeah, I, uh, ordered parts for the servers and hoping they get here in the next couple days. It's handled, don't worry about it. Look, L'zar, whatever you're—"

"Two days."

"Huh?"

"Two days is all I need, Persh'al." L'zar opened his eyes and slowly turned his head to look at his friend. "I'm just waiting for one more sign, and then I'll be out of your house and your…hair." He eyed the troll's mohawk.

Persh'al sniffed and folded his arms. "Just two?"

"That's what I said."

"And you want me to keep everyone out of here for two days, so you don't blow your cover as an escaped convict."

The drow closed his eyes again. "That's a good way to put it."

Persh'al puffed out a sigh and shook his head. "You're a piece of work, you know that? That was a rhetorical question, by the way. Don't bother answering. I got your back for two days, brother. Least I can do to repay the last couple centuries."

"Appreciate it."

With a relenting chuckle, Persh'al went to his computers and sank into the ample executive desk chair. "Log some Zs. I'll keep it down." That said, he popped open another energy drink, stared at a monitor, and started tapping away on an oversized custom keyboard.

L'zar cracked an eye open to look at his friend, then closed it again and let himself fully relax. *One last sign. This has to be it. I finally found her, and there's no way I missed the timing. Just wait for it all to line up the way I was told it would.*

The escaped drow thief fell asleep that night thinking of Bianca Summerlin and wondering if the child he wouldn't get to see would have her mother's curls.

Two days later, the final sign came.

"They're crackin' down," Persh'al muttered, vigorously rubbing his blue forehead covered in orange spots. He leapt from his chair. "I gotta go. You good here?"

"Go do what you gotta do." L'zar finished the last of the energy drink—Persh'al was overjoyed to share his addiction. L'zar tossed the can in the trash.

"Right. Yeah." The troll snatched up his black messenger bag propped beside the desk and slung it over his head and shoulder. He headed for the warehouse exit.

"Hey, Persh'al."

The troll stopped and peered over his shoulder. "What's up?"

"Thanks. It was good to see you."

Persh'al chewed on his bottom lip, his eyes narrowing as he gazed at the drow. Then, he nodded, and they both knew what this meant. "Yeah, you too. I'd tell you not to get into too much trouble, but...that would be pointless." With a wry chuckle, the troll raised a hand in farewell and slipped out the side door.

L'zar waited forty-five minutes before he made his move. He took on the same human form in which he'd brought in the year 2000—in bed with Bianca Summerlin—and opted this time for a pair of jeans and a sweater. He phased through the warehouse and its security wards and made his way back through DC toward Chateau D'rahl, and he did so with inhuman speed.

They weren't looking for this face, of course. The prison staff only knew him as Inmate 4872, six-foot-seven with slate-gray, purple-tinged skin and long white hair. The guards knew him as L'zar Verdys, a drow.

It came as no surprise when, as he stepped through the open chain-link gates outside Chateau D'rahl, the guards stationed there had no idea who he was or what to do with him.

"Sir, you're gonna have to move along. This is a high-security facility, and it's not open to civilians."

L'zar spread his arms and raised them a few inches above his head, then sauntered forward.

"Sir, stop where you are. Go back! Did you hear me?"

The man in jeans and a sweater looked up at the security cameras lining the front of the magical prison. The guards' radios crackled, and a muffled voice came through: "Yeah, we've got a guy out here, trying to walk onto the premises." *Crackle.* "I have no idea what he wants. I'm not gonna invite him in and ask him for his whole life's— What the hell?"

L'zar let go of his illusion spell, and the glamour faded. Their looks of disbelief, then terror, then rage pleased him. He grinned at the cameras.

Just a little something to remember me by. They'll find this when it's time.

"On your knees!"

The three guards trained their weapons on L'zar, two of them loaded with bullets, the third with fell darts. L'zar could smell the alchemical agent on the darts.

"I said, on your knees! Hands behind your head."

L'zar did as he was told, smiling in amusement as the guards headed toward him, weapons at the ready. The closest one—his nametag read Thomas—holstered his firearm to remove a pair of magic-binding handcuffs from his belt.

"What the hell do you think you're doing?" the man hissed as he folded L'zar's arms behind the drow's back with no resistance whatsoever.

"Aw. Did you miss me?" L'zar sucked in a sharp breath when the dampening cuffs clamped around his wrists.

"You're in deep now, convict. Stand up." Thomas jerked the drow to his feet and jostled him toward the prison's front gates, flanked by the two other guards with weapons at the ready.

L'zar glanced at the elevated surveillance booth outside the prison entrance and grinned at the watch guard. He caught the last piece of the radio conversation before the doors buzzed and Thomas pushed him inside.

"O'Brien, you're not gonna believe what I'm looking at right now. It's Verdys. No, sir, I'm not shitting you. Yeah, that's right. He just showed up out of nowhere, and Christ, he turned himself in."

CHAPTER THREE

September 4th, 2021

"Are you kidding me?" Cheyenne lowered her beer bottle to the table, and while she didn't mean to slam it down, she sort of did.

"Nope." Ember leaned back in her chair, smirking, and spun her gin and tonic on the table. "I think you can help. No, I *know* you can help."

"Help with *what*? Em, I didn't understand a word out of your mouth right now. Even if I did, I'm the last person you should be talking to about this." She swallowed, wanting to chug the rest of her third beer and knowing it would just make her order another one sooner than she wanted.

"You're the only person I *can* talk to. Listen. These guys have been pressing in on us for a couple months now, but they just took it to a whole different level. One of them showed up at my friend Trevor's work, Cheyenne. His work. Right there in front of everyone." Ember stopped twirling her glass and leaned closer over the table, lowering her voice. "Trevor didn't do anything wrong, but this stupid orc threatened him with a body bag. And magic."

Cheyenne blinked and hoped she looked clueless. *Is she serious?* "Orcs, huh?"

"Yeah. Big ones."

"And you think I'm gonna sit here and play along with whatever fantasy world you're living in?" Cheyenne was acutely aware of her grip tightening around the beer, her black-painted fingernails against the glass, and she might have felt the bottle give just a little beneath the pressure—at least a tiny crack.

Keep it together, Cheyenne. This is not *the right place.*

Ember squinted at her and shook her head. "What do you mean, 'fantasy world'?"

"You just..." Cheyenne glanced around Gnarly's Pub on East Clay Street and lowered her voice. "You're talking about orcs and magic, Em. I'm not stupid. If you're trying to shock me into believing this crap, you're wasting your time. It sounds like your friend Trevor's dealing with some kinda gang issue, and I'm not gonna touch that, no way."

"Seriously?" With a snort, Ember took a long drink and set the glass down. "I know there's a lot of hush-hush going around, especially with the Borders 'unofficially' officially open now. But I'm not buying it for a second you have no idea what I'm talking about."

"Oh, I get it. This is about money." Cheyenne jerked her hand away from her beer and folded her arms. The thin chains dangling from her wrists clinked against each other, cold against her sides through the lightweight fabric of her black tank top. "I thought we were adults, Ember. If you need to borrow some cash, it's okay."

"Money? You think this is about—" Ember threw her head back and laughed much louder than the conversation warranted. "I don't want—or *need*—your money. I need *what you are*. And so do my friends. People like us have to stick together, and I haven't seen you with any other magicals since...well, since I met you. I can't be your only friend."

People like us?

Cheyenne took a breath, stifling the rage boiling up inside her. That would only make things worse, and it would prove her friend's point better than anything Ember could say. "I don't know how many times I have to tell you," she muttered through clenched teeth, "I don't know what you're talking about."

"Oh, come *on,* Cheyenne." Ember thumped her fists on the table. "Drinking at dive bars and living in a dumpy apartment does a pretty good job of hiding who your mom is, sure. And yeah, it's a good mask to conceal you're the only person I know who's not worried about supporting themselves through grad school. But this..." She gestured toward Cheyenne with one sweep of a hand.

"This what?" Cheyenne's nails dug into her palms.

"This whole Goth thing, girl. I mean, sure, most of the world's not even gonna look past the face paint and the piercings, so good job fooling everybody. But you can't hide who you are. If I saw it freshman year, you can bet other magicals around Richmond with a lot more experience can pick you out of a crowd no matter what you're wearing."

Cheyenne snorted. "Me being Goth doesn't mean I believe in magic or orcs or whatever other bull you're trying to convince me of right now."

"True. But you're a bad actor and an even worse liar." Ember smirked as she lifted her glass in a one-sided toast and took another long drink. "So, are you gonna help your only friend in the world or what?"

"I can't give you what you want." Cheyenne shifted in her seat, then realized she couldn't keep still and snatched her beer bottle off the table. "And I don't know what you're talking about."

"Seriously, Cheyenne, I have no idea what's stopping you or why you're so set on playing this game. Until I met you, I thought halflings were just legends. But the drow's already out of the bag, so to speak—"

"The *what?*"

"Oh, please." Ember snorted. "Don't tell me you've never heard that word either."

The bottle in Cheyenne's hand burst, sending shattered glass and foamy ale all over her hand and the table and the already-sticky, grungy floor. Cheyenne stared at her shaking, sopping hand, and felt the heat rush up her spine and curve across her shoulders.

Just this once. Please, just one time, don't let it come out.

"Cheyenne."

"What?" *Why do I keep breaking things but never cut myself?*

The amusement had drained from Ember's face, replaced by a sympathetic frown as she pointed to the side of her own head. "Your, uh, your ears?"

The chair screeched behind Cheyenne as she jerked to her feet. Before the chair tumbled backward and clattered to the floor, she was already rubbing her black hair vigorously with both hands to cover the changes she knew most people wouldn't believe—changes Ember had apparently picked up on four years ago.

One of the bartenders stopped beside their table with a rag in hand, ready to clean up the mess. "Everybody okay over here?"

Cheyenne's hip bumped against the table corner as she stormed away from him toward the front door. Ember had almost caught her own drink before it also hit the floor, although hers wasn't in shards.

She stayed in her seat and called after her friend. "Cheyenne. Hey, come on. You don't have to *leave.* I'm not—"

The door burst open with a little jingle from that stupid bell some idiot thought would be fun to tie to the handle, then Cheyenne was in the fresh September air. The door bounced shut, and she stalked down the sidewalk in front of the bar, taking deep breaths.

How does she know?

"That's a stupid question," she hissed at herself, shaking her hands out as she stalked toward the alley on the other side of Gnarly's. She slipped between the buildings, pressed against the alley's brick wall, and closed her eyes. "She knows because you have serious anger issues. That's how."

The chains she wore every day, rain or shine, sleeves or not, clinked as Cheyenne lifted her hands toward her face and peered at them in the half-light of the alley's shadows. The blotches of grayish-purple skin dotting her forearms were already fading, leaving nothing but her pale, vampirically white skin. "I have no problem with the vampire jokes. But she wasn't joking, was she?"

She brought both hands up to her head and poked around in her mess of black hair, which now looked like she'd just rolled out of bed and rubbed a balloon all over it. Not that she spent a lot of time on her hair, anyway. But what Cheyenne was trying to gauge with her fingers had in fact been hidden by her mess of hair she'd been dyeing High Voltage Raven Black for the last six years. Her fingers ran up the sides of her ears, brushing over the industrial piercings and the half-dozen rings passing through each piece of cartilage until she reached the top.

Perfectly round human-shaped ears. No pointed tips. Hopefully, they weren't slate-gray anymore. Even if they were, that would disappear soon enough. Cheyenne puffed a sigh and ruffled her thick hair until it covered her ears and all the silver rings again, then she rested her head against the brick wall and stared at the escape ladder and the catwalk on the other side of the alley.

"She could've just been messing with me." The heat of her rage had toned down. "No, she brought up the ears. Out of all the other things, why does it always have to be the ears?"

A few yards down the alley, a dumpster lid clanged against the brick wall. A skinny man in a kitchen apron with a severe case of adult acne lugged a giant trash bag and then another onto the almost overflowing pile. "I can't say anything about your ears, kid, but it sounds like you have some serious issues."

Cheyenne peered at the cook who'd been firing up jalapeño burgers every Tuesday night since last year. She pointed her chin at him, smiling. "Bite me, trash boy."

"Hey, that's more like it." Grinning, the cook—she thought his name was Sam—slammed a hand against the side of the dumpster and pointed at her. "Don't lose that winning attitude, Wyoming."

"Yeah, you think it's cute. I was born here, by the way." She stared at him until he slipped back inside Gnarly's side door, stopping just long enough to shoot her a wink.

Alone in the alley again, her rage gone, Cheyenne was ready to talk to the one person besides her mom who seemingly knew what she was. Shaking her hands out, her chains clinking around her wrists, Cheyenne headed toward the bar's front door. The cold had helped calm her, and she was ready to start over. If Ember knew about Cheyenne's little secret—which wasn't so little but had been easy to keep under wraps, or so she'd thought—it didn't change anything about their friendship.

Except she's apparently a better liar than I am.

If Ember was coming to her with whatever this orc problem was, after four years of never crossing this line into humans-versus-magicals territory, maybe she *did* need Cheyenne's help. Perhaps this half-drow Goth chick could offer something no one else could.

When she was only a few yards from the bar's entrance, the

door burst open with that stupid jingle, and Ember stepped outside. Cheyenne opened her mouth to start the slippery slope into heartfelt apologies, but her friend turned in the opposite direction and hurried down the sidewalk. Ember hunched over, one finger stuck in her ear while the other hand pressed her cell phone against her cheek. "Are you serious? Why would he—" Ember groaned and glanced at the night sky. "Yeah. No, Jackie, *listen* to me. I'm on my way, okay? Just keep him from doing anything stupid. Please. Hey, if anybody can do that, it's you. I'll be there soon."

Shutting her mouth, Cheyenne frowned and followed her friend down the sidewalk. She paused beside Gnarly's front door for a quick glance inside, but nobody seemed to care about the two regulars in a dumpy bar full of regulars, all of whom had their own problems to deal with without chasing down someone else's.

Maybe I should've listened to her. Cheyenne glared at her wan reflection in the door, backlit by all the lights on East Clay Street. The ring through her septum glinted in the bleached lights, and in the warped glass, it almost made her look like she was smiling.

"Sometimes." She glanced down the sidewalk to see Ember turn the corner around the building to cut across the parking lot. Maybe there was something Cheyenne could do to help.

Time to find out what she meant by "people like us."

CHAPTER FOUR

Cheyenne followed her friend down five blocks on the northwest end of Jackson Ward, her hands shoved into the front pockets of her baggy black pants just to keep the chains on her wrists from giving her away. Ember had caught her attention freshman year during their Intro to Cyber Security lectures. Even back then, the girl had sat in her seat like Cheyenne—slumped all the way back, legs stretched out in front of her, arms folded with her chin to her chest, and blankly staring at absolutely nothing. They'd bonded over an inability to focus in that useless class of over two hundred students. Ember had been bored to death, and Cheyenne had taught herself three years ago everything the instructor had to say.

Back to the moment at hand, it wasn't challenging to see Ember was hoofing it. The girl cut a pace above power walking but under jogging, and typically Ember didn't do either of those speeds. Ember strolled.

Cheyenne stuck to the shadows a half-dozen yards behind her friend, never taking her eyes off the back of Ember's brown leather jacket and her light-brown ponytail swinging from side to side.

I'm spying on her right now. My only friend, and I can't suck it up and tell her I'm coming because I wanna see some other magicals to know what that looks like.

Shaking her head, she slipped behind a thick sugar maple on the other side of the sidewalk and realized where they were. *Gangs meeting at skateparks. Low on the originality score.*

Ember turned to glance across the open space of grass and trimmed hedges, then she moved toward the six-foot-high fence around the skatepark. Cheyenne crouched outside the pool of light cast by the parking lot streetlamp. No one else around, as far as she could see; yet, it would take serious effort not to hear angry, hushed voices arising from the cement playground of halfpipes across the park.

Cheyenne stood and crept as fast as she darted across the grass. Luckily, she'd worn her black Vans. She went wide around the tall chain-link fence and the pavilion outside the skatepark. The arguing voices stopped when the gate creaked. Ember stepped inside the open-air structure, leaving the gate open, while Cheyenne crouched on the other side of the closest pillar. From her position, she got a clear view of everyone, including her friend.

"Who's this?" The deep, gruff voice came from a hulking figure the size of an NFL linebacker. He held a pistol pointed at the concrete rise beside the dip of the halfpipe, and Cheyenne could tell his flesh had a dark green tint. *An orc.*

"She's with us." Another guy in a group of three faced the orc and his six cronies. *A lot of 'em. Fantastic.*

Ember joined a man who ran his hand through his tuft of dark-blue hair, and Cheyenne realized his skin was a light purple shade. *Halfling. Earth-sider, definitely.*

"She's human," the big orc snarled and waved his pistol at Ember. "This is between you and me, Earthside-lover. Get her the hell outta here."

"I'm not human." Ember stepped beside the purple guy and

faced the orc. "I'm just smart enough to hide my face when I'm in public. It wouldn't be a bad idea if you all did the same."

"Masks." The orc grunted with disdain. "I didn't cross the Border to betray everything I stand for just to *blend in*. And I sure as hell didn't expect this much shit from a goblin traitor who wouldn't know his place if it bashed him over the head."

Cheyenne narrowed her eyes. *Goblin?*

"Watch it, Durg." The guy with blue hair standing next to Ember pointed at the orc. "I've been minding my own business for years, okay? And I came here to meet with you because I wanna *keep* minding my own business. But you're making that fucking hard."

"Careful, Trev." The woman standing just behind Ember lifted a hand like she meant to pull him away from the orcs, then reconsidered and chewed on her fingernail.

"Careful? I've *been* careful for thirty years, Jackie. And this Border-rider storms in from Ambar'ogúl thinking he runs the place. You know what?" Trevor turned back toward Durg, whose beefy face was split by giant yellowed tusks jutting from his lower lip. "This is what I came to tell you tonight, face to face. Six months and a few terrified gremlins coughing up your so-called protection money doesn't change a damn thing about how this world works."

"Trev." One of the other guys in the small group of Ember's friends stepped behind the goblin and put a hand on his buddy's shoulder. "I don't think this is how you wanna handle things."

"No, this is *exactly* how I wanna handle things. This orc doesn't own me. He doesn't own this city or any of us who came across to make something of ourselves instead of being parasites."

"Your turn to watch it now, you halfling piece of shit," Durg growled, lifting the gun in his hand and leveling it at Trevor's gut.

"Okay, hold on." Ember raised both her hands and stepped forward, throwing Trevor a harsh glare that meant one thing: *shut up*. She peered at the orc thugs who'd called this poor excuse for a meeting and nodded at the loaded pistol. "We don't need to go there, okay? I'm pretty sure there's a way for all of us to get what we want. So let's talk and keep all the weapons pointed elsewhere."

Trevor leaned toward Ember and muttered, "Is she coming?"

"Not now, Trev."

"Not...you said you'd get her to come."

"Hey!" The orc snapped his thick, meaty fingers then pointed at them, his gun still trained on the goblin's gut. "I didn't bring my guys all the way out here to sit in on your little conference, so shut the fuck up. This is how it's gonna go."

Seething, Trevor hissed at Ember through gritted teeth. "I did this because you said we had help."

"And I told you to *wait*. If these guys found out what we are, how long do you think it's gonna take the FRoE to find us? It'll take even less time for them to put us in chains and send us all *back*." Ember shook her head, holding Trevor's gaze with her hard glare. "Right now, Trev, we must help ourselves."

The orc leader issued a harsh, barking laugh and pointed his pistol up toward the sky. He turned toward the half-dozen thugs behind him, who stood there with their beefy arms folded, watching everything with blatant disregard for their own intelligence.

Cheyenne studied them from her hiding place. *Maybe they just want everyone to think they're brainless on purpose?*

"Can you believe these morons?" Durg laughed again as he gestured at Ember and her associates. "Standing up for the little guy. Fighting a fair fight. Like they still think *anything* on this side of the portal is fair at all."

Trevor shrugged his friend's hand off his shoulder and

stepped toward the orc. "Hey, things are good when *O'gúleesh* stop thinking they rule everything over here too. Somebody's gotta change your mind, and if I'm the one who has to do it—"

The orc's crooked grin dropped, and he leveled the gun at Trevor again. "What makes you think I give two undead brain-stems what's good for any of you?"

"Whoa." Everyone in Ember's group stepped back, all of them raising their hands.

Cheyenne inched around the column. Heat flared at the base of her spine. It swelled beneath her skin like hot mercury in a thermometer—a thermometer in a microwave, the red line about to explode. She clenched her fists, unable to show herself, unable to look away.

It's going to be okay. Ember negotiated herself out of homework for two semesters. Cheyenne's chest filled with heated air. *Yeah, this isn't remotely the same. Shit.*

Ember licked her lips and stared at the pistol's barrel gleaming in the moonlight. "It doesn't need to be like this."

Durg's upper lip curled into a menacing sneer above his yellowed tusks. His chuckle lacked humor. "We'll do it the way I say we will, trash." He moved his arm a few inches to the right, swinging it from Trevor to aim at Ember's face. "And I say shut your Earthside-lovin'—"

Electric-blue light hurtled from someone in Ember's group and struck Durg's shoulder. The orc leader staggered sideways, and a gunshot rang out.

"End this!" Durg screamed as he grabbed his injured shoulder.

His thugs barreled forward as one. Spells flashed and exploded on both sides, striking a few targets, mostly making craters in the park's pavilion and skating area. Chunks of concrete flew in every direction, and Ember's friends staggered across the ledge beside the halfpipe, flinging spells and retreating toward the chain fence's open gate.

Cheyenne spotted her friend sprawled on the concrete at an awkward angle, her light brown ponytail splayed out on the ground in front of the halfpipe. A dark stain spread on the back of Ember's shirt beneath the hiked-up hem of her leather jacket.

The mercury of Cheyenne's rage exploded as searing heat flared up her spine, overwhelming the half-drow's senses. She became vaguely aware of her skin turning, taking on her dark elf's gray-purple hue. The tips of her ears lengthened and burned, the rage poured through her, and she roared.

CHAPTER FIVE

"What the hell?" Durg lowered his pistol, grasping his right shoulder, and stared at the shrieking shadow gliding beside the skatepark from the pavilion. "Brul, you were supposed to scout the—"

The shadow was a dark elf, and she surged forward with both hands raised. Black light erupted from her palms, and the chain-link fence between her and the orcs ripped apart in a tumult of tearing, twisting metal.

Durg thumped Brul on the back and pointed. "Whoever the hell that is, stop her."

Brul nodded. "Got it, boss." The orc headed after the attacking drow.

A streak of green slime sputtered past Durg's head. He turned to snarl at the idiot goblin halfling who'd thought he could stand up to him and his boys. He raised his gun again. "You're not getting out of this!"

A blazing purple light flashed in the corner of his eye. Searing agony and purple-black sparks erupted in Durg's right hand, and he bellowed in pain, his dropped gun clattering across the concrete before skittering to a stop at the halfpipe's lip.

"It's a goddamn drow, boss," Brul shouted over his shoulder.

Durg rubbed his right hand and seethed. "I know what the hell it is, you moron. Take her down!"

The dark elf tossed magic in every direction. Snaking lines of black energy whipped from her palms, lashing out to send a pair of orcs flying across the skatepark. Durg glanced at his discarded firearm, growled, and turned toward the stranger. He balled his unaffected hand and summoned a crackling orb of green light.

The drow flung her hand toward him before he could release his spell, and another burst of purple with the darkest black at its center erupted from her fingers. It crashed into his fist and sent his spell in the wrong direction. The black tendrils of energy slapped the ground at his feet and two more orc thugs fell victim to the dark elf's power.

Durg whirled around at the choking, gasping sound behind him and found Hamal—all six and a half feet of him—dangling midair by one of those coils wrapped with deadly intent around his bulging neck. Ceeru screamed as another black tendril whipped around his ankle, jerked his feet out from under him, and yanked him across the concrete.

"Get out!" Durg shouted.

The orc leader turned and darted toward the chain-link fence behind him, shoving one of his own guys out of the way to avoid a blast of that crackling, purple-black energy. The grind rail beside him exploded in steel fragments and cement chunks. A thick piece of it tore into Durg's neck and stung like hell as he leapt up onto the fence and started to climb. Something lashed at his ankles. He thought he'd be ripped from the fence or his thick fingers would be severed by the metal in his grasp since he'd be damned if he let go.

Durg fought through the tug on his ankle and flung

himself over the top. The fence came down with him in a jingle of links and another grating squeal of metal. He pushed himself from beneath the section that had fallen on him as a bolt of searing magic scored the ground two feet away, spraying up dirt and chunks of grassy soil. Durg risked a glance back as he got to his feet at his orcs, who were getting beaten and pelted with purple-black spells. He spotted Brul running toward him.

Durg didn't wait. He took off for the trees and toward a streetlamp on the other side of the park. Brul kept on his heels, yelling for his boss to wait up. A few more gunshots rang out behind them, followed by shouts of rage. More concrete exploded, and the orcs kept running.

Cheyenne lowered her trembling hands and released a shaky breath. The skatepark was empty and utterly destroyed, upturned chunks of concrete and twisted metal here and there, the chain-link fence pulled down in places or ripped open. The closest tree smoked from where one of the orc's spells had lodged itself in the bark instead of her own skin.

And everyone was gone.

Slowly, Cheyenne closed her fists and blinked. The searing rage still coursed through her, but it was less now—so much less and not nearly satisfying enough. Her gaze fell on Ember, and with a grunt, she hurried through the overturned rubble to her friend.

"Em!" She slid to her knees on the concrete, ignoring the ripping of her thick pants and sting as her knees scraped the pavement. "Ember, get up."

Cheyenne's hands were sticky with blood before she even touched her friend. She turned Ember over, noticing the pool of blood on the ground glistening in the moonlight.

Ember groaned and her eyelids fluttered, yet they didn't open.

"No, no, no. Come on!"

Cheyenne's oncoming tears burned as she found Ember's wound a few inches beside her navel. The stain of crimson on her friend's shirt at the small of her back grew by the second. "Okay. Just hold on. Okay."

Sucking in a breath, Cheyenne slid one arm under Ember's shoulders and hooked the other behind her friend's knees. She stood and cradled Ember in her arms and nearly slipped on the pool of blood. Ember hung limp, and Cheyenne stormed back toward East Clay.

She didn't think about how many other magicals—the first she'd seen in the twenty-one years of her life—she'd scattered into the night. She didn't think about how light Ember was or how clearly she could smell her friend's blood. Instead, Cheyenne focused on the faint but audible wheeze of Ember's shallow breathing. She moved as fast as she could toward the university Medical Center's ER.

"They just left you," she muttered, stalking across the street. "How could they just leave you? If you can hear me, Em, you better stay with me. I'm getting you help. You got it?"

A group of college kids parked outside a bar on East Leigh Street laughed and jostled each other until they saw Cheyenne carrying a bloody woman in her arms.

"Oh, my god." One of the girls clutched at the closest guy standing next to her, and they all stared. Yet, none of them offered to help. They didn't even ask if she was okay.

They're useless anyway.

Cheyenne picked up the pace, glancing every few seconds at Ember's soaked shirt. Every time, rage flared up in her anew. Adrenaline pumping once more, she started running. Street-lights flashed by in a blur, punctured by the white streaks of headlights and the red of taillights. A woman stepped from the passenger side of a sedan parked at the curb. When Cheyenne ran past her, the only thing the woman saw was a flash of dark gray and black and white before the shockwave of the half-drow's speed knocked the woman against the side of her car and slammed the passenger door shut.

Darting around the last corner, Cheyenne saw the flashing lights of an ambulance pulling up to VCU's emergency room doors. She reached the entrance before the ambulance driver had pressed the brakes.

A muted *crack* ripped through the air when she stopped. Those few people making their way into the ER glanced about in surprise at the whipping wind. Several gawked at the dark-skinned woman appearing in front of them.

Cheyenne ignored them all, took a deep breath, and carried Ember through the automatic doors. The ER waiting room was filled with humans hacking and coughing, moaning, cradling bloody limbs, pressing ice packs to their faces, and leaning their heads against the wall as they waited to be seen while trying not to lose composure.

Cheyenne fought back panic when she sensed Ember's sluggish heartbeat dwindle even more. As the drow carried her dying friend into the ER, she remembered to lose the dark-gray flesh and returned to her natural paleness.

People didn't see me. They're just staring at all the blood.

She made a beeline to the intake desk. "I need help here!"

The two nurses behind the desk stood abruptly. "What happened?"

"She was shot." Cheyenne stopped in front of the desk and stared at the women. Both of them took in the young woman with wild black hair and eerily pale makeup, the chains, the tears in Cheyenne's pants, and the blood-soaked Ember, who was taller than Cheyenne who seemed to weigh as much as an empty box in the Goth girl's arms. "*Do* something!"

The nurses jumped to attention. One ran around the desk

toward a gurney against the wall and kicked up the wheel locks, while the other grabbed the phone and blurted "ER Code Blue!"

Cheyenne barely heard anything but her friend's slow, whispering heartbeat.

"Ma'am?"

"What?" Cheyenne looked up with tears in her eyes.

"What's her name?"

"Ember Gaderow."

The other nurse patted the gurney. "Here. Lay her down… gently, that's it."

After she lowered her friend onto the gurney, she gripped Ember's hand, everything slick with blood.

"You said she was shot?"

"Yeah."

"Shot by what?"

The half-drow blinked at the nurse. "A gun."

"Any other injuries?"

"Yeah, probably. I don't know. Look, she needs help right now. She's barely breathing."

"Our CPR and Code Blue team are on the way, ma'am."

The other nurse started to wheel Ember through the triage doors but stopped when the force of Cheyenne's grip on Ember's hand nearly pulled the unconscious woman off the gurney. "Ma'am, you can let go. She's in good hands."

Cheyenne glanced at her own hands, white skin beneath all that blood. She let Ember's fingers slip from hers. "Where are you taking her?"

"The OR."

"I'm coming with you." Cheyenne surged forward.

The other nurse rounded the desk and stepped between the half-drow and her unconscious friend. "I'm sorry. You can't—" The nurse staggered and removed her hands from Cheyenne's shoulders. A little gasp escaped her at the force of Cheyenne's last step that had almost knocked her backward across the ER floor.

"Ma'am, please, you have to stay out here. Let's get a look at you too." The nurse was joined by a strong-looking man in scrubs, who smiled and gave off a calming disposition.

"I'm fine." Cheyenne blinked away her tears and watched Ember get wheeled through the swinging doors.

"You're covered in blood, and you're in shock." The woman standing in front of her nodded toward a triage room across the hall from the intake desk. "Come with me, and we'll take a look at you."

Both nurses tried to guide Cheyenne toward the room, the woman with her hand on the half-drow's back, and the man right behind them, still smiling. Cheyenne jerked away and tried to see Ember again through the swinging doors.

She was gone.

"Ma'am, please..." spoke the male nurse, gesturing at an open room.

"Hey, only one of us got shot, okay? And it wasn't me." Cheyenne balled her hands into fists and tried to calm her breathing, but the rage still smoldered. *The last thing I need right now is a repeat of the skatepark. Keep it under control.*

Both nurses blinked at her and offered sympathetic smiles. The woman asked, "What's your name?"

Cheyenne stared at them both, swallowed, then turned and walked out of the ER without speaking another word.

CHAPTER SIX

She nearly barreled right into a woman being pushed through the doors in a wheelchair. The woman moaned and rolled her head from side to side. When both the chair and Cheyenne stopped to avoid crashing into each other, the agonized woman took one look at the Goth girl covered in white makeup and someone else's blood and fell quiet.

Avoiding everyone else's gazes and all the staring, Cheyenne swerved around the wheelchair and stalked outside. *I need air. I need to think. I need...*

A short, vengeful growl escaped her as she moved down the sidewalk outside the hospital. A man with a cane hobbling toward the ER jumped at the sound, glanced at her, and double-timed it toward the doors.

Smoothing the hair away from her face, Cheyenne ignored the old-timer and took a deep breath. "How did I let that happen? I should've just gone with her. Some fucking friends..."

She paced the sidewalk until her rage lessened, then she turned toward the ER again. She approached the intake desk, and the same nurse, whose nametag she read for the first time, looked a little less terrified of the bloodied Goth chick reentering the emergency room.

"Sharon. Can you at least please find out how she's doing?"

"With a gunshot wound and that much blood loss, they took her straight to the OR. We won't know anything for a bit."

"She's in surgery now? Can't you get an update?"

The nurse spread her arms and bowed her head, her gaze darting from Cheyenne's. "I'm sorry."

"What? Why not?"

"Are you family?"

Cheyenne bit the inside of her bottom lip and glared at the woman. "No."

"I can only speak to family. I'm sorry. Do you know anyone we can call?"

"Seriously?"

"Any information helps us help her."

Cheyenne closed her eyes. "I might as well be family, okay? Ember's from...I don't know. Chicago, I think. Her family's all there."

"Do you have any phone numbers?"

"No, I don't have their numbers." The half-drow rolled her eyes. "But I'm telling *you,* there's no one else here—"

"I'm sorry." Nurse Sharon shook her head. "If you're not related to the patient, I can't give you any more information."

"Ember."

"I'm sorry?"

"Her name's *Ember.* Not 'the patient.'" Cheyenne softened her tone.

"Of course." Nurse Sharon gestured toward the full waiting room, her brows flickering together in concern. "I am sorry there's nothing more I can do for you, ma'am. Ember's being taken care of as we speak, and I have to get to all these other people waiting to be seen next. If you'll just—"

Cheyenne pressed her palms on the edge of the desk, then

changed her mind and slammed her fists on it instead. Sharon squeaked in surprise, the ER quieted in a split second, and someone's baby started crying.

The male nurse from earlier poked his head around a partition, then sauntered out. "What's happening, Sharon? Are we good?" He maintained that same disarming smile.

"I'm sorry," she said, looking at his nametag, "Andre. Sharon." She peeped around the waiting room, then stared at the back of the old computer monitor and blinked. "But I'm not leaving until somebody tells me she's okay."

"I get it, you know. Your friend is lucky to have you." Andre looked at Cheyenne's appearance and leaned forward to whisper, "The police are going to want to talk to you. It's protocol with all gunshot victims. Why don't you have a seat, and I'll grab you a coffee."

Cheyenne weighed her answer and nodded at him, then glanced at Sharon, who looked down at the intake forms on her desk and then called, "Mikey?"

Cheyenne removed her hands and stepped back.

A man with an angry gash in his forearm from a splinter larger than splinters had any right to be—which still protruded from the red, swollen skin around it—stood from his chair and walked toward the desk. He'd forgotten his discomfort as he smiled at Cheyenne's piercings. He scanned her lip and nose, then his eyes traveled to the silver ring in her eyebrow. "Cool," he said.

She brushed past him and went to sit in an empty chair. The people waiting in the ER watched her as she slumped. The woman on her right, who'd been hacking up a lung for the last ten minutes, leaned away, then stood and took her cough to the other side of the room.

Cheyenne folded her arms and closed her eyes. Bits of rubble and dirt and Ember's blood were encrusted on her clothes, and her skinned knees stung like a bitch.

I'm not leaving. I'll figure out the police when I have to.

Cheyenne jerked awake when the screaming child was carried through the emergency room doors by a sobbing mother. The nurses at the intake desk managed to quiet them before leading them both into one of the triage rooms, and Cheyenne cleared her throat.

The waiting room now only held about a dozen people, and it still felt way too full. Once the crying mother and her kid were ushered into a private room, Nurse Sharon came out from behind the desk. She stopped in front of Cheyenne and offered her a paper cup of water. "Are you sure you wouldn't like someone to take a look at your knees?"

Her arms still folded, Cheyenne pulled her outstretched legs back toward her and held the nurse in her gaze. "Are you going to tell me anything? If the surgery's done or if she…if she's okay?"

"I can't. I'm sorry, Miss…" When Cheyenne didn't offer her name, the nurse sighed and offered the cup again. "Some water will help."

"Your friend over there," she glanced at Andre, who was speaking to an ill elderly woman and her grandson, "offered me coffee already. Must be how you guys try to…" She shook her head. "I'm good."

The nurse lowered the cup and glanced at the water, holding it now with both hands. "Legally, I can't tell you what kind of treatment your friend is receiving or has received since you're not related—"

"We covered that part already." Cheyenne sniffed and glanced around the waiting room. "I can't leave without knowing if she's okay."

"I understand, but no one's going to be able to tell you

anything." The nurse tried to smile, then looked at the blood all over Cheyenne's clothing and injured knees. The smile wavered. "I *can* tell you to come back tomorrow during visiting hours. If your friend's recovered enough to put you on the approved visitors' list, you'll have more luck." She paused like she was weighing something, then she whispered, "The police are on their way. You have about five minutes."

The words made Cheyenne perk up. "Right."

"My suggestion would be to go home, get cleaned up, get some sleep, and come back tomorrow."

Blowing out a sigh through tight lips, Cheyenne pushed out of the chair. "I have to go to the front lobby for visiting hours?"

"Yes." Sharon's voice was surprisingly level and calm.

"Thank you." Cheyenne eyed the cup in the woman's hand. "Some water might help." Then she turned and headed out the automatic doors.

If I can't get anyone to talk to me here, gonna have to go to Plan B.

Cheyenne Summerlin had been doing that since she was ten.

CHAPTER SEVEN

At the front door of her apartment on St. John, Cheyenne fumbled in her pocket for her keys. It wasn't out of exhaustion or fear for Ember, although those things were swimming through her in equal parts, but because she just couldn't move as quickly as she wanted to. She was exhausted.

Once inside, a glance at the clock over the stove told her it was 3:07 a.m. She kicked her sneakers off and left them in a heap beside the entryway closet, then headed for the bathroom sink. The blood swirled in the water around the drain, and she had to work to get it all out from between her fingers. She peeled off her shirt, still damp with blood, and picked up a tank top from the floor, giving it a brief sniff.

She headed for the fridge. Tonight's options were mustard on the last slice of deli turkey and half a quart of milk. Cheyenne sniffed the carton's contents, shrugged, and guzzled it.

"Time to get to work."

Cheyenne went to the long executive desk that was the only real piece of furniture in her tiny living room. The minute she sat at it and gazed at the dark screens of her dual monitors, her nerves calmed. This was where she belonged, not out in some park blasting away at the first magicals she'd ever seen. The only place where Cheyenne knew what she wanted and how to get it was right here behind her computer. *In* her computer.

She woke everything up. The fans in the tower she'd built from scratch whirred to life, followed by the blinking lights of her private server hidden behind an updated VPN and the entire world at her fingertips. "Maybe she'll put me on the visitors' list. Maybe not. I'm not taking any chances."

The first thing she did was slip into VCU Medical Center's patient database, which took about thirty seconds once she found the right network. It gave her a minor twinge of irritation that hospital records took less time to find than anything she'd searched for in her online classes as an undergrad.

"This is a joke." Shaking her head, Cheyenne looked up everything they had on Ember Gaderow. It wasn't a lot, but it was enough.

'Caucasian female; early twenties; diagnosed GSWSCI at the thoracic level; entry and exit sites both identified; attempted surgical stabilization; possible paraplegia after recovery and decompression.'

Cheyenne swallowed. As far as she could tell—and as much as anyone at VCU Medical Center had bothered to put into the system—Ember was okay. For now. But "possible paraplegia" made the half-drow recline in her chair and give a constricted groan. "She might not be able to walk."

She closed her eyes and pictured Ember in the recovery ward, unconscious, cut apart and sewn back together, and it was all Cheyenne's fault.

Because I keep hiding.

She opened her eyes and pulled up information on the hospital's visitation policy, then accessed a form under Ember's name and added her information. She paused before typing her name. "They're gonna figure it out sooner or later, and they're gonna crap themselves when they realize they didn't let me in to see her when I asked. Can't say I didn't try."

It was her mom's name that made people stop and think twice about how they interacted with Cheyenne. That had given her a good smack in the face when she'd enrolled at Virginia Commonwealth University for her undergrad. She tried to keep Bianca Summerlin out of the equation whenever possible, but it got harder every year for Cheyenne to carve her own path.

Bianca hadn't been a bad parent. That never crossed Cheyenne's mind. It didn't change her mom's voice in her head, whenever she found herself with a clear head facing a problem she hadn't already solved.

"The line between good and bad, fair and unfair, is very thin, Cheyenne. Black and white don't exist. The trick is knowing when to cross that line. Once you understand that, you'll understand everything we do comes with a price. *Everything.*"

Those words had taken on many different meanings since Bianca drilled them into her daughter's young mind. Cheyenne had soaked it up like a sponge, just like everything else. Now, for the first time, they made sense.

"Okay, Mom. I get it." Cheyenne sighed and dragged her hands down her face. "Ember was the price tonight. I tried to keep things black and white. Me versus the world."

Nodding, she dove deeper into her network, using untraceable routes switched out through her VPN with new entry locations every time she dug into the dark web. "Next time somebody asks for my help against magicals, I won't say no."

Saying it felt right, despite no one being there to hear her pledge. She knew other magicals existed; tonight, she'd seen the way the orcs dealt with others. "I'll figure it out. Gonna find the asshole who started it. This *Durg.*"

Over the last three years, Cheyenne had come across

mentions of magicals around the city. She'd gathered a few crumbs about underground businesses, about "the other side." Tonight, Durg had spouted something about portals and Earthside. About *halflings*. What was it Trevor had said? *"This Borderrider storms in from Ambar'ogúl, thinking he runs the place."*

That must mean something. Cheyenne was determined to find out what and how it applied to Ember. And to herself. *"People like us have to stick together."*

Ember had been so certain of that when she'd said it at the bar, but as far as Cheyenne knew, the things they had in common—the things connecting them into a friendship that had only strengthened since freshman year—had nothing to do with magicals and underground markets and portals. Until they did.

She typed in a few searches and plugged them into her encrypted data sources, coded to ping her with any matches that came up. Not that it was ever as fast as Googling something, but Google couldn't find what she was looking for. Cheyenne sat at her desk for another ten minutes, hoping her searches would find something quickly but not expecting anything so soon.

Finally, when she sat back and her tank top cracked and rustled with the dried blood stuck to her chest and stomach, she gave up waiting for real-time results. "You do you, Glen." She pointed at her center monitor and stood from the desk chair. "I gotta clean up."

She walked across her small apartment toward the single bathroom beside her bedroom, stripping off her clothes as she went. Instead of dropping them wherever they fell, she bundled them all up and chucked them in a pile in the bathroom's corner before turning on the shower. Everything felt fine except for the stinging scrapes on her knees, and she gritted her teeth when she peeled off her underwear and flung them onto the pile too. Before she stepped into the shower, she glanced at the clothes.

Blood is the one drawback to wearing so much black. Only place that crap shows up brick-red.

Stepping into the scalding water, Cheyenne hissed in pleasure and pain. The steam felt good. She used a washcloth to scrub her knees before bothering with the rest of the stains on her skin.

Twenty minutes later, her long hair toweled off enough to not soak the giant Slipknot t-shirt she'd pulled over her head, Cheyenne stopped at her desk to check her results. The code for her search scrolled across the black background of the center monitor. She was about to head toward her bedroom when the computer duck-quacked—the tone she'd set for notifications. Cheyenne sat at the desk and reached down to rub her raw, itchy knees. She leaned toward the monitor.

Durg Br'athol; pure O-class, 207 years; entered via Border 7 Reservation, March 2021

"That's it? O-class, huh? What the heck is 'Border 7 Reservation?'" Cheyenne grabbed her thick black hair in both hands, twisted it to make sure it was dry enough for sleep, then glanced at the time. "Ugh. Class in four hours. Durg Br'athol, you'll have to wait a bit. I'm sure you don't mind."

Cheyenne left her searches running and retired to her twin bed covered in gray sheets and a black comforter with a cartoon skull. She grabbed her phone from the nightstand, set her alarm for 6:45 a.m., crawled under the covers, and turned off the small desk lamp.

I'll get my answers. She turned on her side and pulled the comforter over her shoulders. *Whatever Ember meant by "people like us," I can't talk myself out of it anymore.*

Cheyenne fell asleep to the vivid memory of the chaos she'd unleashed on an O-class thug named Durg.

CHAPTER EIGHT

Just under four hours later, Cheyenne hurried through the campus' IT building toward her first class of the day. Her backpack hung loose off her shoulders because only a few folders for her individual classes were in it. The sight of so many undergraduate students on the first floor made her push her memories of the first four years of college aside.

Ember was the only good thing that came out of four years of pretending to be stupid.

Some students stared at her as she walked past, the chains draping from her pockets jangling with every step. She'd braided her hair when she woke up after way too little sleep because she didn't appreciate the wild curls after a shower and hadn't had time to straighten it. And after years of practice at hiding and covering all her bases, it was second nature now to make sure every hairstyle came with a way to hide the tips of her ears just in case.

Cheyenne snorted. *Like that's the first thing people look at when they see somebody's skin turn dark purple. It's the first thing that changes, anyway.*

But just to be sure, she'd put on a long-sleeve shirt today

and pulled the sleeves down past her hands. Three hours of sleep and a friend lying in a hospital bed with a gunshot wound didn't make it easier to keep her temper under control.

She found her first class on the third floor—Theory of Programming Languages, Tuesdays and Thursdays from 8:00 to 10:00. Her schedule tried to pass it off as a lab, but after only having had the class twice so far this semester, Cheyenne had already pegged it as a recap class. She wouldn't learn anything in this "lab" she hadn't been taught in her undergrad classes or mastered by the time she'd tested out of online high school at sixteen.

Just playing the game. It's the second week, and I'm already bored.

When she slipped inside the open door to a computer lab, Cheyenne felt the stares of the other students on her. She picked a seat at a table in the middle row, slid her backpack off her shoulders, and settled in.

"Hey." A kid in a white-and-blue-striped polo and his hair gelled into inch-long spikes took the chair next to her. "This seat taken?"

Cheyenne cast him a sideways glance and raised an eyebrow. "Just as taken as every other empty seat in the room."

"Cool. Cool. I'm Peter."

She nodded and unzipped her backpack to pull out her laptop.

"Mind if I ask you a question?"

Cheyenne shrugged as the dude named Peter kept talking. "'I was wondering if the '90s called and asked for their death gear back. You still have a landline too?" Hushed laughs came from the group of other grad students beside the door.

"Don't be a jerk, Pete." A girl leaned against the wall with some books clutched to her chest. "She's not gonna get the joke. The Goth kids I went to high school with never laughed."

Cheyenne slid her laptop out of its sleeve and centered it on the table in front of her. She pushed aside the provided keyboard to make room and opened her computer.

"Seriously, though." Peter propped an elbow on the table and stuck his chin in his hand. "I wanted to ask when I first saw you, but I figured it was better to wait until at least the second week of the semester, right? When everybody's a little more open to getting to know each other. In grad school. So, what's up with all the piercings? Do they mean something, or are they just supposed to make you look extra scary?"

"If you think *this* is a lot, I used to set off metal detectors at the airport." Cheyenne sniffed and tucked her laptop sleeve back into her backpack. "So, yeah. I guess that scared a few people."

Peter tilted his head, still resting in his hand, then leaned back and put a lot of unnecessary effort into looking her up and down. "I thought the whole Goth thing was a phase."

With a deep breath, Cheyenne lowered her hands from her keyboard, folded her arms, and turned to look at the guy. "Anyone who *grows out* of something that makes them feel like themselves is quitting. I'm not a quitter."

"Huh." The dude's top lip twitched as he decided whether to smile. "That's deep."

Cheyenne turned back to her laptop and shrugged. "I thought the whole asshole-jock thing was supposed to be a phase too. Looks like you don't quit, either."

Peter's mouth popped open, and the group of his friends standing by the classroom door burst out laughing. They spread out to take their seats, and the guy sitting next to Cheyenne nodded and pushed the chair out behind him as he stood. "Nice getting to know you, whatever your name is."

She waited for him to pick another chair at the row of desks in front of her before she typed in her laptop password and sat back again. More than anything, she wanted to sync her laptop with the server at her apartment and check on her running search through the dark web. Nothing else had pulled up in her three hours of sleep, but that wasn't unusual. Cheyenne was just impatient. And tapping into her personal IP using the school's internet was the dumbest thing she could do —especially while running on almost zero sleep.

The lab filled up with the other grad students in their first years of pursuing a master's in computer science, though the room was only half-full. Then the professor walked in, pulling a light-brown briefcase on wheels behind her. The color of the leather made Cheyenne think of Ember's jacket, which now had to have at least one bullet hole in it, if not two.

"See, so I appreciate my grad students so much more," the woman said as she hustled toward her desk at the front of the lab. "If anyone's late, it's gonna be me."

A few chuckles filled the room, followed by the sound of backpacks and briefcases unzipping. Cheyenne took a quick glance around at the others. Most of the students pulled out pens and pencils and notepads, which seemed ridiculous when they were here for programming and code-writing. *Do they write faster on paper than they can type?*

Cheyenne brought her laptop with her everywhere, even for her undergrad classes. She'd bought a new HP Spectre x360 to celebrate graduating with what amounted to a useless bachelor's degree. But even now, at their third class of the semester, she was the only one who'd thought it was a better idea to bring her own laptop instead of depending on what the school called "cutting-edge technology." The thought almost made her smirk.

"So who went the extra mile over the weekend and dug into all the extra fun bits of Python and Java they wouldn't teach you as undergrads?" Professor Bergmann stood behind her desk, the handle of her rolling briefcase still extended to its full height. The woman was tall and graceful, which was the complete opposite of every instructor Cheyenne had had for her classes before grad school. Her hair was black, which contrasted with her olive complexion and striking hazel eyes.

I could be jealous right now. Cheyenne pressed her lips together and pulled up the two coding programs, just to be ready for whichever one their professor would tell them to pull up next. *Or I could just appreciate the fact that she's wearing neon-yellow Chuck Taylors and a tie-dyed skirt. She looks as much like as an IT professor as I do.*

The class was silent. Cheyenne could feel the looks darting all over the place from most of the students sitting in the front row ahead of her. Only two people sat behind her, both of them at opposite ends of the last row of desks. She stared at her laptop.

"Seriously?" Professor Bergmann chuckled and scanned her students' faces. "Oh, come on, people. You've spent four years figuring out how to *do college*. Please don't tell me you're taking on grad-school loans just so I can teach you how to think for yourselves."

A girl with a messy bun tied closer to her forehead than the top of her head sighed and gestured toward the professor. "If you don't give us an assignment before the weekend, how are we supposed to know you wanted us to show you something today?"

"Huh." The corners of the professor's mouth turned down in mock consideration, and she stroked her chin. "I thought you guys wanted to be here. Was I wrong?"

No one said a word.

"It's in the syllabus," Cheyenne muttered, still staring at the black background of her desktop screen. Then she bit her lip just to keep from smiling.

"What?" The woman sitting in front of her beside Peter turned around, the messy bun on her head wobbling a little. She cocked her head and shot Cheyenne a fake smile. "I didn't hear you. Sorry. I think you were mumbling."

Cheyenne just raised an eyebrow and stared at her computer until the other student shrugged and turned around again. "It's in the syllabus." This time, she said it loud enough for everyone to hear. "It's laid out by the week and a detailed summary of what we're going into."

Messy Bun scoffed.

"It's okay if you lost it," Cheyenne added. "I bet that happens a lot in grad school."

"Oh." Messy Bun dug through her well-oiled, expensive-looking designer messenger bag, jerked out a bright-yellow folder, and thumbed through the small number of papers inside. "I didn't lose it." She whipped out the stapled-together syllabus and spread it out in front of her on the table. "But it says nothing about having to do assignments before we learn about it in class."

Professor Bergmann opened her mouth to reply, but Cheyenne just couldn't help herself. "At least your dog didn't eat it or anything."

The heavyset guy sitting behind Cheyenne with the wild red beard who smelled like beef ramen let loose a low chuckle. A few others in the class followed suit. Messy Bun stiffened in her chair but just kept staring up at their professor, waiting for an answer.

"I'm glad you still have that thing." Professor Bergmann pointed at the syllabus, her mouth curled up at the edges. "I spent a lot of time putting that together."

"Is that what you want us to do, though?" Messy Bun asked.

"Hmm. What do *you* want to do?" The professor's hazel eyes glittered with amusement, and she gazed at Cheyenne as if they were in on something together.

"I want to know if I'm supposed to try finishing an assignment before it's even assigned. That's not too much to ask."

Bergmann dipped her head and grinned. "No. Don't beat yourself up too much, though. This is the first time you've asked and, before you feel insulted, keep in mind if I wanted to argue about what comes first, the assignment-chicken or the turning-it-in-egg, I'd be teaching philosophy."

The big guy sitting behind Cheyenne snorted.

"Which I'm *not,*" Bergmann added. Then she glanced down at her desk again, tapped her fingers on the wood a few times, and pulled her grin into a calmer, gentler smile. "I'll return to my original question and ask if any of you took your education into your own hands and dove a little deeper into these programming languages over the weekend."

Messy Bun just shook her head and folded her arms. "Nobody will tell you they did."

I could. Cheyenne fought back a little chuckle of her own. *But saying I did it over the weekend instead of five years ago would still be lying.*

"Well, it doesn't hurt to ask, does it?" Professor Bergmann spread her arms and seemed to make a point to not stare at Messy Bun. "But now you know that in my class, I expect at least a few of you to be working on your own time, with your own brains, even if that means I didn't assign it. If anyone can come up with a workaround to something I've listed in any previous class, a different route or shortcut...hell, even if you fumbled your way into an encrypted box with no way out, I wanna hear about it. It helps me gauge the class overall and where we're headed the rest of the semester. More than that, it helps me gauge the IT nerds I get to work with for at least the next four months."

"I don't think that's—"

Peter nudged Messy Bun with his elbow and shook his head, muttering, "Just drop it, Natalie."

Messy Bun turned her head a full ninety degrees to shoot him the death-glare.

Ignoring the power struggle between the students in the front row, Professor Bergmann clapped her hands and nodded.

"So, my fine-groomed grad students, here's what I'd like you to get crackin' on."

Before the woman retrieved the smartboard remote from her briefcase, Cheyenne felt her gaze settle on her for a few seconds longer than a fleeting glance. The half-drow kept staring at her laptop.

"I like Python as much as the next person who knows what they're doing. I'm sure you guys spent hours making lists of all the pros and cons before you got here, so I won't bore you with the fundamentals. That's another thing you should know about this class." Bergmann straightened and clicked a few items on the smart screen with the clean, sleek white remote in her hand. "Today, we're gonna check out some nifty little tricks C++ can pull that most people overlook."

"See?" Messy Bun whispered to Peter. "Even if we did any work over the weekend, she'd scrap it all and say we're going over something else..."

Cheyenne tuned them out and focused on what Bergmann was showing them; if this class was like the first two last week, that presentation would last about five minutes before the professor told them to scatter and get to work. Not for the first time, she cursed her overactive hearing—Messy Bun's voice was the first living experience she'd had with nails on a chalkboard.

CHAPTER NINE

"I still don't understand why everyone calls these 'smartboards.' Questions before I turn off this giant, dumb computer behind me and let you guys get down to the work that requires actual intelligence?" Professor Bergmann lifted the remote in her hand, acknowledged the lack of questions, then turned off the power and tossed the remote into her briefcase. "Excellent. Time to exercise your practical-application skills and build another light-level algorithm using C++. All the software's already on the lab's computers, *with* updates, so none of you will have to worry about sorting that mess out first. Oh, and just to be clear, I don't want to see anything based on the example I gave you that's over forty percent of the original. You're learning how to build here, not copy and paste."

The woman didn't look at her students again. Instead, she sat and pulled out her laptop. Cheyenne heard the woman's low chuckle—just a few puffs of air through Bergmann's nose.

I can't believe this is an upper-level class.

They'd just been assigned something on the lower side of advanced. Cheyenne had used C++ when she realized she was into computers at the age of eight—she might have manipulated her mom into thinking the coding expansions and non-essential updates were a surprise Christmas present for her—and that had been eleven years ago.

This little project the professor seemed to think would take her students an hour and a half to complete would take Cheyenne ten minutes if she wrote the code from scratch. She already had the bones left over from a pet project she'd mastered and abandoned when she was fifteen.

She opened the program on her laptop—she refused to use the lab's computers—and searched for the little block of code she'd written off as useless once she'd moved on to bigger and better things.

At least, I thought college was going to be bigger and better. If I learn nothing new in the next two years, I should ask for a refund.

That made her smirk, and her fingers flew across her silent keyboard while the rest of the students were still pulling up the program and laying their foundations. Cheyenne could have paid for her entire graduate education ten times over without batting an eye; the money her grandparents had left her made sure of that. That would've been nice to have as a freshman, sure, but she'd gotten a full ride to Virginia Commonwealth University on academic scholarships, none of them manufactured on her end, so it wouldn't have made a difference.

And the way Mom talks about them, her parents were people who didn't think anyone could be responsible for anything until they were twenty-one.

She worked on the assignment until she felt like tearing her hair out in boredom. Then, she remembered a trick she'd learned with closed proxies and threw it in for fun. If Bergmann couldn't open it, all the better.

Cheyenne logged onto the school's slow wi-fi and attached her new code-baby to an email from her personal address. The university's email provider drove her nuts; despite having to work around sending files that were way too big for undergrad assignments, all her previous instructors had insisted on everything being sent that way. Bergmann, however, had provided her new students this semester with an alternate email address unencumbered by a crappy server.

Once she hit send, she reclined in her chair and closed her eyes. *I need to sleep.*

Five seconds later, a little *ding* came from Bergmann's computer. She watched the professor lean forward with a frown of curiosity, click a few times, then her eyes widened. She glanced over the top of her laptop at Cheyenne.

The half-drow glanced away and cleared her throat. She shut her computer and stood, turning toward the door.

"Do you have somewhere to be, Miss..."

"Cheyenne." *If she saw my name on a roster, she knows what it is.*

Bergmann smirked. "Miss Cheyenne."

"Just the bathroom." Cheyenne jerked her thumb toward the closed door. "Unless we're supposed to be locked up until ten."

The professor's eyes narrowed, and her laughter cut off. "Interesting choice of words for someone who opted to keep coming to school."

Some other students raised their heads from staring at the monitors and looked at Bergmann, then at Cheyenne. Most of them kept working, but Messy Bun wasn't one of them.

Cheyenne shrugged, although it took more effort to keep from getting pissed off. "I didn't think I had to raise my hand and ask permission."

"You don't." Bergmann leaned back in her chair. "I just want to make sure you have enough time to do the work before you head off to someone else's class."

Seriously? She just got my email.

"Yeah, I'm good." Cheyenne went toward the door, fighting not to jerk the handle off. That ribbon of tingling warmth was building at the base of her spine, and it distracted her enough she couldn't figure out why the door wouldn't open. "This door get jammed a lot?"

"Only when someone's trying to pull it open."

Cheyenne whipped her head over her shoulder to shoot the professor a confused look. "What?"

"It's a push-out door," Bergmann said. When her gaze darted toward the hair that was supposed to be covering Cheyenne's ears, the half-drow's stomach lurched. It made the heat crawling up her back stronger.

Cheyenne twisted the knob and pushed. The door shot out and banged against the wall. She didn't bother to catch it or close it again as she stormed toward the closest restroom. She didn't stop until she stood in front of the sink, then she splashed three rounds of cold water on her face.

That was the other thing she hadn't had time for this morning. Even with the piercings and the braid of her black hair tied tightly around her head, the chains and the black clothes, Cheyenne hadn't quite recognized herself with the makeup washed off in the shower last night. Even if she'd put any on this morning, she wouldn't have had the presence of mind to think twice about washing it off in the bathroom sink with water that sputtered and burst from the faucet.

Sighing through the cold wetness dripping off her face, she opened her eyes and stared at her reflection. "Shit."

They weren't there, but she'd expected them—the twin points of her half-drow ears poking up from the binding of her hair. She didn't miss the hint of gold light flashing behind her eyes, either. Her skin hadn't done much more than go a little darker at her fingertips and around her nails, but even that was enough for people to start asking questions. "No, it's not a phase," she whispered, imagining Peter's stupid smirk as she glared at the mirror. "This is my fucking life."

Clenching her teeth, she slapped another handful of water on her face, slammed the faucet back down with a dull thud, and almost left the bathroom before remembering she did have to go.

By the time she finished and washed her hands, every trace of her drow heritage had disappeared beneath the mask of a world-weary grad student who still hadn't outgrown her Goth phase. "They shoulda seen me in high school. But nobody saw me, did they?"

"What did you do to your face?"

"You're such a pretty girl. You don't need all that makeup."

"I'm sure your mother didn't raise you to mutilate yourself like that."

Just a bunch of judgmental crap from the few people who'd she'd been forced to meet in her life. Bianca had kept her isolated in their giant lodge off 653 in Henry County, surrounded by more trees and deer and occasionally black bears than people. That didn't mean Cheyenne hadn't gotten out as a kid, just not as much. "And four years in college still hasn't wiped all the weird out of me. Good."

With a nod at the mirror, Cheyenne took a deep breath, snatched a paper towel from the dispenser, and crumpled it up irritably to dry her hands. Without looking, she tossed it at the trashcan on her way out the door—she didn't turn back to see she hadn't missed. She didn't miss even when she tried.

When she stepped back inside Bergmann's classroom, no one stopped what they were doing to acknowledge her return. Not even the professor. Cheyenne quietly closed the door behind her, then went back to her chair in front of her closed laptop, and took a seat. It wasn't 9:00 a.m., and she'd completed all her other various class assignments over the weekend. So she pulled out her earbuds, jammed the jack into her phone and one bud into her ear, and pulled up an album of Rachmaninoff performed by a pianist who didn't look old enough to be out of high school.

Nothing like an angry Russian composer to get an angry chick to calm down. Godsmack wouldn't help right now.

She folded her arms and stared at the back of Messy Bun's head. The other student couldn't have felt Cheyenne's gaze on her, yet she turned around and shot the half-drow a contemptuous glare.

Cheyenne closed her eyes. *I bet she uses the word 'irksome' in everyday conversation.*

One and a half tracks later, Cheyenne didn't need to look at the clock to know class was over. Other students were packing up, getting ready to move onto some other class where they could gobble up more banal attempts at imparting knowledge.

She didn't take her earbuds out until Professor Bergmann stood from her chair and announced: "...if you want to get credit for it. And because Miss Arcady brought up an excellent point about not having been *assigned* the work, I'm telling you all right now that I want these brilliant bits of code in my inbox by eleven fifty-nine p.m. tomorrow night. I hope that's specific enough."

Bergmann smiled sweetly at Messy Bun, who returned a faker smile and jammed her bright-yellow folder into her expensive leather messenger bag. Cheyenne slipped her laptop into its sleeve and let it glide right into her backpack, then paused the Rachmaninoff and wound her earbuds around her phone. She wasn't the last one out, but that didn't seem to matter to the professor. "Cheyenne," Bergmann called, "can you spare a few minutes?"

"Uh..." Cheyenne slung her backpack over her shoulder and blinked, feeling a few curious glances her way, although none lingered long. "I have another class at—"

"Oh, so do I. We're both very busy, I know. It won't take long."

"Yeah, okay."

Cheyenne walked down the row between the long lab tables and stopped to lean back against one. Messy Bun didn't look at her at all as she sauntered past with her messenger bag thumping against her thigh. Peter raised an eyebrow and tried to smile. Cheyenne's deadpan stare saw him out of the classroom. When the last student cleared out, Professor Bergmann stepped past Cheyenne and pulled the door shut.

She turned, nodded, and licked her lips. "We have a problem, don't we?"

CHAPTER TEN

"What?" Cheyenne stuck her hands through the straps of her backpack over her shoulder and eyed her black-haired professor as the woman crossed the room again. "Did you look at what I sent you?"

Bergmann stopped behind her desk and started packing up her own computer and random academic paraphernalia. The handle of her wheeled briefcase still stretched up to its full length, and Cheyenne had an overwhelming urge to slam it back down into place where it belonged.

"Of course, I did."

"There was nothing wrong with my code." Cheyenne straightened away from the end of the lab table and gripped her backpack straps even tighter. "If you looked at it, you'd know that—"

"Only twenty-five percent of it was based on the given directives I laid out in my presentation. Yep." Bergmann nodded and zipped up her briefcase, then straightened. "That it's more complex than anything I've seen a student turn in, and I've been doing this for…well, longer than I'd like to admit. And let me just say that I found your proxy entryway while you were in the bathroom. Threw me for a loop for about sixty seconds, but I did find it. So nice try."

"Okay." Cheyenne stared at the handle of the woman's briefcase. "So what's the problem?"

"Well, hell, Cheyenne. We both know it's not your work." Finally, Bergmann peered at her, stuck a hand on her hip, and laughed. "You might not be able to learn anything from me this semester, seeing as you're already crushing it with the assignments. Only three classes in. Did you find that code somewhere, or are you telling me it really is yours?"

Cheyenne shook her head. "I didn't cheat if that's what you're asking."

"Hmm. No, I didn't peg you as someone who'd enjoy wasting both our time. So, like I said, this class might be pretty useless for you."

"You want me to drop out?"

"Don't put words in my mouth." The professor laughed again and tucked her dark hair behind her ear. "You can stay. Easy A for you, I have no doubt. If you're willing to go through the drudgery of turning in work you already understand. Hey, maybe you'll teach me a few new tricks. But what I *can* help you with is control."

Cheyenne cleared her throat. "What?"

"There's a side of you you don't want anyone else to see. Right?" Bergmann lifted a hand and wiggled the tip of her own ear, reaching for the handle of her roller briefcase without looking at her student. She glanced at her watch. "Boy, I hate schedules. Look, Cheyenne, I'm going to be late for my next class, which I enjoy slightly less than this one. If you're interested, I know I can teach you things that have nothing to do with computers or programming. You know my office hours."

With a fleeting grin, Professor Bergmann nodded and strode toward the classroom's exit, muttering something about always being late. The door didn't slam as it had when

Cheyenne stormed out for her bathroom break, but it was close.

The half-drow, hands tucked through the straps of her backpack, stared out into the hall. Students and professors and instructors passed by the open doorway, and for the first time in a long time, all the chaos and everything Cheyenne would normally have tried not to notice stayed out of her head.

"Seriously?" She lifted a hand to her ears, which still felt round and human beneath the tight binding of her braided hair. Yet, the professor had looked right at them before Cheyenne burst out of the classroom as if the woman had expected to see dark peaks popping up from beneath her hair. And the rest of the changes, she was pretty sure, had happened in the hall.

"How the hell did she know?"

She realized she'd been standing there like an idiot when she had another class to get to. Hissing through her teeth, she tightened her grip on her backpack straps and hurried into the hall. She pulled her phone out of her pocket to check the time, then shoved it back down again.

"Great. Four minutes to get across campus."

Somehow, it felt pointless to be rattled by being late to class in the second week. It wasn't like she was going to miss anything important in the first five minutes. Something felt like it was about to crash down around her all the same.

Although most of the other students seemed to take Advanced Social Media Network Analysis and Security seriously, to Cheyenne, it was a joke. The instructor was some old bald guy with patches of gray fluff sprouting from the sides of his head and ears.

Cheyenne stared at his mouth as he droned on.

Looks like he cut off the end of that beard and glued it over his ears.

The thought made her snort, which earned her a glance from the professor.

For an hour and a half, the man lectured. Everything went in one ear and out the other. *Oh, man.* Cheyenne rubbed her hands down her cheeks and stifled a yawn. *Everything's about ears now.*

She almost missed it when the instructor excused them at the end of class and said something about them needing to prepare for a pop quiz this week, maybe next week.

Her backpack felt heavy as she headed outside to cross the campus one more time. She had two classes on Tuesdays and Thursdays, giving her the rest of the afternoon to do whatever. Ten minutes later, she found herself in line at the food court in the Student Center. She didn't remember walking inside and getting in line, but her stomach's growls convinced her she'd been on autopilot.

Don't get lazy, Cheyenne. Three hours of sleep isn't an excuse.

The guy standing behind the counter nodded at her. "What do you need?"

"A nap."

He chuckled. "I hear most college kids get their beauty sleep in the library, but you're up next to order, so…"

"Sorry." Cheyenne shook her head, then pointed at a plastic container in a triangle shape. "Just one of those."

"Chicken salad sandwich. You got it."

She paid the guy and turned away with her boxed sandwich before he could ask if she wanted a receipt. She slumped in a chair at the closest unoccupied table and popped open the container.

The sandwich went into her mouth, and she didn't taste a single bite.

I don't need some hippy-skirt professor telling me how to hide. *I need to sleep. I need to go home and check my search. I need to find the orc asshole who brought a gun to a...*

The chicken salad sandwich stuck in her throat. She forced down the dry, painful lump and coughed. "Magical fight."

Can a girl get a glass of water?

Cheyenne glanced around when she realized she'd said that last part out loud, then shoved the sandwich container across the table and unzipped her backpack. Professor Bergmann's syllabus was in one of the three unmarked manila folders, clean and stapled neatly together with the woman's office hours on top: 1:00 – 4:00 p.m.

"Control the parts of me I don't want anyone else to see, huh? Yeah, she probably wouldn't still be so willing to help if she'd seen me last night." Cheyenne coughed again on the bread stuck in her throat and wished she'd thought to buy a bottle of water.

But if I knew how to control myself, maybe Ember wouldn't be in the hospital. Maybe she wouldn't have been shot.

That thought sent Cheyenne to her feet again. The chair behind her lurched back with a grating shriek against the floor, and her hand whipped out to catch it before it fell over. She scooted it in with her foot, strapped on her backpack, and snatched up the rest of her sandwich before heading to the IT building to find Professor Bergmann's office.

As she wove her way through the throngs of college students with enough money—or a big enough budget on their meal plan—to spend on the food court, she pulled her phone out of her pocket and glanced at the notifications screen through the earbud cord wrapped around it. No phone call from the hospital. No texts or alerts. If Ember was already recovering and headed home, she would have called or texted or something.

I can spare some time for an IT professor who thinks she knows what I am. Then I'll stop by for their stupid visiting hours.

CHAPTER ELEVEN

The door to the professor's office was closed, but even through the frosted glass window, Cheyenne could tell the lights were on. She'd made it to the office of Matilda Bergmann—typed right there on the removable paper card beside the door—at two minutes past 1:00 p.m. *At least she's not late to her own office hours.*

Cheyenne knocked on the door.

"Come in."

This was a "pull-in" kind of door, or at least it would have been if Cheyenne were standing on the inside of the office. She pushed it open and stepped into the small, tidy space the university had carved out for Professor Bergmann. For a few seconds, Bergmann didn't glance up from her computer at the L-shaped desk, and Cheyenne took a quick look around. "Huh."

"Cheyenne." The professor gazed at her and smiled. "I see the wheels turning, and that one non-word says a lot. What's wrong?"

The half-drow stuck out her bottom lip and shrugged. "Nothing's wrong. I…expected something else."

"You mean, like a sweet setup and a bunch of cool new tech

funded by the money this school doesn't have for its IT professors?" Bergmann laughed and stood, shuffling papers around before lifting herself enough to sit on the corner of the desk this time. "Turns out, I'm a regular professor with a regular office. Sorry to disappoint."

Cheyenne shrugged.

The room fell silent, and the older woman let out a patient sigh. "I'm glad you came. That's what I'm here for. I still can't help but ask *why* you came, though."

With raised eyebrows, Cheyenne stepped toward her professor's desk and stopped to look at the degrees and awards and plaques hanging on the office walls. "I still can't help but ask what you meant by 'controlling the parts of me I don't want anyone else to see.'"

Bergmann's eyes narrowed above a coy smile. "That's a very good question. I'm more than willing to answer it, and whatever other questions you might have that aren't so…academically focused, but I need you to do one thing for me first."

"What?"

"Shut the door, please."

Holding the woman's gaze, Cheyenne lowered her backpack to the floor beside the bench along the wall. She turned and shut the door with a soft *click*.

"Well, at least we know you *can* be gentle. With doors, at least." The professor chuckled at her own joke and gestured toward two narrow armchairs at the far end of her office. "Come take a seat, and we'll talk."

"I'm good right here." Cheyenne folded her arms and studied the woman's inquisitive smile.

"In case you decide I'm full of it and want to make a quick escape, huh?"

"More like in case I fall asleep in one of those chairs."

"You know, I have a hard time believing you weren't able to get enough sleep. How old are you? Twenty-one? Twenty-two?" Bergmann wagged a finger at her and went to sit in an armchair. "And don't tell me you spent all night drinking. From where I was sitting last night, you looked *very* awake."

Cheyenne's stomach lurched. "What did you say?"

"In the bar. With that friend of yours, right? The blonde girl in the leather jacket." Bergmann crossed one leg over the other in the armchair, pulling the edges of her tie-dyed skirt out from under her before letting it fall around her thighs again. "You're not gonna try to tell me that wasn't you, are you? That would be boring, and we both know I'm smarter than that."

With a quick glance at the closed office door, Cheyenne stepped hesitantly across the office toward the armchairs. "You were at Gnarly's last night?"

"One of my favorite awful places. You bet." Bergmann winked. "I was there. I saw *you* and your little bottle-crushing trick. I'm sure it was a mistake, but it caught my attention. We don't see too many halflings these days. Or ever."

Cheyenne's jaw clenched and unclenched as she tried to process what this woman was saying. "Next you're gonna be asking if you can touch my ears."

"Cheyenne—"

"Yeah, this was a mistake. I gotta go."

"No, you don't."

"You're the second person who's called me that in the last twenty-four hours. The first person got shot in the stomach, so it's safer for you if I head out." Cheyenne scooped her backpack up. *This was a stupid idea. I can't get into this now.*

"Cheyenne!"

"Don't worry, I'll be in class on Thursday, and we can pretend I'm learning something. No problem." She wrapped her hand around the doorknob, and a spark of silver light burst beneath her fingers and crackled across the door. Cheyenne jerked her hand away from the electric jolt and stared at the smoking metal doorknob.

She turned around. "What was that?"

"You tell me."

Cheyenne's grip tightened on the strap of her backpack, and she stepped away from the door. "I didn't have to come to your office if I wanted to answer my own questions."

The professor's smile bloomed, and her hazel eyes danced with a light that wasn't the reflection of the track lighting. It looked more predatory than Cheyenne wanted to admit.

"Okay, look." Bergmann folded her hands in her lap and raised her eyebrows. "I told you to stop by, and I meant what I said. We already established you don't need my help with your classes or anything I could offer you toward your next degree, which I sense you'll earn. But I *would* like to cut the shit on this other topic because what you came to my office to talk about is a lot more important than a piece of paper saying you've played the game of higher education. Got it?"

A chuckle of surprise burst through Cheyenne's lips. "That was magic."

"Yes. It was. Wanna ask me what kind?"

"Honestly?" Cheyenne dropped her backpack and headed toward the armchair and her computer programming professor. "I want you to tell me what you think you know about me."

"Sure, let's cut to the chase. After I tell you to call me Mattie."

"Mattie."

Bergmann cocked her head. "Matilda's a name better suited for a cat lady. Or a crone sitting around playing knucklebones with her—" The woman stopped when she noticed Cheyenne's disbelieving frown and waved her last thought aside. "Never mind. Just Mattie."

"Sure."

"And take a seat."

Cheyenne pressed her lips together and lowered herself

into the narrow chair across from her professor. "Ready when you are. Mattie."

"Perfect." The woman grinned and relaxed. "Now, please tell me you weren't serious about walking out."

The only reply Cheyenne gave was a twitch of her head—it felt too heavy to shake any more—as she squinted and chewed the inside of her lip.

"Wow." Mattie's eyes widened, and there was that flash of light that wasn't light again. "You've got me beat with course content, but I get to be the expert on *you*, huh? This'll be fun." She rubbed her hands together. "How much time do you have?"

"As much time as it takes," Cheyenne muttered. "As long as what you tell me makes any kinda sense."

"I like your attitude, kid. We'll work on that too."

CHAPTER TWELVE

"You must help me out a little here, though." Mattie leaned forward and winked. "I know you're smart enough to figure out what the word halfling might mean."

"Half-human." Cheyenne glanced at her hands, then peered at the wall behind Mattie's armchair. "Half something else."

"And in your case, that something else would be?"

When Cheyenne still wasn't forthcoming with the information her professor wanted, the older woman rolled her eyes. "This is a give and take kinda thing, Cheyenne. I need to gauge how much you understand before I spout a bunch of information you may or may not be ready to hear. So what is it? Half-human and half..."

"Drow. I think." Cheyenne cleared her throat.

"Thank you. Drow. That's an old word for an even older race. Do you know what it means?"

Cheyenne shrugged. "Some kind of elf."

"Some kind... Are you not going to take this seriously?"

"Not when it feels like you're trying to drag me around in circles." The half-drow's nose wrinkled, and the chains on her wrists jingled when she reached up to scratch the back of her neck. "I'm waiting to see if coming to you was a good idea."

"When you know nothing and someone who knows about magic comes along and says they can help you, it's a good idea to take advantage of the offer. Unless they're trying to sell you someone else's organs."

"What?"

Mattie shook her head. "Let's table that for later. The drow aren't just any kind of elf."

"Yeah, I know. Dark elf, which is why my skin changes color, and my hair goes all freaky white, and I can't control myself. Next."

The professor pursed her lips. "And you first heard the term 'halfling' yesterday, huh?"

Cheyenne propped her arms on the armrests and shook her head. "It's not like I grew up clueless about what makes me different. When I couldn't figure it out by myself, my mom..." She stopped and frowned. *I need to stop talking.*

"Your mom. Right. Well, it doesn't surprise me Bianca Summerlin would know enough to give you at least a few pieces of the puzzle."

"I don't wanna talk about my mom."

Mattie appeared puzzled. "Why not?"

"She's not... She has nothing to do with this."

More like she has no idea what I can do, and she doesn't know how to use or handle or even recognize magic. Cheyenne pushed her tongue against the back of her teeth and forced herself not to get up out of that armchair.

"That's a little simplistic, don't you think?"

"No." The half-drow shifted in her chair. "Beyond her giving birth to me, she has nothing to do with this. I don't need you to explain to me where halfling babies come from."

"Well, isn't *that* a major relief?"

Cheyenne rolled her eyes but couldn't help a small smile as

she avoided Mattie's gaze. "You're making fun of me."

"Me? No way." Mattie smirked and shook her head. "So your mother told you what you are. Does she know who your dad is?"

"Nope. He has even less to do with this than she does."

"I understand. It's tough trying to make things work in a world most people don't know exists." The professor held up a finger when Cheyenne opened her mouth. "We can get to that later. I'm trying to get to the part about me giving you useful information."

Cheyenne shut her mouth and huffed an airy chuckle.

"You put two and two together, Cheyenne. A halfling is half human and half something else; in your case, half-drow. Most people, magicals included, are shocked and certainly skeptical to see, hear, or even *smell* a halfling."

Ember's words at the bar the night before came trickling into Cheyenne's head. "Because everyone thinks halflings are just a myth, right?"

"Listen to you. Well done." Mattie shifted and crossed her legs in the opposite direction, then spread her arms. "There are plenty of documented magicals here."

"In Richmond?"

"All over the world. That's kept under wraps, for obvious reasons. But, in all the time I've spent on this side of the Border, you're the first halfling who hasn't been a myth. You're very real. Or I've lost my mind. But the point is—"

"What Border?" Cheyenne leaned forward, thinking of the orc and the same thing he'd said at the skatepark. Her lower spine felt warm.

"That's something we can get into later."

"I heard someone else talking about a Border too. And a… portal." Despite wanting to tread carefully, Cheyenne couldn't keep her voice from rising in volume. "What is it?"

"Cheyenne, we need to ease into this."

"We don't *need* to do anything. You said you could help me, and I want to know what—"

"Enough!" Mattie slammed her fist on the armrest, and a crackle of silver light erupted across the fabric.

Cheyenne's skin tingled. She stopped asking questions and stared at her professor's fist.

Mattie blinked, took a breath, and dipped her head. "I'm sorry. I'm realizing I didn't start this off the way I should have. So, you won't like the next thing out of my mouth, Cheyenne, but it must be said. After that, it's up to you whether you want what I'm offering."

"I'm all e—" The half-drow stopped and grimaced at the saying. She sat back in the chair.

"All ears." Mattie chuckled. "The irony's not lost on me, either. You ready to listen?"

Cheyenne gestured with a sarcastic flair toward her professor. The chains on her wrists jingled against each other. "I'm still here. Let's do this."

Mattie studied her student with a predatory glint in her eye. She didn't seem fazed by Cheyenne's sarcasm or her impatient scowl. "Fantastic. You have questions. How could you not? Bear in mind, anything that doesn't apply to you personally, Cheyenne, I can't answer. Whatever you thought you heard someone else say, leave it alone for now. I'm not the person to answer those kinds of questions, and even if I were, I wouldn't consider it until I knew you had a handle on your drow abilities and everything that makes you...well, you. The only thing I *can* teach you is how to control your magic. At least, to the best of my knowledge and your willingness to follow someone else's lead."

Cheyenne blinked. "To the best of your knowledge?"

"Yep."

"Do I have to ask how many other drow you've taught?"

Mattie glanced at the ceiling in amusement. "'Trained' has a better ring to it, yeah? And no, you don't have to ask. I'll tell you. I've met only a handful of drow in my lifetime, and I trained none of them. Beyond that, you're the first halfling I've ever seen in the flesh. Of either color. So this is the perfect opportunity for us both."

"Doesn't sound like it." Cocking her head, Cheyenne tried to wipe the smile of disbelief off her face, but it wouldn't budge. "Taking advice from someone who's never trained a drow or a halfling doesn't sound like my best option."

"How so?"

"Huh. I don't know. Maybe just the *insignificant* fact neither of us knows what we're doing." The half-drow offered an exaggerated shrug, her arms spread wide over the armrests. "And you're not making a strong case."

"Hmm." Stroking her chin again, Mattie feigned consideration and nodded. She stared past Cheyenne's armchair at the blank wall of her office. "You want a strong case? Well, I worked with hundreds of orcs before I came through. Hundreds. So, training you should be a piece of cake."

Cheyenne leaned over her lap, casting her professor a sidelong glance as if she might have heard her wrong. "You did what now?"

"Orcs. And, new rule, we never bring that up again after today."

A huff of surprise escaped the half-drow. "What are the *old* rules?"

Mattie tossed a dismissive hand in the air. "There aren't any. I'm making this up as I go."

"And I'm not an *orc!*"

"Neither am I. Didn't stop me from being the best damn… well, from doing my job."

Cheyenne shook her head and stared at her programming professor. "Show me."

"*That's* what I was waiting to hear." Mattie grinned. "I'm

glad your decision—"

"I've not decided. Not yet." The half-drow squinted at the other woman and looked her up and down from the top of Mattie's wavy black hair to her neon-yellow Chucks. "Show me why you're so sure you can do this."

Mattie's eyes narrowed. She stiffened. "Oh, I can do this. Trust me."

"Prove it. "

Professor Bergmann didn't break Cheyenne's gaze, even when the woman's fingers bent and curled in her lap in a complicated pattern. The air around Mattie's body shimmered, then she changed—same height, same dark hair, same hazel eyes, only backlit by a soft golden light now, the pupils widened and elongated into something inhuman. Like cat eyes. Her lips parted in a feral smile and revealed sharp white teeth. Cheyenne expected a few whiskers to sprout beside that smile. Mattie's flattened nose twitched.

"What *are* you?" Cheyenne whispered.

"What I've always been." Mattie's voice was lower, smoother, and filled with amusement. "And that's none of your business. You're not here to learn about me or how I do what *I* do. Everything you need to know about harnessing your magic and making it do what *you* want, I can and will show you. Believe me, Cheyenne, I haven't survived this long by mere luck. And, as far as I can tell, luck is the only thing on your side right now."

Cheyenne studied her professor's feline appearance. *If I had luck on my side, I wouldn't have missed that stupid orc last night. I would've made him pay, and I would've kept Ember out of the hospital.*

"Luck runs out," Mattie added. "Unless you learn how to make your own." Her hands moved together in an even quicker pattern. She pulled them apart, and the human guise of Professor Bergmann returned.

"That's what you're calling it?" Cheyenne smirked. "Making your own luck?"

"Some people think that's what magic is. I can show you so much more. This is just an illusion for me." Mattie gestured toward her face. "Like wearing a piece of jewelry without ever taking it off. And it's served me well. You, though? Using makeup and nose rings and this whole getup," she eyed Cheyenne's black shirt with the safety pins studded around the collar, "to hide what you are. I'm guessing that doesn't work during intense situations."

"You could say that." Cheyenne rubbed the corner of her eye and fought back a wry laugh. "So, let's begin with you showing me how to do that whole illusion thing."

"No." Mattie folded her hands in her lap again. "Halflings don't need an illusion to hide in this world. You need *control.* Over yourself, your abilities, and your emotions. Without control, you're a sparkler over gunpowder."

Cheyenne snorted. "I don't need a therapist."

"I have enough students coming to me with their problems, trust me." With a sigh, Mattie tipped her head back and peered at the ceiling. A dreamy smile grew on her lips. "You might just be the only one I can teach to get over them."

The office fell silent. The professor didn't move for long enough to make it feel like she'd forgotten about Cheyenne being there.

The half-drow cleared her throat. "So, when are we gonna do this?"

Mattie glanced at her wristwatch and shrugged. "Office hours, Cheyenne. Might as well do *something* useful with them."

A flutter of excitement churned in Cheyenne's stomach. She forced it down and pressed her lips together.

I'm about to start training with drow magic. For real.

"Yeah, now's good."

CHAPTER THIRTEEN

"Now is always the best time to do anything worthwhile." Mattie slapped the armrests with a dull *thump* and pushed to her feet. "Get up."

Cheyenne did as she was told, staring at the tie-dyed skirt whisking around her professor's ankles as Mattie walked to the other side of her office. *It's gonna take a while not to see a cat in a skirt when I look at her.*

"Come on. Show me what you got." Mattie waved her student away from the armchairs into the center of her office.

"Show you *what?*" Cheyenne's feet whispered across the decades-old carpet until Mattie lifted a hand to stop her.

"What you can do." With a curt nod, Mattie eyed her student and gestured at the few feet of space between them. "We already made the mistake of assuming I could teach you anything in class, so let's get on the same page. Show me what you've got a good handle on already."

"Um." Cheyenne blinked and shook out her hands. The chains clanked against each other, muted by her sleeves. "I mean, I can't do what *you* just did."

"Obviously." Startled by her own short laugh, Mattie shook her head but didn't stop smiling. "Go ahead."

She thinks I can just pull this up on command? Cheyenne glanced at her open palms and shrugged. "Sure."

She thought about the orc-thug party she'd crashed last night at the skatepark. About the magic she'd unleashed on all of them without even thinking. But standing here in her professor's office didn't bring a fresh new wave of inspiration. *Sounds like she wants a trick. Just summon a light or something.* Focusing on one hand, Cheyenne curled her fingers and tried to pull up the soft glow she'd used instead of a flashlight to light her forts as a kid, before she figured out computers were a lot more interesting than a tent made of blankets and chairs. *Come on!*

The blue glow pulsed for a second in the center of her palm. A long bulb in the light fixture overhead flared, then burst with a *pop*. Shattered glass rained onto the armchairs. *Okay, screw that idea.*

She lifted her head to look at Mattie and shrugged.

Professor Bergmann studied the glass on her furniture and floor with raised eyebrows, then tapped a finger on her lips. "Huh."

"Hey, it's something."

"It is." The corner of Mattie's mouth twitched. "You can quit playing games now. That should be a new rule too. I know it's hard to trust another magical you just met—officially, at least—so if it helps, I promise I have nothing to gain from this but satisfaction for not being completely useless to you."

"Okay. That's awesome, I guess." Cheyenne glanced away to avoid seeing Mattie's expression when she admitted, "I don't know what you want me to do."

Mattie gave her an exaggerated laugh. "Oh, come on. Do whatever you think will give me enough of an overview that we can lay the missing groundwork. I won't say you *have* to remove all the glass from the floor and my chairs, but it'd be a nice start."

The half-drow chewed the inside of her lower lip and raised an eyebrow. "Got a broom?"

"What?" The way Mattie cocked her head and turned away from her student seemed much like a cat listening to birds in the yard. "Please don't tell me the drow halfling hasn't learned how to cast a spell beyond a flash of light and an accidental lightbulb burst."

"No problem." Cheyenne folded her arms. "I can do more than that."

"So?" The professor gestured toward the open space between them again with a tight, expectant smile. "I'm ready to drop the games."

"Yeah, me too. But this whole magic-on-command thing isn't my style."

"Uh-huh." By the time Mattie finished sighing, the predatory glint in her eyes had returned. "Okay, I get it. You've been doing things on your terms your whole life, and now I'm asking you to do them on mine. I don't want to pressure you into anything. When you're ready to come back and put some effort into learning how to control your magic, I'll be here. Every day. From one to four." She gestured toward her closed office door and dipped her head.

Oh, sure. It's always attitude and willful disobedience from the Goth chick, isn't it? Cheyenne rolled her eyes and didn't move. "I'm ready to put in the effort now," she muttered.

"It looks to me more like you're trying to turn this into a powerplay, and that's not what I'm interested in." Mattie turned away from her and went back to her L-shaped desk. "I'm aware of where I stand in the scheme of things. And I have better things to do with my time than spend it on a halfling who pretends to be, I don't know, whatever the hell you're going for right now."

The warmth at the base of Cheyenne's spine was soft, but it stayed there, a gentle reminder of how far she couldn't let this go. "Hold up. You're the one who came to me." She stepped toward Mattie's desk. "*You* told me to come by your office. Trust me, I have better things to do with my time too, Mattie."

Mattie didn't look up at her as she shuffled through more papers on her desk. "Yes, I know you're very busy with all the graduate work you complete in a quarter of the time it takes everyone else. It must be difficult for you to find time for anything."

"That has nothing to do with it." Cheyenne swallowed. The heat rose. She balled her hands into fists to force it back down. "If I didn't want to be here, I wouldn't have come."

"Show me you want to be here."

"I didn't think I'd be joining the circus and have to perform for you."

"That's not an excuse."

"I'm not giving an excuse. Why can't you show me how to keep anyone else from seeing what I am?" The half-drow's skin tingled, warmth spreading over her shoulders. *Not now!*

"Without understanding the skills you already have? I don't think so." Mattie tucked her hair behind her ear, still scanning the papers on her desk, and snatched a pen from the glass jar beside her computer. She started writing something. "You can forget we ever had this conversation if you can't give me something to work with."

"I don't know *how*!" Cheyenne's hands flew up in front of her face in frustration. An orb of black energy burst from between them and headed for the pen in her professor's hand.

The fingers of Mattie's other hand twitched in a small, hidden gesture, and the halfling's magic orb froze a hair's breadth away from the pen. The professor smiled at the magic hissing and crackling in a churning mass in front of her, then she flicked her gaze toward Cheyenne and stared at the half-drow with narrowed eyes. "I think you do."

Cheyenne released a breath through her clenched teeth. Her nostrils flared. "When I'm pissed off, yeah."

"Good." The pen dropped from Mattie's hand and clattered to the desk. Her empty hand moved beneath the sparking black magic like she meant to grab it. Then her other hand, finger still twisted in command, passed over the top of the static orb. Her lips moved almost imperceptibly. Anyone else in the room wouldn't have heard a thing, or maybe the barest whisper, yet Cheyenne's drow hearing caught the entire spell.

Great. Sounds like magic has its own language too.

Mattie pressed her hands around her student's unintended attack, and the black energy shrank between her palms. The purple sparks flaring inside grew brighter and more violent as the churning mass reduced in size until with a sharp *pop*, it disappeared. Mattie clenched her bottom hand into a fist and straightened behind her desk. "You know what you can do and how, Cheyenne. Looks like we need to work on the when and the why."

When the professor flung her hand toward the half-drow, something dark flew, glinting under the light. Cheyenne moved without thinking and caught whatever it was.

Mattie grinned.

Still fighting against the tingling heat in her back and shoulders, Cheyenne forced herself to open her hand and look down at the metallic diamond shape in her palm, its four points elongated and thinned out to look like a star. "What is this?"

"Call it a souvenir." Professor Bergmann nodded and stepped out from behind her desk. "And maybe a reminder *not* to attack your mentor when things get a little heated."

"Time to drop the games, huh?" Cheyenne pocketed the four-pointed star, then folded her arms and tipped her head back to eye her professor. "You knew that would happen."

"Perhaps. Just so you know, I rarely enjoy getting under someone's skin on the off-chance they might cast a spell with really nasty side effects."

"Sure, you don't."

"You almost blew my hand off. Granted, I was being an asshole on purpose." Mattie pointed at the halfling. "Is that a smile?"

Cheyenne pretended to be a lot more interested in the degrees and plaques on the walls. "No."

"Okay." Rubbing her hands together, Mattie scanned her student and nodded. "Now we know what we're working with."

When Cheyenne realized why the other woman was looking at her like she was a plastic ball filled with catnip, she jerked her head down to see the dark gray-purple flesh of her drow heritage peeking out from the ends of her black sleeves. "Shit."

Both hands flew to her hair, and she spun away from the professor so she wouldn't have to look at the woman and feel for the points of her ears at the same time. She pulled her hair, which had now gone from High-Voltage-Raven-black to drow-bone-white, trying to cover the thing people saw first.

"I think we're past the point of you trying to hide that from me." Mattie chuckled and stepped toward her student. "You can stop."

Cheyenne pressed both palms against her head and turned back around. "It's everywhere, isn't it?"

Her professor licked her lips, smiling, and gazed at the transformed halfling in front of her. "You look like a drow, all right. It's a shame you hide that on this side. We all do, but you?" Mattie clicked her tongue, shook her head, and crossed her office again. "This is how we're gonna start."

"We're gonna start." Cheyenne dropped her hands from her

head and glanced at their dark color again. "This goes away after a few minutes."

"Well, find your angry place."

"I just gotta let myself cool off— Wait, what?" Cheyenne blinked, opened her mouth, then shut it again. *My angry place?*

"Don't cool off," Mattie added. "I'm assuming you can feel it when you're about to transform, right?"

With a snort, Cheyenne rolled her shoulders. "Like being set on fire. So, yeah. Kinda hard not to feel."

"Hmm. Excellent. Stay in that place."

"That's not a good idea."

Mattie wagged a finger at her student and circled her office, taking in every angle of the drow-presenting halfling. "It's the best idea I've had all day. Before you can master keeping your drow blood down, you need to know how to 'get it up,' so to speak." The woman chuckled and shrugged.

"Seriously?"

"It's an accurate metaphor."

"Not really." Cheyenne stared at the ceiling, feeling the professor's eyes on her as the other woman completed her circle of study.

Mattie stopped in front of the halfling and cocked her head. "I'm trying. Help me out a little. Oh, look at that!"

"What?" Another glance at her hands made Cheyenne reach up to feel the rounding points of her ears. She shook her head. "I told you, it goes away after a few minutes."

"Okay. Bring it *back*." Mattie's eyes glinted. "Would it help if I slapped you?"

"It wouldn't help *you*."

"Maybe not. We'll save that method for later. Right now, it's time to work on making yourself angry."

Cheyenne eyed her professor.

She's insane. Maybe that's what I need. "My angry place."

"Your *drow* place. Or at least much closer to it. Go ahead. I'll wait." Once Mattie had taken a few steps back and folded her arms, the office fell silent.

"This is what fish in an aquarium feel like." Cheyenne shook her head. "I wonder if they can get pissed on demand too."

"You're searching for the source of what drives your magic. Let's start with… Oh. Don't think I didn't catch it when you told me about someone getting shot in the stomach."

Cheyenne stiffened. *Ember.*

"On a scale of one to ten, how does that feel in terms of rage fuel?"

The heat flared along the half-drow's skin, and it washed over her like a flash this time. Cheyenne drew a long, steadying breath.

"Okay." Mattie nodded, her smile widening. "I struck a nerve."

"She's my friend."

"That must be hard."

"Ya think?" Cheyenne spat.

"Yep. I'd be pissed if one of my friends got shot. Did you see it happen?"

A low, warning growl escaped the half-drow's throat.

"Right." Mattie tapped a finger against her lips again, studying her student's face. Cheyenne's eye twitched. "And you wished you could've done something about it."

"I *did* something about it," Cheyenne hissed. "Just not enough. The asshole got away."

"Oh, yeah? What'd you do? Tell him to stop or else?"

"You know what?" Cheyenne's teeth ground together, and she glared at her professor. "Maybe I should just think about *you* when I'm trying to get pissed."

"Hey, if that's what works." Grinning, Mattie leaned sideways to watch the halfling from a different angle that didn't make sense, then snapped her fingers and lifted her hand in front of her face, pointing at Cheyenne. "There. Right there. *That's* the black fire in your eyes. Hold onto that."

"And do *what?*" The words came out with surprising effort. Every muscle in Cheyenne's body burned with the heat and all the rage she'd unleashed on a bunch of moronic orcs in the skatepark. She saw Ember in her arms, covered in blood, and heard the soft, slow whisper of her friend's pulse.

"Nothing." Mattie didn't take her gaze from her student's. The smile was gone. "Just keep it there, Cheyenne. Sit with it. Keep thinking of your friend if you feel it slipping. Embrace it. Really feel it."

"I'm gonna make *you* feel it if you don't stop talking about it." Purple and black sparks burst from Cheyenne's fingertips and dropped on the carpet.

Mattie eyed the floor but didn't seem to think the fire-hazard carpet was worth more attention than that. "Can you stay there without me poking the drow bear?"

A thicker spray of sparks erupted from Cheyenne's fingers when she spread them wide. Her chest heaved, and a tremble appeared in her arm before she stomped it down. "I can stay here."

"Perfect." With a sharp flick of her wrist and another quick spellcasting gesture, Mattie sent a soft neon-yellow light into the air in front of them. The light rearranged itself into floating numbers—0:00. A timer began.

Cheyenne grunted and held the rage and the sparks at her fingertips and the fire inside that made her drow—or half, at least. "You started a magical timer. It better just be for this. 'Cause I don't run laps or anything."

Mattie glanced around her office and pursed her lips. "I imagine you'd need more space for something like that. In here, anyway."

CHAPTER FOURTEEN

"This is ridiculous." Cheyenne paced across Professor Bergmann's office, purple sparks occasionally bursting from her hands and trailing behind her.

"Ridiculous and necessary." Mattie sat on the edge of one armchair and crossed her legs, one foot bouncing up and down.

"It's a universal truth that bottling everything up is bad for you." When Cheyenne shook out her hands, another spray of sparks erupted, some of them landing close to the bookshelf against the wall filled with binders and loose papers.

The professor's foot stopped swinging. "That's what you *were* doing. Now you're releasing. Let it all out."

"No, I'm not," the halfling growled. "This is like having to sneeze without being able to."

"And for…" Mattie glanced at the neon timer she'd conjured midair. "Almost fifteen minutes. At least you keep beating your own records."

Cheyenne stopped short, spun toward her professor, and nodded. "I'm ready."

"To keep practicing? Absolutely. The clock's still running."

"No, I'm ready to *do* something. Magic. Training. Let's go."

"That's what you're doing, Cheyenne. This is—"

"Just *stop*!" The half-drow spread her arms, and even more sparks flared. "Stop telling me to *stay here*. If you're gonna train me, train me. I'm in my angry place. Do your job."

"Oh, it's *my* job now, huh?" Mattie nodded. "If you can pay more than my tenure, we'll call it official."

I can, and she knows it. Instead of saying anything about it, Cheyenne cocked her head and released more of her "angry place" into a continuous shower of sparks raining all over the floor. Thin wisps of smoke rose from the carpet. "Teach me how to fight the way I want to. With control."

Mattie's eyes widened at her student's volatile magic. "Okay, okay." She stood and dusted off her hands. Another few gestures with her fingers made the singed carpet around Cheyenne's feet hiss within summoned puddles of water. The smoke cleared and filtered into the air. "Good thing I turned off the smoke detectors."

Cheyenne glanced at the ceiling. "Sorry."

"Don't worry about it. So." The professor stopped in front of the dark-skinned, white-haired, and eager student with drow magic humming through her. "If you want control over your abilities, you need to give it up."

"Yeah, that didn't work so well."

"Right." Mattie spread her arms and stepped back. "So, what were you *trying* to do when it didn't work so well?"

"I was trying to fry the asshole with a gun in his hand." Cheyenne hissed out a disgusted breath. "I almost had him. I think."

"You think. Huh. Do you even know what you were thinking?"

"My friend got shot by an orc," Cheyenne growled. "Was I supposed to be thinking about something else?"

"Yes. You need to think of everything else. And nothing. Got it?"

"Just tell me what to do."

Narrowing her eyes, Mattie performed another series of gestures, then raised her hand behind her and flicked her wrist. The jar of pens on her desk rattled and floated through the air. It stopped a few feet away. "Put something in the jar."

"What?"

"In the jar, Cheyenne. A pebble. A hair. Those cute little sparks."

"Cute?"

"Focus." Mattie held the halfling's gaze and tilted her head. "Put something in the jar."

Cheyenne's nostrils flared, and she turned her attention to the floating jar of pens. In one swift motion, her arm came up, and a column of purple and black sparks exploded from her hand. It shot over the jar by two feet and smashed against a framed certification on the back wall. The glass shattered, the frame thumped to the carpet, and the paper certificate burst into flame.

"Okay. Time to call it." Mattie sent the floating jar back to her desk, then muttered another spell and shot a stream of water onto the burning paper and frame against the wall. "You can come back tomorrow."

"I'll try again." Cheyenne nodded at the professor's desk, thrumming with energy and a need to get *something* done. "I can do it."

"I know you can."

"So pick up the jar."

"No. It's almost four, anyway. I have a life too, believe it or not. And you need to take a break." Mattie stepped toward the halfling and set a gentle hand on her shoulder. "Time to leave the angry place."

"Seriously?" The corner of Cheyenne's mouth twitched. "I

don't need a break. I've been standing here getting ready to do something, so let me do something."

"You've done enough." Mattie removed her hand and glanced at the soaked and charred mess. "Hey, look at that. Seventeen minutes and twenty-one seconds. New record."

"You're making me leave because I burned a stupid piece of paper?"

"Burn all my stupid pieces of paper, Cheyenne." Mattie turned and pointed at the office door. "Tomorrow."

The sparks in Cheyenne's hands fizzled out. She took a deep breath and glanced away from the professor. "I can't leave like this."

"I guess you'd better figure out how to look like a Goth grad student again, huh? You have as long as it takes for me to pack my things." With a lifted eyebrow, Mattie turned toward her desk and started piling papers into stacks.

"That's the part you said you could teach me."

"We'll get there." The professor jammed a stack of binders into her wheeled briefcase and paused. "Try thinking of a happy place instead."

"You just told the Goth to find her happy place. I'm *in* my happy place." Cheyenne's back and shoulders still burned, but it was lighter now. Softer.

"Call it whatever you want, then. Rainbows and unicorns, maybe. Sunshine?"

The half-drow almost choked on her disbelief. "You do not understand what you're doing."

"Neither do you. Not yet, anyway." Tucking her dark hair behind her ear, Mattie zipped her briefcase and grabbed the raised metal handle. "You did better than I thought you would."

"Super encouraging."

"Don't let it go to your head." With a wink, Mattie stepped around her desk and pulled the briefcase behind her. She stopped for a last glance at her student and tilted her head in cat-like consideration, then glanced at her watch. "Okay. You can't leave looking like that."

"Hey, thanks. That's helpful." Cheyenne turned her dark, slate-gray hands over and scoffed. "Hadn't thought about that."

"Take your time. Just don't shut the door until you're ready to leave for the night. I've rigged this place to cut the lights and lock itself. And there's an alarm."

"Anybody gonna show up looking for you?"

Mattie was already halfway out the door, and she didn't stop as she called over her shoulder, "Office hours are done. Says so outside the door. Nobody ever looks for me here after four o'clock."

Then the programming professor was gone, her Chucks squeaking on the linoleum floor of the hall, which echoed with the rolling hum of the briefcase's wheels.

"Great." Cheyenne turned away from the door and stalked toward the back of Professor Bergmann's office. *Some training. Might as well just teach a dog to throw its own ball.* When she looked up, her gaze settled on the jar of pens on Mattie's desk. *I can just do it myself.*

She pointed with careful aim at the jar. A stream of purple light darted from her finger, missed the jar, and blasted a dime-sized crater in the thin office wall behind the desk.

"Or I can take a break." Cheyenne sighed and went to ruffle her hair before remembering she'd braided it. "After I cool off and lighten up." She glanced at her dark-gray hands.

After two minutes of pacing, she realized she had to take her mind off being in Bergmann's office with nothing to show for it. She shoved a hand into her pocket and took out her phone, then removed her earbuds cord and looked at the screen. No missed calls or messages. She took a chance and called Ember's phone. Her friend's voicemail greeting played by the time she stuck one earbud into her ear, so she ended the call. *All that means is that she's still in the hospital. Or...*

Cheyenne shook her head and jammed the earbuds into her ears. "Don't go there. She's still in the hospital."

With a few swipes, she pulled up more classical music, this time by Liszt, and tapped play with the volume turned all the way up. *Only way to drown out everything else.*

For a few seconds, she stood in the office, eyes closed, arms folded, listened to the symphony blasting through her earbuds. She took a few deep breaths, then glanced at her hands. Pale, human skin. Snatching up the end of her braid, she pulled it forward over her shoulder to see the dyed black color seeping back into the thick white strands. "It worked! Great."

Cheyenne kept the earbuds in and dropped her phone into her pocket. After slinging her backpack over her shoulder, she took a last glance at her professor's office. *If she can't teach me how to keep the drow under wraps, I'm gonna have to glue headphones into my ears. Or wear a hat.*

She stepped into the hall and pulled the office door closed behind her. A tingle crawled up her fingers just before she released the doorknob. The lights went off, the lock turned on its own, and the office locked itself.

"Yeah, nice trick."

CHAPTER FIFTEEN

Cheyenne left the music on and one earbud in as she stepped into the main lobby of the VCU Medical Center. It was still a hospital, still sterile and depressing, but at least it wasn't the ER. And it wasn't as full of people. The man sitting behind the front desk didn't have a lot of tact in watching her approach.

"Shoulda seen me last night," she muttered, raising her eyebrows.

"I'm sorry. What?" He blinked and leaned forward, but he just couldn't seem to take his eyes off the ring of safety pins studded through her shirt collar.

"I'm here to see a friend."

The guy's eyes lifted and settled on her lip ring before he cleared his throat. "Your friend's a patient here?"

"Yeah. Ember Gaderow. They admitted her last night."

"Sure." The receptionist met her gaze and nodded.

Guess they don't see the same kinda horrors over here as in the ER.

Cheyenne pointed at the outdated computer monitor between them. "I don't know what room she's in, so could you..."

"Huh?"

"Look her up? Please and thank you."

"Right. Right, sorry." The man blinked and got to typing.

Wow. People still get jobs typing that slow?

"Ember…what was the last name?"

"Gaderow." Cheyenne shifted her weight onto one leg and folded her arms.

"Date of birth?"

"Really?"

Her reaction startled him. "Well, I mean, I need it for the system."

Cheyenne glanced at the ceiling and tried to remember. "Yeah, it's March twenty-sixth. Two thousand one."

The keys clicked with agonizing slowness beneath the guy's not-so-nimble fingers. His eyes widened when he pulled up the next screen.

Here it comes. Say it.

"And your name?"

"Cheyenne." She unfolded her arms and stuck her hands in her pockets, but they both knew he was waiting for her to give him her full name. "Yeah, Cheyenne Summerlin. I know you're looking at my name right now. So, can you just tell me what room she's in?"

The receptionist cocked his head and looked from his screen to Cheyenne and back again. His mouth opened without sound before he found his voice on the third or fourth try. "Room 218."

"Cool." She nodded and stepped away from the front desk.

"Would you like a map, Ms. Summerlin? Or directions to—"

"You know what…" Cheyenne leaned toward the desk to read the name on the badge that hung from a lanyard around his neck. "Toby? I'm good."

"Well…"

She made haste, not wanting to let that mess of a conversation go on any longer. *My last name doesn't make me any less capable of reading the freakin' signs.*

And the signs were everywhere, pointing with large, colorful letters down the various branching hallways. Cheyenne double-timed it toward the ICU. She passed room after room, the doors closed for privacy. Then she stopped in front of Room 218, also with a closed door, and took a heavy breath. The handle turned beneath her fingers, and she slipped into a room darkened by drawn curtains over the windows.

The bed was against the right-hand wall, just like all the monitors beside it, blinking their different-colored lights and reaching out with cords and tubes and cables like so many fingers. *Just to keep her lying there like that.*

Cheyenne didn't need to look at the heart rate monitor or study the rise and fall of the green light flashing across the screen. She could hear her friend's heartbeat, still slow but stronger than it had been the night before.

She crossed the room while staring at the thin form beneath the hospital-issue sheets. Ember looked more dead than alive, lying on her back with her head sunken into the pillow, both arms straight at her sides above the comforter. Cheyenne caught the glint of a metal contraption peeking out from beneath the covers and refused to inspect it. The oxygen tube in Ember's nose made Cheyenne think of her mom's next-door neighbor—if they could call twenty acres between houses *next door*. Ms. Master had been a smoker for forty years and did all her gardening, grocery shopping, laundry-hanging, and general existing with a tube like that strapped to her nose. She wheeled the oxygen tank around with her everywhere.

Ember looked worse.

Swallowing, Cheyenne took another few steps toward the bed. "Em?"

The door opened, spilling light from the hallway into the dim hospital room. "Oh. Hello."

Cheyenne eyed the blond doctor, who appeared to be somewhere in his late thirties—tall, rail-thin, with huge, round lenses in thick black frames. "How's she doing?"

"I'm Dr. Andrews." He stepped forward, tucked a clunky laptop under one arm and extended a hand.

Cheyenne's eyebrows flicked together. "I know she went into surgery. So how is she?"

Dr. Andrews lowered his hand and nodded. "The surgery went well. Stopped the internal bleeding, got her vitals up where we want them. She hasn't spent a lot of time awake. And she still has a long road ahead toward recovery."

Cheyenne wanted to yell at him to just spit it out and tell her what she suspected. She could smell his discomfort. *I should've gone online to check their notes. This guy's not gonna tell me anything.* "Full recovery?"

"We hope so." The doctor nodded and stepped toward the bed to check the monitors. He shot her a hesitant glance before opening the computer and clicking around. "She has everything she needs."

"But you're not sure about a full recovery?"

"I'm sorry. Are you related to Ms. Gaderow?"

"No." *These people and their family rules.* "Just a friend who's on her visitor's list."

"Sure. Well, I can't discuss anything else about your friend's condition without her—"

"Without her permission, I know. And she's not waking up to sign paperwork." Cheyenne studied the slow rise and fall of Ember's chest beneath the thin, dark-blue comforter. "Look, she doesn't have any family here. They're in Chicago, and I don't know how to get ahold of them."

"I see." Dr. Andrews nodded, typed a few more things into the hospital laptop, and closed it. "Are you the only person who knows she's here?"

"I'm the only person who tried to help her." She swallowed

the thick, dry wad of frustration in her throat and considered sticking the other earbud into her ear just to keep herself under control. "I brought her into the ER last night."

"Then you saved her life." The man offered a small smile. "And I don't say that to everyone who brings a friend into the ER."

Cheyenne's mouth quirked. "Okay, listen. I saw what that bullet did to her. Where it came right back out. It looked close to her spine."

Dr. Andrews bit his lower lip and nodded, glancing at Ember, but he offered nothing else.

Sighing, Cheyenne clenched her eyes shut and pulled the other earbud out so she could focus on being polite. "What's she gonna wake up to?"

"I'm sorry. I can't—"

"Please." The sting of oncoming tears burned in Cheyenne's nose, and she blinked. *You can cry later. Get him to talk first.* "If she's not gonna be able to walk again after this, please just tell me. It's not like I have anywhere to broadcast it or anything."

The doctor's eyes widened, and he tucked the laptop under his arm again before rubbing his hairless chin. "It's easy to forget that people without a medical degree can put two and two together and nail the issue right on the head."

Turning away from the doctor, Cheyenne stared at Ember's light brown and blonde hair matted on the pillow. That was as close as she could get to looking at her friend's face. "I was right."

Dr. Andrews cleared his throat and cast her a sidelong glance. "I hope you understand I can't share any more than that with you."

"Yeah, I get it. It's enough just to hear what I already knew." She turned away from the bed and nodded at him. "Thank you."

"She'll be thanking both of us when she wakes up. And we

won't be able to gauge the full extent of the damage until then. Whatever happens, it will take time. If you're the only person she has close by, she'll need you."

"I know." Cheyenne stuck her earbuds in her pocket and scratched the corner of her mouth, trying to keep from losing it in front of the doctor who'd not quite but almost broken a confidentiality oath. "Do you need to look at anything else? I can get out of the way."

"Nope. All good. You came to visit your friend, and I'll let you get to it." The man paused like he was about to say something else, then went to the door and stepped into the hall.

Cheyenne's lower lip trembled. She walked around the bed and picked up the stiff, uncomfortable-looking armchair from beside the window. She positioned it beside the hospital bed and studied Ember's face. "I'm so sorry, Em."

The only reply was the rhythmic rise and fall of Ember's breath and the repetitive blinking from the monitors. The half-drow lowered herself into the chair and stared at her friend's limp hand. She reached out, hesitated, then grabbed Ember's hand and cradled it in both of hers. It was surprisingly warm. "This is my fault. We've been friends for a long time, and I should've listened to you. Believed you when you said you needed me."

The hospital room felt way too quiet, but Cheyenne couldn't just get up and leave. Not yet. "I don't even know if it would be different. You know, if you knew why I didn't want to get involved. Why I'm still trying to hide who I am."

Her thumb passed over the back of Ember's hand, and she stared at her own fingers as she sought the words to tell her friend what she'd told no one else. "But you deserve to know because my issues got you into this mess. I, uh, I know I haven't told you much about my mom or where I grew up. There are already enough people out there talking about her, so I don't like to add to it. But, you know, she told me the same thing you did. More than once. That I won't be able to hide forever."

A wry chuckle escaped her, and Cheyenne hung her head between her outstretched arms. "Except my mom *was* trying to hide me for as long as possible. Raised me in our own private wildlife preserve—a halfling in her natural habitat. I mean, I could've started college when I was fifteen, but Bianca Summerlin doesn't budge an inch when she's decided something. I enjoyed being away from the city and so many people and all the noise. And I had tutors. Jiu-jitsu instructor. My mom was born mingling with the Washington elite. That didn't change when she grew up. I got to sit in on the random consultations she had with whatever senator or political figurehead wanted her advice enough to come all the way out to the middle of nowhere just to talk to her. And it was easier to be whoever I wanted when it was just us. So..."

Cheyenne grimaced and sucked her teeth. "I feel like I'm rambling."

She looked at Ember's hand, still limp in hers, then glanced at her friend's face. "Okay, Em. The point is, I've spent my whole life knowing what I am. Knowing there are others out there, kind of like me, but never having met them. Well, maybe not halflings, but magicals. I didn't have anyone to talk to about how to be a drow. Or halfling, or whatever. I don't know who my dad is, and if my mom knows, she hasn't unlocked that door yet. Instead, she drilled into me what I am will only make things worse for *me*. That no one else can see it, because no one else knows. Bianca Summerlin's little secret. But that's...that's not what I wanna be."

After sighing, Cheyenne patted Ember's hand. Her vision blurred with new tears. "I promise you, Em, I won't keep hiding. Not the way I have been. I won't let this happen to anyone else, and if I could go back and make sure it didn't happen to you—"

She swallowed a sob and sniffed, turning her head to wipe away the tears with her sleeve. "Whatever's happening with your friends and that orc bastard, I'll figure it out. I'll help. It's too late to keep you from getting hurt, but—" She wiped her cheek against her shoulder one more time, then Cheyenne took a deep breath and pressed her lips together to keep them from trembling. "Yeah. I'll make sure the same thing doesn't happen to anyone else. Plus, wringing Durg's neck is gonna be satisfying, so I'll come back and tell you all about that. Okay?"

Nodding, she stroked the top of Ember's hand and gave it a little squeeze. "I'm gonna go, but I'll be back. You work on all that healing stuff, and you better call me when you—"

The softest, slightest pressure of Ember's fingers closing around hers made her stop. A gasp of disbelief escaped the half-drow, and she blinked the last few tears away before pulling herself back together. "Yeah, sounds like a plan."

She slipped her hand out of Ember's, which she set back on the hospital bed, then patted the comforter. "I felt that. So don't think you can deny it later. You're gonna be okay."

Cheyenne pushed herself to her feet, wiped her damp cheeks, and slipped out of the hospital room. She had both earbuds in and Diva Destruction playing full blast before she'd gotten halfway out of the ICU. A few of the nurses on staff slowed on their way to other patients just to stare. The half-drow felt their gazes on her, and she shoved her hands into her pockets before picking up the pace.

Guess I have to make my angry place and my happy place the same thing. And then I'm gonna kick that orc's ass.

CHAPTER SIXTEEN

"Ow!" Cheyenne jerked the forkful of microwaved lasagna out of her mouth and glared at it. "Either still frozen in the middle or burn-your-tongue-off hot. Someone's gotta make a microwave that does what everyone expects. Or I should quit buying these."

She blew on the food and stuck the whole thing in her mouth. A quick slurp of energy drink cooled it off enough to keep most of her taste buds, and the rest didn't matter. "Okay. Time to hunt some orcs."

The dark-web searches she'd had running all day had pulled up four different hits. None of them mentioned Durg, but they all had O-class in them somewhere. One of them came from a forum called Borderlands, which had a lot of rabbit holes Cheyenne had to fight not to dive down right now.

"Man, what is this? Facebook for racketeers?"

The forums with names so stupid—like Fight the Power—had to be blind fronts for law enforcement just hoping to crack down on as many morons as they could find. Just distractions for the angsty teenage hacker trying to find meaning in places most people didn't know how to access. She moved through these, scanning the titles and discarding the ones that had more than a handful of comments. This wasn't about hopping on the most popular discussion for wannabe badasses or way more conspiracy threads than she could count. "Where's that O-class?"

Five minutes later, she'd found the OP's bulletin entitled 'Third-Quarter Projections' and snorted. "Sounds boring."

She sent a polite enough message asking for access to the comments. The reply was immediate from a handle she hadn't seen before.

gu@rdi@n104: Welcome, ShyHand71. Friendly admin reminder—Users with first-time access keep their opinions to themselves for the first 48 hours.

"Aw, bummer." Cheyenne rolled her eyes.

ShyHand71: No problem. Thanks for the open door.

gu@rdi@n104: Looking for anything specific?

Cheyenne jammed another steaming forkful of lasagna into her mouth and washed it down with Blueberry-Buzz-flavored energy. "Hey, somebody's bringing back old passwords." Her fingers clacked on the keys.

ShyHand71: Wouldn't tell you if I were.

The cursor on the private message blinked a few seconds, then the admin's message came through accompanied by a thumbs-up emoji and an A+.

gu@rdi@n104: Have fun.

"Oh, yeah. Loads of fun. You could save me time and give me that orc's head on a silver—"

The private message disappeared from her screen, and the entirety of the Third-Quarter Projections forum rearranged itself into a different conversation. "That's more like it."

Grinning, Cheyenne scrolled through the message board. They were ordered by race, apparently—G-, GM-, N-, O-, and T-class labels. "Guessing it would be D for drow if they had any. At least it's alphabetical."

She dove into the G-class boards first. No one explicitly said anything about goblins, but it was implied. *Gobbling as Free Market Trade. Gobs Pushed Off Rez. G Biz Needs an Interpreter.*

"Obviously not for English if they're writing in it." She clicked on that last one, took ten seconds to read the bulletin, then scrolled through the comments. "Jackpot. Goblin businesses being hit by orcs. Sounds like the same problem that Trevor guy had. Except for the O'gúl threats. Whatever those are."

There wasn't an address listed for the place, which would've been stupid. If she wanted to hang around the forum to monitor things, she wouldn't be able to send anyone anything for two days. "Yeah, since they're monitoring everybody in here, good thing I can be invisible."

The VPN decryption she'd built a few years ago still worked the way it needed to, although it didn't have any fancy code attached to make it look pretty. Which was the point. "Nobody's looking, anyway." Cheyenne released the thing and let it sniff its way through the OP's backtrail. It hit four different rerouted IPs before settling on the fifth and bringing it up on a map of Richmond and the surrounding areas, flashing in a bright-red circle.

"Bloodhound found the scent. Good work. My turn."

The lasagna called her name, so she shoveled the rest of it in her mouth with her usual efficiency. Until tonight, that efficiency meant she had more time to poke around in all the dark places she'd learned to navigate from behind her desk. Now, it meant she was out of her apartment two minutes later to locate that last IP address and hunt an orc in the flesh instead of through symbols on a screen.

After a twenty-minute drive across town, Cheyenne parked a block away from the building she'd traced. At 7:00 p.m., the sun had almost set, and the street was completely empty. *It's not Stony Point.*

She locked her Ford Focus and slid a fingernail beneath a piece of chipped, matte-gray paint she hadn't bothered to redo since she'd bought the thing. Then she stepped onto the sidewalk and made her way toward this goblin business.

When she reached the address with the number on the front of the building, she stared at the marquee over the front door—Robe Up, Dress Down. Her mouth twitched into a smirk.

What are goblins doing with a consignment boutique? Different strokes, I guess.

She stepped up to the front door, shaking her head, and pulled on the handle. It was locked. The hours of operation on the front window listed 8:00 a.m. to 5:00 p.m., but she could tell someone was inside. The lights were on, and Cheyenne might have been the only person around, magical or otherwise, who could hear tense voices coming from somewhere in the building. They were muted, but it sounded like whoever they were had anger issues to rival hers. *Yeah, when I was twelve, maybe.*

The half-drow cupped her hands around her eyes and pressed her face against the window. The front room was unoccupied. Knocking on the door wouldn't get her anywhere, either, so she stepped back, glanced up and down the street, and headed around the side toward the back.

The narrow road between buildings led to a rear parking area lit by a streetlamp that blinked on as soon as Cheyenne stepped behind the building. She froze at the sudden light, then reminded herself that was what streetlights did when it got dark. Sticking her hands into her pockets, she gave the two pickups parked behind Robe Up a quick, sweeping glance. One of them with the business logo printed on the side in bright pink. *If I knew any goblin clichés, I'd still say that breaks 'em.*

A dark-gray van sat on the other side of the parking lot, far enough away to be separated from the trucks but close enough to belong to someone inside any of these commercial buildings. The air smelled like magic in a way Cheyenne didn't recognize. Something was off.

"You can't *do* this!" The shout came from the goblin business, all right.

Cheyenne turned toward the back door. Someone hadn't shut it all the way.

She heard a *thump,* followed by a muted growl. "That's not what we agreed! You said we— Hey! What are you doing?"

That must be what goblins versus orcs sounds like. Cheyenne padded to the cracked back door, slipping around the pool of light from the streetlamp. She pressed her hand against the wall.

When she closed her eyes, she applied the same trick she'd been using for ten years to spy on her mom's consultations in her private office at home. Now her ability granted Cheyenne sight within the building. Four figures lit up in her mind's eye in different wavering colors, one of them blue, the other three a dark, muddy green. The three circled the blue guy, their height and bulk overshadowing their target.

Or victim. Please let these be the orcs from last night.

Heat flared at the base of her spine and drowned out the breeze on her skin, the glow of the streetlamp behind her, and the low, thick voices from inside. All she felt was that burning, tingling flame licking its way up her spine. Cheyenne's fingers brushed a small, cold object in her pocket—the four-pointed star Professor Bergmann had made from Cheyenne's accidental magic.

A souvenir.

She closed her fist around the trinket and thought about her brief and frustrating *training* session with Mattie. *Feel it. Check. That's the easy part.*

Her breath quickened. *Embrace it.*

She thought of Ember on the concrete of the skatepark and in the hospital bed connected to monitors. Her skin prickled, the heat spreading over her shoulders and down her arms and climbing up her neck.

Hold it. Stay in my angry place.

Somewhere behind her, a car door opened, then another. Boots crunched on loose, scattered gravel on the asphalt, then two doors shut.

Yeah, I got it.

"Valdu," a gruff voice muttered at the other end of the parking lot.

"I told you to wait in the van and let me handle this." That voice came from inside.

"There's someone out back."

"Well, get rid of him and stay the hell outside until I'm done!"

Cheyenne's eyes flew open, and she peeped over her shoulder to see a huge orc in a business suit and a creepy smaller guy with blue skin and a long, pointed nose. They headed straight for her. When they saw her face—the dark-gray skin, white hair, and golden glow behind her eyes—the pair paused. They both blinked in surprise before exchanging hesitant glances.

Screw this. I'm taking these orcs down.

The half-drow, who now looked full drow and pissed, sneered at the magicals before she whirled toward the rear door and kicked it wide open.

CHAPTER SEVENTEEN

The door burst open and cracked against the inside wall as Cheyenne stormed inside.

"Hey!" the orc from the lot shouted from behind her.

Inside, an orc turned his head and snarled. "We're closed. Can't you see?"

The orc who'd been messing with the goblin owner of the shop—and now had his fists around most of the guy's shirt collar—didn't take his hands away from the terrified magical with blue skin. "Come back tomorrow."

"I'm here now." Cheyenne spread her arms, and a hissing spiral of sparks churned in her palms. "Where's Durg?"

The biggest orc turned from the goblin to look at her. "Who the hell are *you*?"

"Tell me where he is!" Her sparks flared higher, and then the orc and the blue-skinned guy with orange eyes burst through the open back door.

"Don't move."

Cheyenne heard them breathing behind her, punctured by a crackle through the air and a burst of magic she felt on her skin while it was still in the other magical's hand. "You first."

The orc with a fistful of goblin ran a thick gray tongue over his top teeth, then glanced at his two companions, who'd done a piss-poor job as lookouts. "Take care of her."

He snarled and almost lifted the goblin off his feet before pulling the store owner through the back and away from the half-drow intruder. The other two orcs who'd come to strongarm the business owner—one of them missing an eye, the other covered in mud-brown tattoos—slammed their fists into their opposite palms at the same time. Green light flared at the contact, and the orc behind her with the blue-skinned friend, whatever he was, stormed forward.

A full furnace blast of drow magic washed over her. "Let's do this."

The orc from behind let off a burst of magic at the same time Cheyenne dropped into a crouch. A spiraling red light with razor-sharp edges wheeled over her and cut a path between the two oncoming orcs before slicing into the far wall of the backroom and sending up a puff of plaster and drywall.

One-Eye and Tattoo barreled toward her, overturning the table between them.

Cheyenne launched black and purple sparks at the orc in the suit and caught him in the upper chest. He roared and staggered sideways as his blue associate slammed the back door shut. One-Eye flung shards of something green that reeked of burnt wiring toward her.

Rolling sideways, Cheyenne came to her feet, whipped her hand in a circle, and sent a crackling black orb at One-Eye. It hit the overturned table instead, destroying it in a rain of huge splinters.

"I don't have it!" the goblin shouted from somewhere in the front.

Cheyenne jerked her head up at the sound. The tattooed orc bounded over a stack of supply crates and crashed into her, knocking her backward. They both toppled into the metal shelving unit, sending rolls of paper towels and boxes of lightbulbs onto the floor. With a shrieking bellow, the half-drow brought her elbow up against the side of the orc's face.

One-Eye shot off a few hissing green charges at them both, but Cheyenne ducked aside. Tattoo wobbled on his feet and reached for her again, swiping with both hands and letting out a strangled growl. She sent her entire foot into the center of his broad chest and kicked him back. One-Eye's magical attacks crashed into Tattoo's back as purple and black energy hurtled from Cheyenne's hands. Both orcs slammed into the ground against the opposite wall.

The non-orc with blue skin stumbled across the scattered paper towel rolls, then found his footing and made himself an open target. Cheyenne snarled and summoned black and purple power into both hands.

The blue guy pulled a gun from his hip and leveled it at her.

"Seriously?" Cheyenne cocked her head, her nostrils flaring. "What is it with you people and guns?"

"Let's see if you can stop a bullet." The blue magical breathed heavily, and Cheyenne picked up the sound of the three others in the building, all breathing faster than the two she'd rendered unconscious.

"You wanna try?" She didn't look at the gun, didn't look away from the orange eyes in that blue face. Professor Bergmann's words came to her.

Put something in the jar.

Right.

The blue-skinned magical squeezed the trigger, and time slowed. Cheyenne heard the scrape of metal pulling back against metal and the slow hiss of the guy's exhale. The chamber ignited behind the bullet just as the purple and black energy of her drow magic burst from her hand. She stepped sideways much faster than she'd realized she could, and then the world skipped to normal speed. The bullet left a hole in the wall behind where she'd just stood, while the blue guy screamed and doubled over as he dropped his gun and clutched his injured hand to his chest.

Cheyenne knew the orc in the suit had made it behind her. She heard air being sucked into his lungs and the press of his rubber-soled shoes against the linoleum floor. She dropped into another crouch and twisted around toward him. Black, snaking tendrils lashed from her fingertips and coiled around the orc's ankles. Her hands clenched into fists and pulled, jerking the orc off his feet and sending him flying across the back room of the shop. He let loose a grunt of surprise before his head cracked against the doorway into the front, and he passed out.

Cheyenne stood and peered around.

From the next room, she overheard: "We made a *deal*, Radzu."

"That didn't include destroying my shop!"

Cheyenne crunched across the broken lightbulbs and slammed her fist into the side of the blue-skinned guy's head. He dropped, still cradling his arm, and she kicked his gun under a shelving unit. She stepped over the smashed table and the scattered supplies, slipping into the front room with her skin on fire and more drow magic coalescing around her hands.

She came around the corner and saw the huge orc looming over the goblin owner, who was cowering in his office chair, obviously forced to sit by the orc leaning into his face. Cheyenne caught the glint of a knife pressed to the short goblin's violet throat.

The shop owner caught sight of her and lifted a finger. "She wasn't part of the deal, either."

The orc jerked the blade away from the shop owner's throat and turned. "No, she wasn't."

"I think we all agree the deal's off," Cheyenne said, spreading her arms. "Whatever it is."

The squabbling magicals exchanged a confused glance, and the orc grunted. "She's not one of mine."

"Seeing as I just put four of your guys down for a nap in the back, it would suck if I was." Cheyenne held up a finger. Everyone listened to the utter lack of noise. "Yeah. They're out."

"What do you *want?*" The orc raised his blade and pointed it at her, half in warning, half in invitation. "I don't do business with drow."

"You do now." Cheyenne nodded at his weapon. "You can put that thing away and tell me where Durg is...or I'm gonna take that knife and use it on you until you talk."

"K'shul?"

"You." The orc jabbed a finger at the goblin without taking his eyes off Cheyenne. "Shut it."

"Can you guys at least take this outside?" The goblin glanced at the main room of his store and grimaced. "I can't do anything with a—"

K'shul let out a mixed bark and battle cry. He leapt away from the goblin and started circling Cheyenne.

She lifted a handful of crackling, churning magic. Purple sparks flew from her palm. "If that's how you want it, I'll play."

The orc could only move back and forth in a half-circle around her, seeing as she stood between him and the entrance to the backroom. He came closer each time and slashed at the air with his blade. In his other hand, he conjured a humming ball of silver that vibrated above his palm. Cheyenne cast it a dubious glance before K'shul came at her.

She went on the offensive, ducking a knife swipe and sending a lash of black sparks out. She would have hit home, but the silver orb in his hand flashed and the air in front of him shimmered, deflecting her attack and sending it careening across the shop. A mannequin crashed to the floor, jewelry and a snapped strand of beads skittering across the floor.

"Come *on*," the goblin shrieked.

Cheyenne released two more attacks, one at K'shul's feet and the other at his head. The silver orb's shield deflected them both, and she dropped her hands to her sides with an irritated shrug. "Fine. Your way."

The orc took two lunging strides toward her and slashed out with the knife. She dodged it, slipping to the side and out of his reach. He shouted in frustration, spittle gleaming on his huge lower lip between his protruding tusks. The blade came down again and again, and Cheyenne let off another attack just to be sure. It bounced off the shield and nearly singed the goblin, who leapt shrieking from his chair.

The halfling let the knife-wielding orc close in on her. The next time he swung out with the blade, she caught his forearm between both of hers, shoving down on the inside of his elbow and jerking his wrist in the other direction. K'shul stumbled forward with a grunt, and Cheyenne grabbed his shoulders and lifted a knee into his gut. The silver orb toppled from his hand and disappeared before it hit the floor.

Doubled over, K'shul swiped out with an empty, meaty hand. She caught his arm in her armpit and clamped down on it with her elbow, then kneed him in the face, and jabbed her other elbow down onto the back of his neck. The orc's shoulder crunched, and his massive weight crumpled. K'shul roared in pain, his arm dislocated at the shoulder.

Cheyenne stomped down on his thick, muscular back and pulled even harder on his arm.

"Goddamnit!" K'shul grunted, fighting for breath and drooling on the floor. "What the hell do you want?"

"Durg." Cheyenne dug her fingers into his skin and leaned down toward his face, keeping her entire weight on his back. "I thought that was clear the last time I said it."

"You're insane. I don't know who—" He bellowed when she jerked on his arm. Cheyenne felt and heard something snap. *"Aiggh! Bitch!"*

"Then what orc do I have to bring down who *can* tell me where he is?"

"You think..." K'shul gasped. "You think we all know each other?" He forced a laugh, although pain was his primary concern.

She pulled back a little and blinked. *Might've been too quick to assume that one.* "Just give me a name."

"You're in deep shit, you know that?" He laughed, his back bouncing up and down beneath her foot. "You got no idea what you're messing with."

Cheyenne dropped to her knees on his back, making him grunt again. Then she grabbed both sides of his head and bashed that thick skull against the shop's floor. When she let go, his face hit with a *thud.* She climbed off the orc's back.

"You didn't have to go there." She growled in frustration and shook her fists. "It wasn't a trick question or anything."

She lowered her glare at the goblin, Radzu, who slumped into his chair and stared with wide eyes at her. He then took in the destruction in his shop.

Cheyenne gritted her teeth and flexed her fingers, straightening to her full height of five and a half feet. "Hey."

The goblin jerked his head to look at her.

"You know an orc named Durg?"

The shop owner shook his head. "No. But I know these guys. They're gonna come back for me after this, and I couldn't pay what they wanted before. Now, when the whole place is..." He gripped the sides of his purple head covered in greenish-yellow hair. "I'm screwed."

"No, you're not." Cheyenne glanced at the unconscious K'shul. "They won't come back."

"Oh, yeah?" The goblin snorted, then his eyes widened, and

he leapt from his chair. "No! You're not turning this place into a chop shop. I won't hold it against you that you kicked their asses, but if you try to—"

Cheyenne rolled her eyes and squatted beside the fallen orc. This time, she grabbed the arm she hadn't dislocated and draped it over her shoulders.

"What are you doing?"

"Cleaning up." She pulled the huge magical's chest and upper torso off the ground and dragged him back through the shop, his pants mopping up the floor behind him.

The goblin stared at her. "Drow." He shook his head and moved after her. "Your kind are surprisingly strong. Oh, look at this place!"

By the time Radzu reached the back room, Cheyenne was out the back door of the shop and dragging K'shul toward the dark-gray van in the parking lot. She dropped him on the asphalt and opened the sliding door into the back, then got to work pushing and pulling him inside.

"So, is beating up orcs in consignment stores a regular thing for you, or..."

"Huh." Cheyenne grabbed the bundle of zip-ties in the backseat cupholder and had to link a few together to get them around both of the orc's meaty wrists. Then she jumped out of the van and stalked past the goblin. "Just yours. So far."

"Okay." He followed her back toward his shop. "But why'd you come here? Is there somebody watching me? I've been doing everything right. Followed the code. K'shul and his... whatever they are make their rounds, but I didn't think I'd put out enough of a signal to bring a—"

"Look." Cheyenne turned on him and gestured toward the van. "Did you want help getting these assholes off your back or what?"

"Well *yeah*."

"Great. So you get what you want, and I still have to find the orc who put my friend in the hospital." She stormed back inside and went to the blue-skinned dude. He had a goose egg on his temple where she'd struck him. His hand looked worse, mangled, charred, and raw halfway up his wrist.

Cheyenne knelt and picked him up. He was much lighter than K'shul.

"Hey, wait." The goblin stepped over the destruction in the backroom. "Did gu@rdi@n104 send you?"

She paused for a split second, then tossed the blue guy over her shoulder. "No."

"Oh. 'Cause, I mean, I don't know how anybody else would think to come here. Just for orcs. If he sent you, I *have* money for—"

"Never heard of the guy." Cheyenne grunted when she stood, carrying a magical who weighed close to twice her size. She headed for the door again. "Never heard of you, either. And I don't need your money."

The goblin blinked. "Are you kidding?"

"Nope. Do you know this guy?"

"The troll?" The shop owner shook his head. "Just another thug trying to take from the rest of us who *follow* the accord."

"Right." *Great. We got trolls now.*

Cheyenne stepped outside and headed for the van again.

"Wait. Did the FRoE send you?" The goblin hurried after her. "I thought they would've sent more people. I mean, not that you couldn't handle it, but—"

"Stop." Cheyenne dumped the troll into the van and grabbed another zip-tie. "I came to help with your problem and maybe get some answers. That's it. You need to cut it out with the questions, dude."

The goblin took a deep breath and paused, then just couldn't help himself. "I'm just trying to understand why a drow would..."

Cheyenne straightened and turned with a raised eyebrow.

The still-burning heat in her body filled her palm with another whirling storm of sparks.

The shop owner swallowed. "Uh. Got it. I'm Radzu, by the way."

"Good for you." Cheyenne walked around him for her third trip depositing unconscious magical thugs into their magical-thug van.

"You have a name?"

"Yep."

Radzu stopped asking questions after that.

CHAPTER EIGHTEEN

Cheyenne slammed the driver-door of the orc van shut and dusted off her hands. Whether the five idiots knocked out in the back woke up anytime soon wasn't her problem, but they'd have a few—mainly untying each other and figuring out which ones among them had to drag their vehicle out of the ditch by the river.

She stepped away and surveyed her message, which she'd written in melted chocolate from a bar she'd found under the seat. It was smeared on the inside of the windshield so they'd see it first thing, but seeing it backward from the outside wasn't any less satisfying.

'Back Off.'

They probably won't listen to that kinda warning. Not even from a drow they don't know is a halfling.

Either way, she'd done her part, which was more for the goblin named Radzu, consignment boutique owner, of all things. She still hadn't found Durg, and she was saving her worst for him. That didn't mean she didn't feel a sliver of pride when she studied the van.

Her skin tingled with her drow blood coursing through her.

I broke my record for holding it all together like this. With a smirk, Cheyenne flashed her middle finger at the orcs and their van, then took off down the street toward the consignment shop and her car.

"Yeah. My happy place."

The fifteen-minute drive from the shop to where she'd ditched the van took her a little over five minutes on foot. She stopped twice to catch her breath, once in a dark parking lot, and the second time on a side street. She was exhausted, and she still had to drive home.

By the time she made it to her apartment, the anger and heat in her veins had cooled. The pale-skinned, dark-haired, human version of Cheyenne Summerlin stepped out of her Focus, and it was only 10:08 p.m.

"Who said fighting a bunch of orc jerks had to take all night?" She snorted. "No one ever. But now I have a few more names."

Once in her apartment, Cheyenne kicked her shoes off by the door and dropped her keys on the counter. She took a bottle of water from her fridge, then sat at her computer and put her hand on the mouse to wake her monitor. The first thing in front of her was a message from gu@rdi@n104.

You like what you find?

It was time-stamped 9:31 p.m., which would've been right around the time she'd climbed into the orc van and booked it out of the lot behind Radzu's shop. She narrowed her eyes. The goblin had mentioned this guy by name.

She responded as ShyHand71. **That's a little nosey. Thought I had to keep my opinions to myself for 48 hours??** Cheyenne sat back and waited for a reply, which took about five seconds.

gu@rdi@n104: Took you long enough. Have fun?

"What the hell? Why does he assume it was me?" There was nothing tying her handle on this forum to her car or her phone or the fact that she'd had them both with her when she stopped by a goblin-run boutique. She sucked on her teeth. This was not good. "Maybe… Could he have somehow hopped through my VPN and saw I pulled up the address?" She groaned. "Dammit."

She chewed on the inside of her bottom lip and figured she should play the game a little longer. She needed to find Durg and give the orc what he had coming.

ShyHand71: Yeah. Took a long shower and put on my fuzzy slippers.

gu@rdi@n104: Hope you cleaned out those pointy ears.

"Shit!" Cheyenne jerked her hands up off the keyboard and rolled backward in her chair. "Bastard. He hopped on my bloodhound bot. That fucking goblin can't keep his mouth shut."

She took a deep breath and shut her eyes.

Maybe this gu@rdi@n104 is just good at lucky guesses.

Or the community of magicals between here and Washington and this stupid Borderlands forum were a lot more interconnected than she'd guessed. *Gotta be more careful. Step away for a bit, let it all cool down.*

That was impossible, though, with Ember in the hospital and Durg still running around doing to other magicals what he'd done to her. And now this? "No, I can't stop now."

Cheyenne slid her chair forward when she got another message.

gu@rdi@n104: The 48-hour rule still applies. But you can look as much as you want. Just don't forget we're watching.

She went for the prickly hacker persona, mostly because she did not understand who these people were, and as far as the rest of the world knew—magicals and humans—halflings were a myth. So, she'd be one.

ShyHand71: While I'm in the shower? Nice try.

gu@rdi@n104: When people want their pets to stay close, they keep 'em on a leash. Maybe yours got away. Don't worry. Nobody's gonna call the pound on you. Yet. You have a few more tricks up your sleeve.

She frowned. "Oh, now he's cocky. Hate this."

Cheyenne closed the chat window. Whoever gu@rdi@n104 was, he wouldn't be screwing with her like this if he wanted an answer. Which meant he thought he knew who she was and what she was doing. "Yeah, but the only person who knows who I am is lying in the hospital. Not like anyone else can be able to pick me out of a lineup or anyth—"

A chuckle bubbled up her throat. She dropped her hands from the keyboard, stared at the frame of her monitor, and grinned. "That's the best part. The Goth grad-level programmer looks nothing like a drow vigilante beating up magical asshats. Huh. Good thing I never considered wearing a mask."

She slapped the arm of her computer chair and gave a bombastic shout-slash-laugh. "Okay. One more point for the halfling. Let's go score some more."

After another two hours of looking through Borderlands for mentions of Durg or K'shul—now that she had one more name that might connect her to something—her searches still turned up dry. Cheyenne glanced at the clock. Midnight, and she was still wired. "There's no way I'm gonna make my first class tomorrow."

Sure, she was worming her way through the dark web looking for one very specific orc, and she'd already gone out once tonight to put a few in their places, but no one could call Cheyenne Summerlin irresponsible. It took her fifteen minutes to go over the syllabus from her Applied Cryptography class, put together a few lines of code way beyond what the professor of this class would have even considered asking of them, and pulled up an email.

Professor Dawley,

I'm not coming into class today, but based on the structure you laid out on Monday about enciphering with block ciphers, the next logical step would be deciphering them again with block ciphers or block cipher modes or both. So I'm attaching a file with the code I built to address deciphering with both. This should show it won't be necessary for me to provide any other work you might ask for today.

Cheyenne Summerlin

She would've emailed that to any of her current professors, but it gave her more satisfaction to send it to Professor Dawley, the short, thin, red-faced man who thought screaming out every code character he outlined on the whiteboard would make his grad students understand better. "And he needs to update his course material. He's totally stuck in 2015."

Cheyenne closed her email and knew she wouldn't check it again for a reply. Beyond everyone seeming to know who her mom was, there was no way Dawley could argue with what she'd sent him. He'd have to ask someone else to explain it to him.

Cracking her knuckles, Cheyenne scooted forward in her desk chair and got back to work on the forums. Despite gu@rdi@n104's not-so-subtle warning-turned-invitation, it didn't dampen the energy she had after holding her drow form for over an hour and a half.

And she'd promised Ember she'd set things right.

She'd find Durg and whoever else was with him in that

skatepark. If she ended up helping a few magicals getting their asses handed to them by a bunch of other magical jerks, all the better. Maybe that was the price to pay for finding the orc she wanted.

Cheyenne was more than willing to pay it.

CHAPTER NINETEEN

Just before 2:00 a.m., one of her original searches pinged with an entrance to another forum that had nothing to do with Borderlands. Cheyenne finished her third water and couldn't help but poke around.

The site was called F-ed Up Realm, which made little sense at all until she found a post there that made her stop.

FRoE Alert Updates.

Both Ember and the goblin shop owner had mentioned this FRoE, though in different contexts. "What the hell is it?"

Cheyenne squinted at her screen and scanned the post. Most of it only made sense if the person reading it knew what all the terms meant—Reservation Patrol, FRoE Raid and Return, O'gúleesh Assimilation, Ambar'ogúl Rehabilitation and Reform. She clicked on that last one, caught by the first word she'd seen.

The document was password-protected. She snorted and ran through her decryption programs. She'd built three of the five she had. The other two had been gifts from another hacker she'd met online when she was fourteen. More like counter-hacker. Their little group of like-minded computer nerds had worried about the guy when he'd dropped off the face of the earth. But Pandora2k had found GRND0's identity in the real world—a ninety-eight-year-old hacker who built decryption programs had died in his sleep a week after sending Cheyenne two of them.

Two of her programs and one of his beat against the site's security until they unlocked the password protection and let her in.

"Thank you, Ground Zero. Wherever you are. Enjoying unrestricted access to all information everywhere." She snorted and killed the other programs before they left too much of a trail.

The document in front of her now made no sense. It was written in English, all right, but it looked more like a dossier than anything else—some convict escaping from a max-security prison called Chateau D'rahl, plus a whole outline of updated protocol and guard qualification requirements.

"This has nothing to do with—"

There it was. Her last name.

B. Summerlin—suspected interaction with Inmate 4872. Exact date and time unconfirmed.

"Uh, what?" Cheyenne blinked and shook her head, but the words were the same when she opened her eyes again. "What the hell is Mom doing in a prison incident report?"

She paid a lot more attention to the rest of the document, but B. Summerlin wasn't mentioned again. There was, however, an addendum to the writeup dated January 3rd, 2000.

Project FRoE started at 1100 hours. First successful operation for Border control at Rez Alpha 1 and Rez Charlie 4. 72 non-human entities detained, cataloged, and entered the exchange system. Results still pending. *See Reports C-182 and CM-014 for further analysis.

"You've gotta be kidding me." Cheyenne scrolled through the initial report, then went back down to the addendum and had to get up out of her chair. "FRoE and Bianca Summerlin on the same report about non-human entities and escaped convicts. What did she *do*?"

The only thing Cheyenne could do was pace around her small living room while trying to put the pieces together —her mom, Inmate 4872, the FRoE, which started the year Cheyenne was born. "That makes it sound like she was gettin' it on with a convicted non-human. Jesus, was that what happened?" She spun around and stared at the back of her monitor, then brushed it off and kept pacing. The chains on her wrists clanked against each other in succession as she shook out her hands and studied the carpet that hadn't been replaced since before she was born.

"Beyond turning into someone else for a night and gettin' freaky with a drow, what could she have to do with Border patrols? And these reservations, and the damn FRoE. Man, I had to dive deep into this."

A wry chuckle escaped her, and she mussed her hair on the back of her head, trying to get rid of the jitters that hit every time she put the pieces together of a big puzzle. "She'll tell me. She has to tell me. Maybe I just found the right question to ask..."

Cheyenne jerked her phone out of her pocket and texted her mom. Although it was almost 3:00 a.m., she had no issues with texting. The woman kept the cell phone in her office and didn't take it to bed. Urgent calls were to go to the house number, the landline. *I don't wanna talk to her right now. She'll find it in the morning.*

Call me when you're up. I have some questions. Big ones.

She'd get a call, most likely at 8:00 a.m. sharp. Bianca Summerlin might have retired early from the political spotlight, but she still kept pristine office hours out of her home, having done so the past twenty-one years.

"I need to get out." Cheyenne shoved her feet into her Vans, grabbed her keys off the counter, and rooted around in her backpack for her wallet. Then she locked the door behind her and headed to the convenience store on the corner.

The gas station was open twenty-four-seven, which had helped her through many a sleepless night. Plus, they carried every single package of junk food and instant meal she'd fallen in love with way more than she should have during her freshman year at Virginia Commonwealth University. She had Ember to thank for most of it. *And it's not like anybody expects grad students to be eating organic, locally-sourced, sustainably-grown meals made by their in-house chef every single day. Nope. I got to leave all that behind me at the Summerlin farm.*

She caught her reflection in the glass door of the gas station. *I look insane. The last twenty-four hours have been insane too.*

The electric bell by the checkout counter dinged when she pulled open the door. Katie looked up from her yoga magazine and jerked her chin up at her latest customer in the middle of the night. "Hey."

"Katie," Cheyenne muttered, giving the convenience store's night-shift employee a nod and a fleeting, distracted smile. She headed for the chip aisle, craving Funyuns.

"Got anything interesting going on tonight?"

"Not really." Cheyenne didn't think she could look at the girl who was her own age. Sometimes, she'd spend a few minutes telling Katie about the random programs she was building or the ridiculous things some people thought they could hide on the internet. Not like Katie understood any of it. But Cheyenne didn't mind someone else her own age, with no connection to her life beyond the fact that she worked at the closest gas station to the half-drow's apartment, to talk to in two-minute bursts before not having to think about her again. At least until the next time she came in to stock up on food that would make her mom scowl.

She snatched the family-size Funyuns off the shelf and turned toward the beer cooler. It didn't matter what kind she picked. She didn't even look. *I just need to cool off. Figure out what I'm gonna do next with this FRoE crap.*

Katie bobbed her head behind the counter, one earbud stuck in her ear as she pulled the six-pack of beer and the onion-flavored junk food toward her to scan them. "You know Moon Hooch?"

"No."

"They're great. Wanna listen?"

"I'm good." Cheyenne tried to smile again, but it got lost in translation and even felt like it didn't look remotely friendly.

"You okay?" Katie raised an eyebrow and turned the card reader toward Cheyenne.

"Just a weird night."

"Weird like you took something?"

"What?"

The girl behind the counter lifted one shoulder in a half-hearted shrug and smirked. "Just 'cause, you know, my brother comes by sometimes after he drops acid. And you kinda have the same look. Not gonna judge. I just didn't think you were into that kinda thing."

"I'm not."

Katie chuckled. "Not what?"

"On anything. Or into it."

"Okay. Sure. Just curious."

Cheyenne ran her card to pay for her beer and snack, and the girl's inability to quit smirking was contagious. Then Cheyenne managed a genuine smile, however small. "Are you?"

"I mean, I guess it—"

The door opened, and a guy in a hoodie with his hands shoved in his pockets and hood pulled up stormed into the convenience store. Both women glanced at him, then Katie pulled down the corners of her mouth and sucked in a breath. "Yikes. Looks like it's a weird night for everyone."

"Yeah, maybe." Cheyenne grabbed her purchases and nodded. "Thanks, Katie. Have a good night."

The other woman lifted a hand and wiggled her fingers, then glanced from Cheyenne to the dude in the hoodie, who was standing in front of the chips with his shoulders hunched. Nothing too weird about that, except Cheyenne could hear the dude's heart hammering in his chest. *He's on something, or he's about to do something stupid.*

When she reached the door, she turned around to nod at Katie and push the door open with her back. It gave her a second to look at Hoodie again, and she found him glaring at her from beneath the hood shadowing most of his face. He looked away, antsy, sniffing, and shoved his hands deeper into his hoodie pocket.

She heard a click, then she stepped outside and let the door close behind her. *He's gonna do something stupid.*

CHAPTER TWENTY

Cheyenne rushed around the side of the gas station, dropped the beer and the Funyuns, and closed her eyes. *This is the part where going drow on command is necessary. Right now. Come on.*

She imagined Hoodie pulling a gun on Katie and shouting for her to open the register. She saw the gun that idiot troll had pulled on her. The gun Durg had pulled on Trevor first, then used on Ember.

Too many damn guns.

The searing heat flared at the base of her spine. Cheyenne didn't have to let it build. She slipped into her anger and her power in two seconds and sucked in a deep breath as her ears tingled at their pointed tips. "People need to stop being so stupid."

Whirling away from the side of the gas station, the halfling with dark-gray skin and white hair stormed toward the front door. She flicked her hand, the security cameras sparking and sputtering to a lifeless blackout.

She yanked on the handle a second after Hoodie pulled the gun she'd known was in his pocket and pointed it at Katie.

Another quick flick of the hand before the cameras inside could record a drow on the premises.

"Empty the register." Even though his voice was low and he didn't shout, it squeaked at the end. "Do it."

Katie stared at the gun with wide eyes and couldn't move. The electric bell chimed, and Hoodie whipped his head toward the door.

"Put it down."

The wannabe robber's chest heaved as he weighed the drow halfling standing with her hands out, palms facing him and fingers splayed.

"What the fuck?" he said.

"I know. Sorry to crash your party. But seriously?" Cheyenne nodded at the gun in his hand, still aimed at Katie but trembling. "Chill out, man. Put it down."

She sensed Hoodie's heart going a mile a minute. Katie's, too.

The guy glanced at the gas station employee, whose face had turned deathly pale, then he put his other hand on his pistol and trained it on Cheyenne instead.

The guy wasn't a magical, or he'd be shouting something about a drow having no business breaking up his attempted robbery.

"Man, just drop the gun. I don't wanna hurt you. Well, I kinda do, but I know I shouldn't."

"What's wrong with your *face*?" Hoodie's voice cracked.

Cheyenne snorted. "You know, I get that a lot."

The guy's hands were shaking so much, it amazed Cheyenne he could hold the weapon. To prove to her that he could, he fumbled the hammer back and swallowed. "Get away from me!"

"I thought you were here to rob the place. Don't make it personal."

Hoodie squeezed the trigger. Nothing happened.

Panting, he turned the gun over to stare at the safety. He fumbled with it, but before he could finish sliding it off, Cheyenne came at him in a blur. The air *popped* when she stopped, and the shockwave of her drow speed blew his hood away from his face and sent a stand of giant lollipops off the counter to scatter all over the floor.

The guy shrieked as the thin woman with bleached white hair, slate-gray skin, and glowing golden eyes unexpectedly invaded his personal bubble. He swallowed and simply gave his gun to her.

"You gotta cut this out." She took the weapon, thumbed the safety on, and placed it on the counter. "Grab that," she told the cashier.

"Sh-sure." Instead, Katie's eyes rolled back in her head, and she slithered to the floor, knocking her chair backward.

Cheyenne and Hoodie turned to see the girl pass out, then Hoodie started hyperventilating. He glanced at Cheyenne and barreled past her toward the front door. The bell dinged.

"Huh." Cheyenne glanced at the gun and shrugged. "That was a little disappointing. Katie? You okay—"

The chime for the open door dinged again. Two guys stepped in, one after the other. Neither bothered to pretend they were looking for snacks. They both pointed guns.

Cheyenne narrowed her eyes. "Your guy didn't pass his test, huh?"

The men in matching denim jackets opened fire on the drow halfling. Cheyenne ducked and found herself once more moving faster than bullets just to dodge them. Plaster and metal grating from above the cooler and glass from a shattered security camera rained down along the far wall.

She straightened in the middle aisle between the snack stands and unleashed black tendrils of her magic at the closest gunman. The dark coil whipped around the gun and pulled Denim Guy 1 forward, yanking the weapon from his grasp. His momentum sent him head-first into the beer cooler door, and he struck it with a *thump*.

Denim Guy 2 looked like he'd just woken from a bad dream. He turned toward Cheyenne and saw her in a different spot. He went to aim at her, but she threw purple and black sparks at his face. He howled in pain and dropped the gun to bury his face in his hands. She stepped toward him and glanced around the convenience store for something to tie these guys up with. Prepackaged shoelaces hung on a hook below the counter.

The screeching burglar fell to his knees, clutching at his face. Cheyenne headed for the shoelaces, then spared a quick glance toward the beer cooler. Denim Guy 1 wasn't where she'd seen him fall.

His running shout came a second before he slammed into her from behind. Cheyenne's head whipped back as she fell toward the edge of the counter. She stopped herself with her hands and spun to the side as her attacker's fist whipped through the air where she'd just been. Her hand shot toward his neck, which she caught with the edge of her palm. The guy choked and staggered back, hands to his throat, staring at her in disbelief and desperation.

These are just regular, stupid criminals. No magic. I can't let everything out on them.

"Just give up, man." She shrugged. "I'm not even trying."

Denim Guy2 with the burned face sobbed into his hands.

Then Guy1 released a choked, garbled shout and charged her again. Cheyenne stepped out of the way and let him run into the beer cooler door a second time. She grabbed him by the back of his stupid denim jacket, both the top and the bottom, and yanked him away from the glass door.

She'd only meant to shove him down the aisle, maybe make him trip on himself or his friend and get them both on the ground. Learning how to stay in her happy place made it hard to gauge how much strength she needed to use, though. The halfling ended up lifting the guy off his feet and tossing him clear over the tops of all three rows of snacks, instant meals, protein bars, and expensive sample-sized packets of over-the-counter pain relievers. He landed on top of the ice-cream cooler beside the door. The glass beneath him cracked, and his flailing feet kicked over a rack of sunglasses.

Cheyenne stifled a laugh. "Whoops."

The guy on the ice cream cooler groaned.

"Stay there." She darted around the aisles and stopped in front of him with another *crack* in the air. It took all the cookie packages off the shelf at the end of the aisle and scattered them around her feet. The half-assed burglar took a swing at her anyway, which didn't help his precarious balance on the cooler.

She leaned back at normal speed and avoided the blow. "Why?"

He swung again, missed again, and tried to leap off the cooler. His legs didn't get the memo, and he wobbled and fell on the floor, crushing the packaged cookies.

"Stop." Cheyenne reached for his shoulder, but he slapped her hand away and grunted. "You probably have a concussion, so..."

He swung at her again and glared at her with glazed, unfocused eyes.

"Oh, boy." She stepped back a few feet, and the guy kept coming. His foot came down on a knocked-aside bottle of allergy pills, and he lost his already questionable footing. The guy's chin hit the floor with a crack, and Cheyenne wrinkled her nose. *This was not what I was going for, but Katie's not shot, and nobody got robbed. So there's that.*

She grabbed the back of the guy's denim jacket and made sure she lugged him with a little less force to where his buddy was now hunched all the way over his knees in front of the counter, sobbing and groaning and still clutching his face. His unconscious partner thumped on the floor beside him, but it didn't stop his whining.

With a sigh, Cheyenne snatched two packages of extra shoelaces from the hook and stripped off the paper with one quick jerk. When she grabbed the crying guy's wrists to pull them down from his face, he screamed even louder.

"Hey!" He stopped short at her tone, and she put a little more pressure on his wrists. "You already know what I can do, so cool it."

The guy held his breath, and she jerked his hands away from his face to reveal a blistered, puckered mess where eyes, a nose, and a mouth should have been. Cheyenne couldn't help moaning in surprise and disgust...and maybe some sympathy. *Maybe.*

"That's what you get for shooting up gas stations like an idiot." She jerked his hands behind him, wrapped the shoelaces tight around both wrists, and made sure he couldn't slip out of them. She did the same with the triple-concussed guy on the floor and stood. "Rethink your choices. Or something."

The guy with the mangled face was still holding his breath. Whatever it was, it lasted long enough to make him pass out—or maybe it was just the pain. Either way, he slumped beside his friend, and Cheyenne blinked at the two beat-up humans in matching denim jackets tied up inside a ring of smashed chip bags and spilled Rolos.

"Yeah. Weird night."

Katie groaned behind the counter, and Cheyenne hurried toward the door. She couldn't let anyone else see her like this, and she hadn't mastered the part of her magic that required turning *off* the drow whenever she wanted.

The Cheyenne Katie knows left, like, ten minutes ago.

"Oh, my God." Katie pulled herself to her feet and gawked at the destruction in her place of work.

"You should call the police," Cheyenne called over her shoulder, and the door shut behind her.

Somebody had already made that call after hearing gunshots and a grown man shrieking inside the gas station. Blaring sirens headed toward the corner. At the side of the building, Cheyenne stopped to grab her beer and Funyuns, and even in the gas station's low light against the wall, it was obvious she wasn't human-colored yet.

Blue and red lights flashed at the end of the street, and she strode toward her apartment building. *No one's gonna know what the hell just happened in there. That was ridiculous. Maybe I will leave fighting humans off the table for now.*

CHAPTER TWENTY-ONE

Cheyenne would have slept in a lot later if her phone hadn't woken her up at 8:00 a.m. on the dot. Grunting, she slapped her hand on the bedside table, then on her phone. She grabbed it, eyeballed the incoming call, and accepted it.

"Mom."

"Morning, Cheyenne. What kind of big questions?"

Rubbing her eyes, the half-drow turned onto her back and blinked at the ceiling. "Great. You got my text."

"I have to admit it made me curious." Bianca Summerlin paused on the other end of the line. "Should it have made me concerned, too?"

"I'll leave that up to you, Mom. 'Cause I don't know." She sat up and rubbed her face. *Four hours of sleep again. Awesome.*

"I'm listening."

"You ever heard of the FRoE?"

Another pause was followed by one of Bianca's sharp breaths that meant she was planning the most level-headed, clear-cut response. Today, it was simply, "I have."

"How about an Inmate 4872?"

"Hmm. Would you mind telling me where this is coming from?"

Cheyenne rolled her shoulders, stretched a little, and stood. "I came across a few things last night, and you can imagine my surprise when I saw my mom's name pop up."

"I see. Well, I'm glad you came to me about it first."

"That seemed like the best thing to do. So what can you tell me?"

Bianca sighed. While her voice carried a hint of relief, she spoke with her well-crafted, businesslike flair. "What you found is about your father."

"My father." Cheyenne paused in the doorway of her bedroom and stared at the dual monitors in her living room. The silence stretched.

"I'm willing to have this conversation whenever you want, Cheyenne. Absolutely. Just not over the phone."

"Right." The halfling closed her eyes and nodded. *Someone's always listening.* "Okay. I've got a few things to take care of today—"

"Like *school?*" She made it sound like a hopeful request and something of a condemnation all at the same time.

"Sure. What are you doing tonight?"

"I have a meeting tonight I can't reschedule. How about tomorrow? I'll clear my calendar for the day."

Cheyenne leaned against the doorframe and took a deep breath. "It won't take all day."

"True. Why don't you come home when you're finished with class tomorrow? We'll have dinner and open a bottle of wine."

"Wine. It's that kinda conversation, huh?"

"For me, yes. I'll pour you a glass too, and you can take it or leave it."

With a wry laugh, Cheyenne nodded. "Okay. Sounds good."

"Wonderful. Thank you, Cheyenne."

"For?"

This is where things always get sticky between us. Drow don't mix well with Mom's politics or her ambitions.

"Thank you for coming to me first. We both know you're dedicated and skilled enough to have found your answers somewhere else. I realize I've been sitting on this conversation for a long time, and I'm glad you felt comfortable enough to bring it up again."

"Well, I found your name, Mom. Who else would I go to?"

"That's my girl. See you tomorrow. Love you."

"Love you too." *Despite everything, I love you.*

Cheyenne ended the call and dropped her hand. *I had to find incriminating evidence before she tells me all about it. Bianca Summerlin sure knows how to keep a secret.*

Her gaze settled on the tall dresser against the far-right wall of her bedroom. She focused on the shiny copper box next to the picture of their German Shepherd, Maxine. The dog had been gone six years, yet that photo was one of the only personal things, beyond her tech and her clothes, Cheyenne had brought with her into the city from her mom's family plot in the hills. That and the box.

Cheyenne crossed her room and stopped in front of the dresser. The copper box, cool in her hand, shimmered in the light poking through the blinds. "You only left her two things, didn't you? Me and this box that doesn't open."

She turned the thing over a few times, perusing the etched symbols she'd studied for twenty-one years. She set the box back on top of her dresser and rubbed her eyes before shuffling out into the living room. She'd go to her mom's house—Cheyenne's childhood home—tomorrow night and have the conversation she'd wanted to have since the first time she'd asked Bianca why she didn't have a dad.

"That still leaves me with a whole day to find answers on

my own. You taught me that too, Mom. Never rely on just one source for the most accurate information."

After inputting a few searches on the dark web and letting her torrents do the rest of the data-sifting and compiling for her, she grabbed the bag of Funyuns she'd opened last night. *Food is food.*

Now that Cheyenne knew she'd found something in that operations report with her mom's name on it, she couldn't just load her backpack and sit through two classes today. She had work to do.

Much like the one she'd sent Professor Dawley, she emailed her professors, informing them she wouldn't be in class today, but based on the trajectory of their course for the semester, here was the work she'd already performed and provided now to show she was on track—or way ahead of it.

"This is such a waste of time." She crammed another handful of Funyuns into her mouth. "I thought grad school was supposed to be harder, at least."

The hard part now wouldn't come from school on the Virginia Commonwealth University campus. No, the hard part was having patience with her searches and whatever holes they dug for her around the FRoE and this Chateau D'rahl and Inmate 4872. *My dad. It has to be.*

Nothing pulled up with her keywords or sub-level terms for over an hour. Although she had more to work with now, Cheyenne was antsy. She popped into the Borderlands forum to look around. *Maybe a unicorn needs help with a dragon problem.* She snorted. *Yeah, right.*

The first few topics were mundane. *New Arrival Support* and *Guidelines and Regulations Not Outlined in the Accord.* She might have gone back to look through those if every other thread turned out to be as useless first.

The next title made her stop: *We Have a New D-class Resource.*

It was the first time she'd seen D-class mentioned, but the D had to stand for drow. *Dragon's out of the question. I would've heard about one of those by now.*

Cheyenne opened the forum thread and took a deep breath. "This is not good."

Our friend HahaRadz444 had a visit from a D-class berserker last night. She helped him out with a greenskin power struggle. So far, things are looking up. Use this thread as a board for requests. If she's looking, she'll see them.—

The original thread post came from none other than gu@rdi@n104, which shouldn't have surprised her. They were all watching now for sure, or looking for her at the very least.

Cheyenne pushed back in her chair and shook her head. "He made me my own bat signal. On a dark-web forum for magicals who need help with…what? Not being extorted? Oh, my God, this is not what I signed up for."

Still, she couldn't help poking around through all the comments addressing their new D-class Resource. Most of them just referred to her as D. *Cute.*

A few trolls wanted someone to sit in on their business meeting with a warren of Nightstalkers, whatever those were, to discuss Ambar'ogúl produce smuggling.

Someone else was asking for money to help them pay the bills for the next three months.

One person, whatever they were, wanted the opportunity to meet her in person because "I crossed through when I was a child and never had the chance to see one with my own eyes."

"This is insane." Cheyenne kept scanning requests. None of

them hinted at anything on the same level as the goblin Radzu needing somebody to get orc thugs off his back and out of his store. "I'm not gonna find anything about Durg or the people going after Ember's friends on *this*. They better not start sending me fan mail."

No one knew her real name or where she lived—or that she wasn't a D-class resource. Not the way they thought she was. These people wouldn't expect their shiny new drow in the system to be just a halfling.

A private message from gu@rdi@n104 blinked on in the corner of her screen.

gu@rdi@n104: There's a lot of fluff to sift through in places like this. But something might show up that's worth your time. I've heard good things.

Cheyenne typed back that whatever the guy had heard, he was mistaken and should leave her alone. Then she deleted it before sending, stood, mussed the hair on the back of her head, and went to take a shower.

This was what Mom meant when she said everything has a price. I try to do a few good things to help some people out, and now I have to deal with everybody asking for everything.

What Cheyenne needed was to focus and not let herself get distracted by wondering how much this gu@rdi@n104 knew. Her data searches could do the rest. She'd gotten this far without a bulletin board for how to contract a drow berserker.

CHAPTER TWENTY-TWO

Without needing to get to class and sit through the most boring part of grad school so far—which was *all* of grad school —Cheyenne had the time to do her hair the way she wanted and put on the makeup she hadn't bothered with yesterday. Pale ivory foundation everywhere. Thick black eyeliner blended into the dark gray on her lids. This forum thing with gu@rdi@n104 calling her out as some kind of drow superhero put her in a don't-screw-with-me-mood, so she added black lipstick to go the whole mile. She saved that for special occasions and not being mistaken for a savior of every Border crossing—whatever that Border thing was—magical.

Metallica's *Master of Puppets* blasted from her Bluetooth speaker. Cheyenne walked circles around her desk, pausing every few rounds to check for pings on her searches. The music drowned out that blaring duck quack whenever a notification came up, but the music helped her think and stay calm.

She took a break to clean the kitchen and wash what few dishes she had. Then she made her bed, stuck some laundry in the wash, and got out the compressed air can to spray the dust out of her computer tower and the server box and used lint-free wipes on the monitors.

When her apartment was as clean as she could stand to make it, she ended up lying on the floor in front of her desk, trying to summon even a trifling spell without seeing the changes in her skin crop up. "Just a tiny spark. Something!"

She snapped her fingers for what felt like the hundredth time, and a silver flash ignited between her fingers. The second it happened, her skin tingled and took on the purple-gray color of her drow heritage. "Well, at least it's getting faster. That doesn't help me right now."

The last of the Funyuns went into her mouth, and then she stood to check her searches and the time. Still nothing, and it was almost 12:45 p.m. "Bergmann better have her office hours open."

If the halfling couldn't spend her afternoon sifting through the information her search programs hadn't found yet, she might as well spend her time doing something useful. She rolled up off the floor, paused, then darted into her room and snatched the copper box from her dresser.

Whatever she is, the woman knows more than I do. Maybe she knows more about this too.

Professor Mattie Bergmann's office door was wide open when Cheyenne stopped in the hall. She reached out to knock anyway, but Mattie beat her to it.

"Door's open, Cheyenne. Just come on in." The woman didn't look up from her desk and whatever work had most of her attention, but her mouth quirked in a private smile. "But feel free to—"

The door clicked shut behind the drow halfling. "Shut it? Yeah, I figured."

Finally, Mattie looked up at her student, those hazel eyes glinting. "I'm glad you came back."

"You didn't leave me *that* much to work with yesterday."

"Well, you know what they say. It took more than one guy to raze Rome and all that."

Cheyenne snorted. "That *is* what they say."

"So." Mattie folded her hands and thumped them on her desk. "How have things gone for you in the last twenty-four hours?"

"That's kind of a loaded question." Cheyenne stepped across the office toward her professor's desk. "The whole 'find my happy place' thing came in handy a few times, though."

"Good for you. I guess you just needed to know it was possible, huh?" Mattie sat back in her chair and nodded. "And you're able to let all the drow fall away just like that, huh?"

Cheyenne squinted and fought back a laugh, running her tongue along the inside of her cheek. "I kinda redefined that *happy place.*"

Mattie's eyes widened in confusion.

"I can slip into drow mode pretty much whenever I want. So far. And I broke the record I set with you yesterday."

"Wow." The programming professor smiled and rolled her chair back away from the desk. "By how much?"

"A long time. Hey, is there any way for me to use my magic *without* going full drow? You know, like if I wanted to, I don't know, knock something out of someone's hand without them seeing the skin and the hair and everything."

"I don't think so." Mattie blinked at the ceiling in thought. "Not unless you can cast a full illusion spell."

"Like yours."

"Yes. Like mine."

Cheyenne leaned toward the woman's desk. "So you can teach me *that?*"

"I can, but not yet. If you haven't perfected your ability to shift in and out of your dual forms, Cheyenne, an illusion spell will be useless to you."

"Right. No playing the system on that one."

Mattie chuckled. "Definitely not. It's a build-as-you-go kinda deal."

"Okay. How about this?" Cheyenne set the copper box on the professor's desk with a thunk and folded her arms. "You ever seen one of these before?"

Professor Bergmann looked down at the box, licked her lips, and cocked her head with a quick jerk. "Where did you get this?"

"Someone gave it to me. Technically to my mom, I guess, but if I'd been born already, she wouldn't have had to keep it for me." Mattie had not taken her eyes off the box, and Cheyenne nodded at it. "You know what it is?"

"This came from your father, didn't it?" The woman tapped a finger on her lips and frowned.

"Yeah, great guess. Care to tell me why?"

"These are drow runes." Mattie gestured to the symbols etched into the copper and cleared her throat. "I recognize only a few, Cheyenne, but even if I knew them all, I couldn't tell you what they mean."

"Why not?"

"This..." The professor took a sharp breath, then met her student's gaze. "Someone intended whatever's inside this box for you and no one else. I'd be doing us a disservice if I tried to solve this one on your behalf."

The halfling stared at her professor and shook her head a fraction of an inch. "What do you mean, 'solve' it?"

"It's a puzzle box." Mattie shrugged. "For lack of a better term. The drow call it something else, and I'm not important enough to have that kind of information. It's your legacy, Cheyenne. For whatever that's worth."

"I'm supposed to get it open?"

"Hmm." With a tight, regretful smile, Mattie stood and tapped the surface with her fingers. "You weren't exaggerating when you said your mom wasn't involved, were you?"

Cheyenne raised her eyebrows and grabbed the box again. "More like an understatement."

"Fair enough. When it's time for you to open that box, you'll know what to do. Or so I've heard. It's not a commonly practiced ritual anymore."

"Neither is knocking up a high-profile research economist before disappearing and leaving her to raise a half-magical baby by herself. Probably."

"True." With a knowing smirk, Mattie walked around her student until she stood at the other end of the office in front of the armchairs. "I'm assuming you didn't come here just to talk about drow artifacts most people have completely forgotten. We both have better things to do with our time, don't we?"

Turning the copper puzzle box in her hands, the halfling nodded and set it back down. The chains on her wrists jingled when she shook out her hands again, and then she turned from the desk to face her magical mentor. "So, teach me some stuff."

"All the stuff." Mattie chuckled and folded her arms. "Show me how much easier it is for you to bring out the dark elf."

Casting her mentor a sideways glance, Cheyenne stifled a smirk and closed her eyes. She opened her hands at her sides and thought about guns being pointed at anyone. Heat bloomed at the base of her spine. She counted to three as it washed up and over her, then she opened her eyes and met Mattie's gaze.

The other woman clicked her tongue. "Very nice. You look grounded in it today. How about—"

A line of purple and black sparks erupted at Cheyenne's fingertips, and she wiggled her fingers, letting her magic play in the electrified air around her hands.

"Okay. Show-off."

The drow halfling grinned. "Get the jar."

A surprised laugh burst from Professor Bergmann's mouth, and she blinked. "What was that?"

"The jar." Cheyenne nodded sideways toward the desk. "Bring it out. I can do it this time."

For a few seconds, Mattie studied her student with indecisive curiosity, then reached out and twisted her fingers in a brief gesture toward the desk. "Did you do something I should know about?"

"Probably."

The jar of pens floated off Professor Bergmann's desk and into the center of the office. It hovered in the air between them.

Cheyenne lifted her hand and reached toward the floating container. "I don't care about what other people *should* know. Just what I can do."

Sparks flared at the tip of her outstretched index finger, lighting the room and both women's faces with a deep violet glow. *Just like dodging a bullet. That's how it's done.*

The crackling hiss of her magic slowed to intermittent bursts. Mattie Bergmann's heartbeat stretched on, with multiple seconds between each percussion tap in Cheyenne's ears—at least, what felt like seconds. Cheyenne focused on the jar and sent a burst of purple and black magic toward the open rim. The light arced from her finger like water from a fountain.

With a hiss and a loud *crack*, every pen inside the jar flew out, striking the bookshelves and the walls and falling all over Mattie's desk. Inside the glass, Cheyenne's magic crackled with a droning buzz—purple and black lighting captured in a bottle.

"Well," Mattie's eyes gave off a feral light, "you get half points for that one."

Cheyenne dropped her hand. "You never said not to take anything *out* of the jar."

"You're one of *those* prodigies, aren't you?" When

Cheyenne's eyebrows flicked together in confusion, her professor laughed. "You're right. I didn't say what *not* to do. Just so we're clear, I hope that won't be something I have to remind you of too often."

"What not to do?" Cheyenne stepped toward the floating jar and shrugged. "Don't worry. My moral compass isn't that broken."

"Very reassuring." Mattie snapped her fingers and, before the halfling could grasp the jar humming with drow energy, the clear glass pulled away from Cheyenne and zipped into the professor's hand. Peering into the opening, Mattie blew into the jar like blowing out a candle, and the sparks buzzing inside snuffed out. "Did you spend any time working on returning to Cheyenne the Goth?"

Cheyenne watched her professor cross the office to put the jar back on her desk, although the woman didn't bother to pick up the pens scattered all over the place. "That part's not as fun."

"I wasn't joking." When Mattie turned around, amusement glinted in her eyes, but it was curtailed by a seriousness Cheyenne hadn't seen in her before. "I'm pleased to see you appreciating where you come from and what you can do. That's important."

"There's a but, isn't there?" The halfling pressed her lips together and leaned against the bookshelf, folding her arms.

"That surprises you?"

"No, it's just annoying."

Mattie rubbed her hands together as she paced her office. "In some ways, we're all a little annoyed about being here, but it's way better than where we came from. Most of the time. But all of us on *this* side, Cheyenne, do whatever it takes to live our lives within the parameters we're given. Everything after that is up to us. Just like it's your responsibility to get a handle not only on using your drow magic but on putting it away when it doesn't serve you. Believe me, there will be times when it won't serve you."

Cheyenne sniffed and watched her professor's slow, aimless steps. "This side of what?"

"I'm sorry?"

"You said, 'all of us on this side.' That's the Border, right?" The halfling leaned her head against the bookshelf. "I'm guessing the Border is the same thing as the portal. Maybe even the reservations. I know they're connected."

Mattie pointed at her student and dipped her head with an intense gaze. "New rule. The next thing I teach you is how to put together all those puzzle pieces you somehow snatched out of thin air. *After* you're able to shift from human to drow whenever you want. Until then, don't ask."

Cheyenne studied her teacher. *She's serious. But it's better than trying to find anything online with gu@rdi@n104breathing down my virtual neck. And it's more than Mom can tell me.*

"Okay. Fair enough. Then teach me something."

Professor Bergmann pointed her index finger at Cheyenne, then turned away. "Don't push it."

CHAPTER TWENTY-THREE

"How is this supposed to help me?" Cheyenne cocked her head, and her shoulders sagged. It took ten minutes to cool from the heat of her drow magic, and now she stood on the other side of Mattie's office, looking like a regular human grad student. *Maybe just a regular human.*

"Come on. Don't tell me you couldn't use a little more money thrown at you—oh." Professor Bergmann laughed and tossed the tray of loose change in her hand. The coins clinked together, sounding much like Cheyenne's wrist chains. "That's funny."

"I'll ignore it as long as you tell me the point of this."

"And ruin all the fun?"

A penny flew across the room and thumped against the half-drow's collarbone. "Ow."

"Oh, please. We both know you have a higher pain tolerance than that. It's in your blood." Mattie picked out another coin. "On *both* sides, if I had to guess."

"So, just because it's not excruciating, it means I should get used to being hit with— Hey!" A dime popped her in the forehead and fell to the carpet. Cheyenne frowned and rubbed her head.

"Look at that! Right in the middle. I still got it." Mattie shimmied a little and wiggled her eyebrows before taking careful aim with another coin. "And yes, this is exactly what you should get used to."

"This is stupid." The next coin bounced off her chin. "Did you do this with all those orcs you won't talk about?"

"Ha. They got fellfire and a couple of bursts of… You know what, that was different. I trained orcs not to feel pain. I'm training you not to give a damn."

"Yeah, that's not what I want."

"It is when you're trying not to unleash the beast within."

"Good god." The next coin headed straight for Cheyenne's ear. She jerked her head away at the last second, and the penny pinged the far wall. "This isn't gonna work."

"Oh, it will." Mattie picked up one coin at a time and began flinging them at her student. "Is this annoying?" *Fling.* "Stupid and pointless and juvenile, huh?" *Toss.* "Doesn't it make you wanna come over and stop me?"

Cheyenne snatched the next coin from the air and clenched it in her fist. "Stop."

"Uh-huh." Mattie lifted her chin and stared at Cheyenne's forearm, the coin still in the halfling's fist.

When she looked down, Cheyenne saw dark-gray patches blooming on her pale skin. A few of them grew, but it was slow. She swallowed.

"Happy place," Mattie reminded her. "Or whatever's the opposite of how you bring out the drow."

"The opposite." Cheyenne took a deep breath and stared at her forearm. It felt as if she could will the dark splotches away if she focused hard enough, breathed slow enough.

Another penny struck her shoulder.

"Ugh! I almost *had* it!" The halfling chucked the penny

across the office, and her drow transformation swept over her before the coin left her hand. It cracked into one of Professor Bergmann's framed certifications and bounced on the carpet. Then, the office fell silent.

"'Almost' isn't good enough. Not in this situation," Mattie said. "And you know it."

"I also know I'm never gonna be target practice for a carnival coin-toss booth. Outside of your office." Purple sparks crackled along Cheyenne's fingers. She clenched her fists and dampened them.

"That would be hilarious, wouldn't it? But you *may* find yourself trying to get some sleep or study or focus, and some dog two doors down won't stop barking. Or how about toddlers on an airplane? The ones that don't make the flight more entertaining for everyone and end up doing the opposite. Maybe somebody rear-ends you at a stoplight, and you have to deal with that mess." Professor Bergmann spread her arms and leveled a bold stare. "What are you going to do then? Pull over and scare the poor bastard off when a gray-skinned woman with pointy ears tries to exchange contact information and blows his car up instead?"

Cheyenne glared, then she let out one continuous, irritated sigh.

"I'm throwing coins at you because that's what I've got today as a Virginia Commonwealth University professor. We're not ready for a magic duel just yet. So if you want to learn, this is part of it. Target practice goes both ways."

"You mean I get to chuck things at you after this?"

Mattie lifted a finger. "Not *that* way. You're the target, Cheyenne, because accessing and using your magic can only happen when it *counts*. When there's no other way to handle things in the guise the rest of the world sees you in, then and only then, do you let the illusion drop."

"What about all the other people walking around without illusions, huh?"

"What?"

"I've seen, I don't know, half a dozen orcs and a spare troll and goblin in the last few days. None of them tried to look human. Why should I have to?"

Mattie swallowed and shook her head. "The rules are different for you."

"Why? Because I have drow blood? Or because of who my mom is?" Heat flared in Cheyenne's veins, and she did not have the patience left to contain it. "Trust me, the rules have been different for me all my life. If I'm to play by some rule that doesn't apply to everyone else, the least you can do is give me a straight answer, something that isn't bullshit."

"Cheyenne." Professor Bergmann's tone was sharp and authoritative, but she didn't move a muscle. "We'll talk about that after you handle getting hit with pennies longer than I can handle throwing them."

"Nope. If you want me to hang out and follow your screwed-up training techniques, I need to know why. I've made it twenty-one years without any of this. I can go another twenty-one." The halfling's nostrils flared, and she spread her arms. "Go ahead."

"I know you understand politics," Mattie said. "Your mom taught you plenty, I'm sure. The world I came from—the world your *father* came from—has its own politics too. And they are…complicated."

"Whatever." Cheyenne whirled toward the professor's desk and headed for her copper puzzle box. "You know, most people see my name and assume I'm Bianca Summerlin's entitled brat, and I couldn't care less about that. But *this*?" She lifted the box toward Mattie and shook it. "I *am* entitled to know these things. They're mine."

"It's not my place to open that door for you until we both

know you're prepared to use the information the way it needs to be—"

Cheyenne scoffed. "*You* won't open that door. Cool. I'll just open this one."

She went to the professor's office door and jerked it open. The door squealed out of the frame, and the brass knob popped off in her hand. She glanced at it, tossed it behind her shoulder, and took one step toward the hallway.

The door slammed shut and would have knocked her sideways if she'd been any closer. Cheyenne whirled around to see Mattie flick her fingers toward the door again. The knob that had never hit the floor whizzed past the half-drow and clicked back into place before reattaching itself.

"You can't do that," Cheyenne snarled.

"I just did." The professor lowered her hand, her jaw clenching and unclenching as she stared at the door.

"Tell me why the rules are different." The words sounded more like a growl from the drow halfling's throat. She held her professor's gaze and wondered if she'd let herself use magic on the only woman who knew enough to tell Cheyenne anything she wanted to know. "Or I'll find someone who isn't a spineless—"

"Because you're a halfling, Cheyenne." Mattie huffed out a sigh like she'd been holding that sentence in for way too long. "Most magicals haven't seen a halfling in their lifetime, which is why they treat those of you who exist like a myth. But the FRoE knows. I don't know how long they've been aware, and I'm sure they've come across only a few. They know about a halfling's magical blood manifesting certain traits when that halfling feels…*intense* about something. They know a halfling's natural state makes them look human. And they just don't care."

"Then it shouldn't be an issue."

"They don't care about *you*. If you don't learn how to

control your magic and hide who you are on a deeper level than black hair and makeup and studs, the FRoE *will* find you. If you make any trouble on this side where humans can see, where there's the slightest human whisper about magic, they'll come for you."

Cheyenne shook her head. "Yeah, that doesn't scare me. I can handle somebody trying to take me down."

"Not these people, Cheyenne. They're way more prepared than even I know. All I *do* know is if they come for you, they will book you and tie you up and ship you out to the closest Border reservation. They'll haul you back across and dump you in the middle of a world that wants nothing to do with humans and has no problem destroying a halfling just because that halfling happens to *look* like one."

Professor Bergmann closed her eyes, swallowed, and bowed her head for a few seconds. "I know that only brings up more questions. And I'm sorry. Believe me, the way this plays out for you if you don't get a grip on covering up your magic is the worst-case scenario. And it *will* happen."

Cheyenne chewed the inside of her lip. "The FRoE's just another kind of border patrol."

"Yes."

"And they don't want magicals on *this* side?"

Mattie dipped her head. "Not if those magicals refuse to follow the law, which is still tenuous and somehow all the more enforced because of it. Things are better than they were in some respects when the FRoE was organized and the reservations opened up to the general magical public. They still have a lot of room for improvement. And that's an understatement."

"You mean, like Native American reservations?"

The corner of Mattie's mouth twitched. "More like the model *for* Native American reservations. Trust me, the ones created for magicals on this side have been around much longer."

"Okay." Cheyenne rolled her shoulders and stretched her neck out. *Might as well take a chance on making a few more connections. She doesn't know I found that report.* "And this whole FRoE thing started when?"

An uncertain look crossed Mattie's face. "Sometime in two thousand. At least, that was when they made the official announcement in what few channels we had for communication. I'm sure the idea and the planning started a long time before that."

At least she knows that much. Cheyenne nodded and muttered, "Twenty-one years ago."

The programming professor let out a dry laugh and shrugged. "Hell of a way to usher in the twenty-first century."

"Yeah. Seems so. For a whole bunch of people." *Like my parents. And magicals all over the place who wanted to be* here *for some reason.*

"Now you know at least that much." Glancing at her watch, Mattie set the tray of coins on the shelf and went to her desk. "It's three fifty-seven. Might as well call it a day. I'll be here tomorrow, in case you were wondering, and I'm still willing to keep throwing things at you until you don't lose it on me." She glanced at Cheyenne as she packed her wheeled briefcase, stuffing it with folders and loose papers.

The half-drow shrugged. "No one else has stepped up to take the job, so I guess you get to keep doing it."

"Yes. I'm just that lucky." Mattie chuckled, straightened, and grabbed the metal handle of her briefcase. "I'll help you as much as I can, Cheyenne. But what you're looking for is beyond my knowledge as a professor or a trainer or even as another magical who crossed over."

"What do you think I'm looking for?"

Professor Bergmann nodded at the copper-coated drow artifact in her student's hand. "A way to open that box. And how to use what's inside."

With a curt nod and a half-effective smile of encouragement, Mattie wheeled out of her office and into the hall. "Lock up when you've cooled down."

The runes etched into the copper cube flashed beneath the lights when Cheyenne turned it every which way again.

A puzzle box. I just have to put the right pieces together. Or...

She gritted her teeth and tried to twist the top of the box off. Maybe they were the sides. Her dark-gray skin tingled a little at the effort, and then a bright silver light erupted from within every single rune and sent a painful electric jolt up her arms.

"Whoa." Cheyenne released one side of the box and held the thing in her palm as far away from her as she could stretch. "You little shit."

CHAPTER TWENTY-FOUR

The first thing she did when she got back to her apartment was call Ember's cell. It was one thing for Cheyenne to insert herself onto her friend's approved visitors' list at the hospital, but filling out a new form giving the place permission to call her with updates on Ember's condition would have taken it a little too far. Plus, while it wouldn't have been impossible, she would have had to pretend to be Ember Gaderow and forge her signature. Which might be suspicious.

Ember's phone went to voicemail right away, which meant it was dead.

Cheyenne went to her desk, dropped her cell beside her main keyboard, and went for a little hunt through VCU Medical Center's patient database. Before she could click into Ember's file, a duck quacked on her screen, and the yellow notification lit up in the bottom right corner.

"Oh, good. As soon as I *try* to do something else..."

With growing curiosity, she clicked on the notification and opened the first search result that had come through. It wasn't just one, though. Her deep search had flagged four listings as a match to "border," "portal," "O-class," and "crossing." From four different IP addresses. There was no way to tell if the listed addresses were real or decoys, but the command report explained why it had taken her programs so long to come back with anything useful. They'd had to break through over a dozen layers of encryption to put the hits together, compile everything, and return the info.

Somebody doesn't want people digging around in their sandbox.

Cheyenne clicked on the first result and opened it.

Too bad. I'm digging anyway.

The first file didn't make much sense on its own, but it contained cross-references with the second and more with the third and fourth. Reading them one right after the other felt like a transcript of a private message someone had split and rearranged. Cheyenne reassembled them as best she could, layering one over the other to find common phrases.

They had embedded the conversation with un-closed code lines, chopped somewhere before the end. Which meant the other end—and the rest of the conversation in any order that made sense—was still *in* the files.

It took her an hour to run the series of overlapping tests to find which severed end of code matched the other. *At least I know I have the glass slipper and the foot in the same place. Probably.*

When the pieces clicked into place, another notification quacked on her screen, and a bright-red warning message popped up in the center.

Unauthorized Access Detected.

"No. Ya think?" Cheyenne cloaked her trail and cut a few corners around the security wall. She didn't override the system so much as made it think she was part of it, and then she was past the last bit of encrypted security and could read the combined conversation.

"Jesus." It came out as a whisper while Cheyenne read the document she'd dug up and assembled. It discussed four locations and four people, all operating on behalf of the FRoE, whatever that meant. The document outlined a series of operations over the last six months by magicals smuggling other races over the Border and bypassing the reservations. She uncovered surveillance and cataloging records of magicals who came across, and the ways they blended in with the humans on this side. Lists of businesses. Lists of families. Account balances and debts owed to this trafficking organization. Locations squeezed for protection money. New targets made of a dozen magicals and their businesses across the country, all of whom had been on this side, living with humans, for years—decades, even.

The most interesting part was the detailed instructions for avoiding FRoE detection and slipping under the radar of an organization created to regulate the magicals on this side and keep them in line. Hotspots of FRoE activity and where the magical-policing agency had overlooked its own blind spots.

"Illegal magical network." Cheyenne blinked in raw amazement at her discovery and leaned toward her monitor. "How long have these people been *doing* this?"

She read over the detailed lists and the gathered information three times before she found a reference to the next operation on the network's list of scheduled "meetings." It was easy to miss when they referred to it as "an on-site update with real-time communication." What the hell? They weren't talking about software or servers at that point. They were talking about meeting in person to make some kind of nefarious deal.

Tomorrow night.

Cheyenne leaned back in her chair and rubbed her face. "Jesus. I need to find out who's gonna be there."

All the hints and vague descriptions pointed to something big. Not only big, but harmful to a lot of magicals with established lives on this side. Beyond that, she knew if she could tap into *this* network and find their databases beyond a few conversational updates and operating plans, she'd find Durg. The whole thing stank as much as the orc who'd shot Ember.

If I don't find him, I can at least keep this deal from being made and help who knows how many magicals by crashing their giant party.

Cheyenne set up bloodhound programs to sniff out the actual IP addresses from all four pieces of this messed-up correspondence, then she pulled the encoded location sites from the list and ran those through a decoder that would match them with corresponding GPS coordinates.

"This hole keeps getting deeper." The halfling stood, double-checked everything was set up to do the heavy lifting, and nodded. "I'll get to the bottom of it. It's just gonna take a minute." She stretched her arms overhead, then made a sour face and sniffed her armpit. "Gross. Time for a shower."

She passed the time after her hot shower by practicing her shifts from human to drow and back again. The first one was easier now with every attempt, but the cooldown was still a big issue. Cheyenne stood in front of her bathroom mirror with a towel wrapped around her, staring at the reflection of her purple-gray face and golden eyes flashing in the vanity lighting.

"I found the trick to letting this part out." Her skin tingled with heat and magic. "So, what's the trick to calming down?"

What an oxymoron of an assumption—that humans were calmer than anything non-human. Calmer than magicals. It was likely true only because humans had no idea these Borders letting magical beings into their world even existed.

Think of something. Cheyenne brushed her still-wet, bone-white drow hair away from her face and ignored her pointed ears. *Something that makes this go away.*

With a deep breath, she stared into the mirror and found herself thinking of the Virginia woods around her mom's twenty-acre plot of land. Their *family's* plot of land. All the maples and the rivers, the wildflowers bursting across the meadow in violet, yellow, red, and white. She thought of the family of deer she'd found in the thicket just over the hill behind the farm. Two fawns and their mother, lying in the dappled sunlight coming through the leaves. She'd been so quiet, moving through the woods on bare feet because it always felt better, more natural. She had paused a few yards away from the animals as they rested in the mid-morning sun. The doe had lifted her head and observed Cheyenne crouched behind the trees. No fear. No concern for her fawns. Just recognition that the girl who looked human but wasn't—not quite—existed in this place with her.

The gray coloring filtered away from Cheyenne's skin, and her eyes lost their golden glow as second by second, she returned to the form most people recognized but never truly *saw*—black hair, blue eyes, pale skin, full Goth.

Cheyenne studied her reflection for a few seconds, letting herself think about the doe and her fawns and the silence of the forest that had raised her as much as Bianca had. Her fingers drummed on the counter around the sink.

"Well, it's better than singing *Kumbaya*."

She tried again to shift to drow form.

She went through four rounds of shifting between human and drow, forcing her mind to flit from orcs with guns to a family of deer in the woods. The duck quacked in the living room. "That was fast."

The message on her computer had nothing to do with her decoding programs or the original IP addresses from that encrypted conversation. It was a personal message, without a user handle or any way to identify who it was from.

It took up her entire screen.

We found your back door. Call off your search.

"Huh." Cheyenne tried to minimize the message, but this asshole had frozen her monitor. She pulled everything but the new message up on her second monitor and made sure it was still running. She also copied the data that had come back with GPS coordinates and locations already and sent them to three different places on her server, just to be safe. "Might as well keep this guy occupied for a few more minutes."

She typed a reply, amused to find her own handle appeared before her message.

ShyHand71: Congratulations. Sorry if I'm a little skeptical of someone who takes over my screen and won't identify themselves.

Whoever it was, they'd opened this dialogue with a rude seizure of her system and no introductory etiquette. "So we'll cut through all the politeness and get right to the point. My favorite way to do this."

What you found doesn't belong to you. You do not understand who you're dealing with.

Cheyenne snorted. "Please."

ShyHand71: Sounds scary. So tell me who I'm dealing with. If it sounds like a good enough reason to call it off, maybe I'll listen.

You only get one warning. Don't make us have to find you again. Shut it down.

She was ready to tell the ghost messenger to go to hell, but the blank screen of the message without a handle flashed and disappeared.

CHAPTER TWENTY-FIVE

For a few seconds, Cheyenne's fingers paused over the keyboard in disbelief. Then, she laughed. "Oh, it's on. You want someone to back off a search on the dark web, buddy, you don't seize their system and start making vague threats. Especially me."

Huffing out another laugh, she shook her head and logged onto a private server she used to share with the group of hackers she'd met through GRNDO. Turned out he'd started the system way before she was born and had kept it alive until his death. Then the rest of the group he'd brought in over time had taken it over and turned it into a space for mentoring young, eager hackers who thought they wanted to do this forever. The name hadn't changed, though: Y2Kickass.

It sounded like a superhero fan group, but at least an awful name kept them off the radar. Whoever managed to find them knew what they were doing enough to be worth the group's time.

Cheyenne sent a message to the guy she only knew as Todd, and that was enough.

ShyHand71: I need a favor.

The instant reply didn't make it like seem the guy sat in front of his screen twenty-four/seven just waiting for someone to chat with him. She almost rolled her eyes, then realized she was the same way at times.

T-rexifus088L: Look at this. You don't call. You don't write. And now you need a favor.

ShyHand71: Yeah, okay. Missed you too.

T-rexifus088L: What's up?

ShyHand71: I need you to hold some information for me. Some douche canoe's riding my ass and probably won't stop until it looks like I stopped first.

T-rexifus088L: Whose Frosted Flakes did you piss in?

ShyHand71: They won't tell me. I just need a storage space for 48 hours. You cool with that?

T-rexifus088L: ShyHand71 needs my help. Always cool. Is this monster in a cage gonna bite me if I open it?

ShyHand71: Probably. My guess is you wouldn't even know it until it killed you.

T-rexifus088L: Thanks for the warning. Send it over. I'll feed the beast for as long as you need.

ShyHand71: I just need you to keep it locked up. But give me a key.

Todd sent a thumbs-up emoji, followed by a link to a terabyte of storage on his own private server—or maybe the one that still belonged to Y2Kickass in general.

T-rexifus088L: Anything else I need to look out for?

ShyHand71: If you get any alerts that the programs finished doing their job before I do, just let me know.

T-rexifus088L: Got it. Hey, we have a couple new recruits wanting to learn from the best. You interested?

Cheyenne closed her eyes and couldn't help smiling.

ShyHand71: Maybe later. Good to see there are still people like you willing to mold impressionable minds into the shape of delinquency. You're good at it.

T-rexifus088L: You're better. Catch ya later.

Closing out the chat, Cheyenne opened the provided link and dumped everything she'd found—the results of her searches, the decrypted conversation from four origin points, and the still-processing GPS coordinates—into the server space. The minute she hit upload, everything disappeared, including the link Todd had sent her. "He'll get me something else when I need to dive back in."

After that, she scrubbed everything off her server to make it look like she'd taken the hint from the anonymous jerkoff who'd tried to scare her away from digging deeper. "We're not done, whoever you are. Just wait."

After two packs of Ramen noodles and another round of meditating on guns and deer families, Cheyenne went to bed sometime before midnight and got more than four hours of sleep.

The next morning, an email from Professor Dawley sat in her inbox saying he expected her to be in his Thursday class after her absence on Tuesday, because "no one gets their graduate degree by skirting the system and insulting their professor's intelligence."

"Whatever. Like I owe him some kind of professional courtesy."

Still, she resigned herself to sitting through a day of classes to placate the old jerk. She did care about getting her master's and completing the program, after all. It looked good on paper if she wanted to open the pool of high-level careers that offered options for a life that didn't bore her to death.

She pulled her long-sleeved fishnet shirt over a black tank top—the one that was mostly ripped to shreds—and painted on black lipstick again. "How's that for professional courtesy?"

The chains on her wrist clinked as she snatched her backpack and slipped on her shoes. "Time to go play the game. At least until I figure out where that meeting's going down tonight."

The drive to the Virginia Commonwealth University campus gave her plenty of time to imagine finding Durg at this illegal meet-up of magical gangs and wringing his thick neck. She thought about baby deer in between each satisfying daydream.

The image of the doe and her fawns was a lot harder to keep in the front of her mind when she walked through the campus and across the quad for her next class. People were staring at her. Not like that was anything new, and Cheyenne was used to unwanted eyes on her, trying to put together the pieces of an expressionless Goth chick storming across the school to sit in her classes and pay attention. But that wasn't what she felt this morning.

Someone's watching me.

A few times, she turned around on the path to search the faces turned toward her that turned away when people realized she was looking for something. Just a bunch of college kids using their dulled imaginations to judge her based on how she dressed. Nothing else.

There's no way anyone online figured out who I am. Not after I've kept that secret since I learned what a computer was.

Still, the feeling of being watched and followed didn't go away. It didn't help that Cheyenne almost knocked over a kid running across the path after a giant bouncy ball. She cursed and leapt out of the way.

"You need to watch where you're going." The kid's mom glared at her with an impressive mixture of scorn and fear as she jogged after the toddler.

Right. Because two-year-olds belong on a college campus.

Her first class was with Professor Bergmann, which didn't feel as awkward as Cheyenne expected. The woman spoke with her usual flair of apathy despite how excited she was to pick apart the aspects of the assignment she'd had them do on Tuesday. Mattie didn't meet Cheyenne's gaze more than once or offer any sign she also agreed Cheyenne didn't need to be here. Except for when Natalie and her messy bun showed up fifteen minutes late and knocked the keyboard to the floor with her oversized, over-prized messenger bag.

"They leave those cords here for a reason," Natalie muttered as she stepped over the keyboard and the dangling cords. "So we can *use* them."

"Nice apology." Cheyenne eyed the other student with a blank expression as Natalie sidestepped a row of tables and took a seat in the front. *What is she even doing in this class?*

A small tingle of heat flared beneath her skin, and Cheyenne sank farther into her chair, stretching her legs out under the table until they knocked against the fallen keyboard.

"All right, Ms. Arcady." Professor Bergmann eyed Natalie and offered a tight smile. "While I appreciate you bothering to come to class today, I expect you to be on time. That's something you should've covered before the last time you graduated."

"Sorry. I had to stop for—"

"Excuses are for undergrads," Bergmann interrupted. "I don't care why you were late. I *do* care that you want to be here, and for that to be convincing, you need to be here at eight o'clock. Preferably before then, so everyone's ready before I get here. So. Who learned something while you were building the programs you started on Tuesday?"

A lanky dude with a bushy red beard, who insisted on sitting in the last row, started talking about the next level of code he'd injected into what their professor had given them to work with, and Cheyenne had no problem tuning him out. Instead, she tried *not* to think of anything related to a gun when she heard Messy Bun whisper to Peter, "She can't talk to us like that. That's harassment."

For the first time in two weeks, Cheyenne turned on the university-provided computer in front of her, pulled the keyboard onto the desk, and sneaked into the sadly vulnerable school servers to connect with Messy Bun's computer. She pulled up the notepad and typed a little message to get the girl to shut up about lawsuits and getting Professor Bergmann fired.

Reminding you you're an adult isn't harassment.

It took a few seconds for Messy Bun to see the message. She glanced at her screen and stiffened, then stared at the professor at the front of the room. She tried to figure out how the woman had gotten a message into her computer without touching it *and* while talking to the class. Not to mention how she heard her.

Cheyenne fought back a giggle and sent one more note.

But I can harass you all day from anywhere.

Messy Bun stabbed the power button on the monitor until the screen blinked off, then she slumped in her chair and folded her arms.

The big guy named Peter leaned toward Natalie. "You okay?"

"I'm trying to pay attention." The girl gestured weakly toward Professor Bergmann, then folded her arms again.

Cheyenne heard Messy Bun's heartbeat racing between short, shallow breaths. That girl wouldn't make it through a programming career if she had no interest in figuring out who'd sent her the message.

"And that's what I…can I help you?" Mattie paused in answering somebody else's question to lean sideways toward the door into the computer lab.

"Sorry. Wrong room." The guy didn't sound sorry or flustered for having stepped into someone else's class. He didn't sound anywhere near the same age as the other grad students, either.

A prickle of suspicion rippled along Cheyenne's neck, and she turned in her chair for a look at the guy. But he'd already left, and the door shut again.

Mattie cocked her head with a confused smile. "Gotta love the second week of class. I swear, it takes first-graders less time to get used to a new schedule." The students chuckled, and Professor Bergmann continued lecturing.

Cheyenne didn't miss the look her professor shot her, even as Mattie kept speaking with zero indication anything might be wrong.

Why do I feel like something's about to blow up in my face any second?

That feeling of being watched, either in person or through any computers she had access to, came back stronger. Cheyenne signed out of everything on the lab's computer and turned her laptop off too.

CHAPTER TWENTY-SIX

Through her second class, she still felt watched. It made her itchy, and more than once, she found herself zeroing in on the memory of deer in the woods instead of trying not to fall asleep while her professor droned on about cybersecurity and why it was important. *They should be teaching people how to hack into these systems instead of coloring inside the lines. You want a high-profile technology firm to protect their assets and keep their private data locked up, you hire the best hacker you can find. Nobody seems to get that.*

None of her professors bothered to ask her to stay after class to discuss why she was skipping during the second week of grad school. They didn't have an argument, because the work Cheyenne had sent via email *before* being absent was perfect. They all knew it.

She stopped at the Student Center for a lamb gyro and two bottles of water. Even here, with students and administrators of every age and academic subject milling around in a haze trying to get used to being in school again, the drow halfling couldn't shake the feeling someone had eyes on her. She couldn't find a single person who appraised her with anything more than superficial judgment.

There's no way I'm just imagining this. Paranoia isn't my style.

Her stomach had different ideas. Cheyenne wrapped the rest of the gyro and shoved it in her backpack, then downed a bottle of water and bagged the other one before heading to the IT building and Professor Bergmann's office.

Useless classes and less-useless training. However, Mattie's been on this side long enough that she's bound to know something about how magicals find each other here. If there is someone following me.

It took her by surprise to see Mattie Bergmann behind her desk wearing yellow sweatpants, a navy tank top, and sneakers with her hair in a high ponytail. She looked more like another college student than a woman getting paid to teach them.

"Right on time." Mattie stood when Cheyenne stepped through her office door. The professor clicked out of something on her computer.

"Going to the gym or something?" Cheyenne closed the door behind her but didn't drop her backpack yet.

"What?" The professor glanced down at her out-of-place attire and chuckled. "Oh. Well, I might. I've got the rest of the day to do whatever I want. After office hours."

"So you changed just in case."

"It's not *that* weird." Mattie eyed her student before offering a halfhearted shrug. "I don't suppose you'd be up for going on a run with me, would you?"

Cheyenne grimaced. "I thought I already told you I don't do laps."

"It's not a lap when it's across campus and back."

"Yeah, the only way you're gonna get me to run is if you blast magic at me." The halfling smirked. "So, I don't suppose you're ready for that duel, are you?"

"You're a pain in my ass." Mattie grinned, wagged a finger at her student, then stepped away from her desk. "No duels and no run."

A few seconds of silence stretched between them, then Mattie's eyes narrowed.

"Everything okay?" she asked.

"Yeah." Cheyenne bit her lip and tried to ignore that itch of suspicion crawling across her back. "Hey, did you know the guy who walked into the lab this morning?"

Professor Bergmann's joking smile faded, and she cocked her head toward Cheyenne. "Just another lost college kid. Why?"

Not the answer I was hoping for. "I'm allowed to be curious."

"But you look suspicious. Of me."

Cheyenne shook her head and smiled to push the other woman's curiosity out of the room. "You look like a cat and hide it with an illusion spell. Why would I suspect you of anything? *Pfft.*"

"You're trying to diffuse this with a bad joke?" Mattie lifted one foot behind her thigh to stretch her quad, then did the same with the other. "Probably should leave the bad jokes to me. Just so we're on the same page, if there's something going on in your personal life that makes you suspicious of random students stepping into the wrong classroom, whatever that looks like, I'm putting it on the record you can talk to me about it."

"I thought you didn't do therapy sessions."

Mattie puffed out a dry laugh. "Point taken. I'll back off. So. After yesterday's little display with the jar, I can't imagine you haven't picked up something new to show me. Let's see it."

"It's not as impressive."

"Please. Modesty is wasted on someone who knows how good they are."

Cheyenne smirked and shook her head, dropping her backpack at the foot of the bookshelf beside the door. "I'm still in training."

"Oh-ho! Are you giving me credit for what you're about to do?"

"Don't get used to it." The drow halfling shook out her hands, her chains dangling, and rolled her neck from one shoulder to the other to loosen up. *Guess it'll be easier to slip into drow when I feel like there's a hidden camera on me somewhere.*

It was. She pulled up an image of a gun pointed at Ember to get herself into that space. Her back sent a barrel roll of heat across her skin, and she took on her dark drow coloring, hair shifting black to white from the roots to the ends. She opened her golden eyes.

The corners of Mattie's mouth turned up in surprise. "You look bad-ass. You've been practicing."

"It's not like I timed myself or anything."

Mattie tapped a finger on her lips, which were still curled into a small smile. She nodded. "Keep going."

Blowing out a long breath, Cheyenne imagined herself in front of her bathroom mirror, practicing for hours to pick up her human form again. She closed her eyes. *Just a bunch of deer in the woods. Might not be the happy place, but it's as calm as—*

Something hit her in the neck. She opened one eye beneath a raised brow.

Mattie spread her arms and grinned. "Had to test it. Just to make sure it was real."

In front of the woman's hand, another penny from the tray on the shelf floated midair.

Cheyenne glanced down at her hands—super-pale and black-painted fingernails, no hint of drow gray. "It's real, all right. And this means—"

The penny shot across the office and pinged off her eyebrow piercing.

"Come on."

"Look at *you*." Mattie bobbed her head in a mix of encouragement and mockery. "It's like I'm throwing pennies at a regular human."

Cheyenne kept her human appearance without letting her annoyance get the better of her. "As annoying as that is, we should step it up."

"Oh, you think you're ready for some real pressure, huh?" The professor nodded and tapped her lip again. "What did you have in mind?"

"Got any guns around?"

Mattie's smile disappeared. "That's not funny."

"I wasn't trying to be funny."

"No, Cheyenne. I don't keep guns in my office on a university campus." Mattie's eyes narrowed, and she turned to pace in a large circle on the other side of the room. "But we *can* try something else."

"Yeah. I'm ready." *Just keep thinking about deer. Little Bambi and his mom.* Cheyenne snorted when she remembered that movie opened with deer and guns.

Okay, not Bambi.

"Good." Mattie whirled to face her student and her hand whipped out. A brief silver light flashed from the woman's fingertips, and an unseen force shoved the drow halfling sideways into the closed office door.

Cheyenne pushed herself away and turned to face her professor. "What the hell?"

"Didn't see *that* coming, did ya?"

Deer. Deer. Deer.

"Nope." Opening her clenched fists, Cheyenne took a deep breath and let it out. "You're gonna have to do better than that if you're trying to hurt me."

"Hurt you? Ha. Trust me, halfling, if I wanted to hurt you, I wouldn't have to *try*." Mattie's dark ponytail swung back and forth as she shook her head, which made Cheyenne think of

Ember's ponytail the night her friend had met up with those orcish thugs.

Think of the woods. The quiet. Keep it down.

"And if anyone else wanted to hurt you…" Mattie lashed out with the same invisible spell and sent her student flying back against the wall. "You'd never see it coming."

With a grunt, Cheyenne pushed herself to her feet and rolled her shoulders. "I'm trying to work around that part."

"What?"

"Nothing." *Crap.*

Mattie folded her arms and held Cheyenne in her feral gaze. "I don't want to ask you again if everything's okay, but that last remark made it sound like you think someone is trying to hurt you."

"I don't." Cheyenne waved for her teacher to come at her, squaring her feet and leaning forward a little to brace for impact. "Do it again."

Mattie didn't move. "Not until you tell me what's going on."

"I said, I'm fine." *Or I will be when I figure out where those magical mobsters will be tonight.*

"Cheyenne, I'm trying to help. I told you more than I should have yesterday, and I can't help feeling responsible for you because of it."

The heat of her magic flared, but she pushed it down. "The only person responsible for me is me. You're responsible for teaching me how not to lose my shit when someone keeps pushing me."

A ripple of gray passed over Cheyenne's skin, visible for a split second on her arms and chest beneath the fishnet shirt. It faded, and the half-drow wished she could keep from breathing so hard. *At least it's better than shifting.*

Mattie studied her, both eyebrows raised, and lifted a hand toward her student for a quick, acknowledging gesture. "Looks like you're getting a good grip on that part."

Cheyenne glanced at her arms. *All human.* "Guess so."

"There's one more thing I think we should try. If you can master that, I'll hold up my end of the deal."

Answering my questions about the FRoE and Borders and portals. Except now the questions I have will give away what I'm trying to do. "Yeah, okay. Let's do it."

"Okay." Professor Bergmann stepped toward her desk and leaned against the edge. "We're gonna work on your speed going back and forth. Human to drow. Drow to human."

"I already covered that."

"*And* letting off a spell or two in between. If you *have* to use magic and it isn't an option to let everybody see your lovely drow locks afterward," Cheyenne snorted, "you need speed on your side. Something tells me you wouldn't just walk away from a situation where you could have stepped in but chose to stay hidden instead."

Cheyenne's last reserve of calm faded. *Because that's what I did with Ember, and it put her in the hospital.*

She shifted to her drow side. "No. I'm not walking away from anything."

"Good." Mattie nodded and studied her student with a wary gaze. "Show me how important *that* is to you."

Purple and black sparks shot from Cheyenne's fingertips, and she hardly thought about where she was aiming or why before those sparks launched across Bergmann's office. A loud *rip* filled the room as her spell tore through the upholstery on one armchair. It didn't register until almost ten seconds later. That was how long it took her to bring up her memory of the woods and let her drow magic fade into the background again.

She frowned at the armchair, blue eyes instead of golden narrowed. "Sorry."

"Don't be." Mattie cleared her throat. "I was waiting for a good reason to replace those. You have your new target. Try it again. Faster."

Cheyenne shook out her hands and got ready to repeat the process. "There aren't any stories going around about halflings shifting themselves into, like, a puddle of goo or anything, are there?"

Her professor shrugged. "Stories are just stories. If you feel 'gooey,' that's a good sign it's time to take a break."

"I hope you're learning something from this too." Cheyenne centered her focus on the armchair, shaking her head as her professor chuckled.

"Oh, yeah? Why's that?"

"So the next halfling you train won't be constantly reminded you're not an expert on halfling training."

"I *will* be after this."

"Right." Cheyenne embraced her drow magic and the heat and her anger, her skin tingling into slate-gray even as she unleashed another small attack on the armchair. It felt easier this time to imagine walking barefoot through the woods.

CHAPTER TWENTY-SEVEN

"Two seconds." Mattie nodded and grabbed the handle of her briefcase on wheels. "Not bad."

"Yeah, for only three days of your weird training methods." Cheyenne wiggled her fingers in front of her face. Her skin still tingled from the aftereffects of shifting and using so much magic with intent, although she looked human.

"It's working well for both of us."

Cheyenne huffed out a laugh. "Yeah. Thanks."

"All right. Now I'm heading to the gym. I'll see you tomorrow. Let me know if you change your mind about a run."

"I won't."

Mattie laughed and stepped through the door. "Just lock up—"

Cheyenne had her backpack over her shoulders and the doorknob in her hand before her professor could finish. "I'm leaving too."

Casting the halfling a sideways glance, Mattie hid a smile as they walked down the hall together. "You know, you might fool most people with the makeup and your apparent mastery over complete lack of expression. But you look pretty pleased with yourself."

"That's what smiles are for." The corners of Cheyenne's mouth twitched in what most people wouldn't call a smile. When Mattie laughed, the halfling let herself join in for a few seconds. "Hey, I have a question maybe you can answer."

The programming professor stopped in the hallway and glanced around. It was empty. "Is it a question we should discuss in my office and not out here in the middle of a public hallway?"

"Hey, when it's four o'clock, you don't even stop to make sure your students are gone and your office is locked up all the way." Cheyenne shrugged. "I'll make it quick."

Mattie sighed. "It better be. I downed an energy shot while you were blowing up my furniture."

Cheyenne ignored the comment and lowered her voice. "If a certain…organization of people like us, more or less, wanted to *find* a specific person…like us…how would they do that?"

Mattie frowned.

"An organization that starts with an F."

"I know who you mean, Cheyenne. My answer is that it depends on the person they're trying to find. Are there records in the system? Are they registered? Do they carry a high profile on this side, or *did* they carry a high profile on the other side? Anything that can be found and any connections that can be made *will* be found and made in covert ways." Mattie tilted her head at her student. "If there's nothing in the system, I wouldn't say this organization is above more old-school routes of finding someone."

"You mean, in person?"

"Something like that."

Cheyenne ran her thumbs under the straps of her backpack and glanced down the hallway behind them. "Any chance you know how to get into that system?"

"None." The professor's grip tightened around the handle of her wheeled briefcase; Cheyenne heard the handle creak in Mattie's grip. "And I wouldn't want to. I'd also advise anyone who thought *they* wanted to that staying *out* of that mainframe might save that person's life. If that person wanted to avoid being found and locked up and shipped out, if you catch my drift."

"Yeah. I do."

"They're doing their jobs, Cheyenne. As long as that's what you keep doing, too, you won't have any problems." Professor Bergmann studied her student with a concerned frown. "Anything else?"

"Just have fun on your run, I guess."

"Right." Mattie walked away and down the hall. "See you tomorrow."

Cheyenne stayed where she was and watched her professor disappear around the corner toward the front of the IT building.

She's way too afraid of these people to believe that the FRoE's supposed to keep everybody safe. How bad can they be if a bunch of other black-market magicals have been gaming the system and screwing with their own kind? Not bad enough to stop them, that's for sure.

It seemed likely someone with no political ties to the FRoE or this "other side" or any of the gangs strong-arming magicals like Ember and her goblin friend Trevor would have more room to operate under the radar.

Someone like me. What's badder than an unlisted drow halfling no one can find?

Cheyenne pulled out her phone and gave Ember another call. Straight to voicemail again. *Still got time to stop by the hospital before heading out to Chez Summerlin.*

A nurse was stepping out of Ember's hospital room and closing the door behind her when Cheyenne arrived. "How's she doing?"

"Oh." The nurse jolted and glanced up from the iPad in her arms. "Hi. Are you here for a visit?"

"Yeah. Is she awake yet? I mean, like, able to talk or..."

"Well." The nurse tried to cover her surprise at seeing a young woman Gothed out in the middle of the recovery ward. "She's—"

"Jeanette." Dr. Andrews turned the corner and walked toward them. "Can you take these files back to my office? I have a follow-up appointment a few doors down, but that's in two minutes."

"Of course." The nurse took his files from him, smiled at Cheyenne, and took off at a brisk pace toward the end of the hall before disappearing around another corner.

"Ms. Gaderow was awake for almost fifteen minutes earlier this afternoon." Dr. Andrews glanced at the door to Ember's room. "She didn't speak as far as I know, so it's plausible she's still in shock. She's sleeping again."

"Hmm." Cheyenne stuck her hands in her pockets and eyed the door, wanting to be there if Ember woke up again. Cheyenne wouldn't be able to leave her in time to get to her mom's. That wouldn't go very well for her later, but if Ember could talk to her, her mom could wait. "Is that normal?"

"I'm sorry?"

She kept her gaze on Dr. Andrews. "Not the shock part. I get that. I mean, all the sleeping."

"Sometimes. Everyone handles trauma differently. But we've found nothing alarming. As long as her vitals stay within normal range, and she's responding well to the surgery and any other treatments, we'll let her come out of it in her own time."

"Has anybody else come to see her? Like her family?"

Dr. Andrews opened his mouth and closed it again with a sympathetic frown. "That's one of those things I don't have the liberty to share with you."

"Right. 'Cause I'm not family. I get it."

"You're more than welcome to visit for a bit." The doctor glanced at his wristwatch. "You still have about an hour and a half."

"Okay."

He nodded at her with a reassuring smile and headed a few doors down before stepping into his next appointment. Cheyenne approached the door to Ember's room and peered inside, cupping her hands around her eyes at the narrow, rectangular window. She couldn't see her friend's face, but Ember's hair was fanned out behind her on the pillow as she lay on her side facing the window.

The halfling stepped back and stuck her hands into her pockets. *Rolling over's a good sign, I guess. And I should leave before I miss my chance at cocktail hour with Bianca. I can't screw this one up.*

She shut the door and went toward the front of the inpatient wing. Just before she reached the automatic doors, a tingle of being watched crawled along the back of her neck. Cheyenne moved faster, grateful the doors opened so she didn't run through them.

Either I'm losing my mind, or there's someone tailing me. If that's it, they're good.

She waited until she'd crossed the parking lot and was halfway to her car before turning around to reassure herself. A tall man in a VCU baseball cap was a few yards behind her. She met his gaze like he'd been staring at her the whole time as they crossed the lot together. He flashed her a smile and veered toward another car.

If it's even his.

The double-beep of the car being remotely unlocked echoed across the parking lot. Cheyenne sighed.

I swear I'm not overreacting. What am I missing?

CHAPTER TWENTY-EIGHT

That feeling of being watched faded after the first ten minutes in the car. Cheyenne let herself settle into the familiarity of the route out of the city and pulling up in front of the house that represented her childhood.

Twenty-something years ago, Bianca had moved to the family farm that used to belong to her parents, who'd both passed in early 2000.

Just in time to miss the scandal of Bianca Summerlin's pregnancy out of wedlock.

Cheyenne pulled off the freeway onto the dirt road and headed farther into the Henry County countryside. Her mom hadn't told her much about her first few months up here on her own, although the halfling knew more about those events than she knew about her father. A young, aspiring research economist with a promising future in politics retiring to the backcountry on a whim.

Bianca Summerlin never stopped working to have her only child, and she'd raised Cheyenne as best she knew how within the six-bedroom lodge home. Nothing stopped her from giving Cheyenne the best education available and access to every luxury Cheyenne hinted at wanting when she was younger, although it wasn't much since Cheyenne had never been a materialistic child.

"It's nice to be back here in the woods." Cheyenne proceeded up the gravel drive toward the main house and scanned the manicured lawn at the edge of the forest.

I'm looking for deer right now.

Shaking her head, she turned her attention toward the reason she was coming here. The conversation would not be a surprise for either of the Summerlin women, not this time. "I need to be ready for whatever she tells me."

She glanced at her backpack in the passenger seat, knowing what she'd brought with her could make the conversation go one of two ways. Either it would convince her mom to lay everything on the table, or it would make the woman clam up. Cheyenne hoped she wouldn't have to pull it out over drinks on the back patio and shove a blast from Bianca's past under her nose, but if it came to that, she would.

She hoped her mom would respond with option number one.

The Focus crunched to a slow stop on the drive in front of the large French doors at the top of the wide, curved steps leading into the house. Cheyenne left her keys in the ignition. No one out here to steal a car. Steal anything. A thief had to drive over an hour off the highway to get to the Summerlin home. No point locking up.

Slinging her backpack over one shoulder, Cheyenne closed the driver's side door and breathed in the September air. Purple asters planted in the front garden kept their bright blossoms all the way through October. Birds chirped, a few of them having roosted in the awning above the doorway, and the breeze rustling through the trees was still warm enough to be pleasant.

Home. It feels a lot more like an escape now.

She headed up the curved steps and pressed the doorbell. Five seconds later, the door opened, and she was looking into the smiling face of Bianca Summerlin's housekeeper.

"Cheyenne!" The woman grinned and opened the door even wider. "So good to see you."

"Hey, Eleanor."

Eleanor wrapped Cheyenne in a crushing embrace. The woman had been running her mother's household for as long as the halfling could remember. She tried not to wheeze under the pressure of Eleanor's bear hug, and she smiled when the woman released her and held her by the shoulders at arm's length. "You look beautiful. New workout routine or something?"

"Oh, stop."

Eleanor gave her employer's daughter a playful slap on the arm. "You haven't been away long enough for either of us to have changed that much."

The door shut with a soft click, cutting out the rustling leaves and the chirping birds outside. The huge, empty house was way too quiet.

"She's waiting for you on the back veranda. Can I take your bag?"

Cheyenne squeezed Eleanor's arm and shook her head. "I'm gonna keep it with me. You joining us for cocktail hour, or does she have you running around doing more important things?"

The older woman pursed her lips and tried to look stern. It hadn't worked when Cheyenne was a kid, and it didn't work now. "Is that an invitation?"

"From me, yeah."

"Oh, she's already invited me too. I'll be tidying up a few more things, but if you're still here when I'm finished, maybe I'll bring up an extra bottle from the cellar."

That brought a chuckle from them both, and Cheyenne

stepped across the foyer to move through the massive, decorated living room toward the back of the house. "And an extra glass, right?"

"That's what I said." Laughing, Eleanor went in the opposite direction.

The woman had already put dinner on in the kitchen, which Cheyenne passed without stopping to snoop around. She hadn't quite gotten used to smelling every single ingredient in a meal, but she knew enough about how her heightened senses worked to distract herself from the instant growl of her stomach.

Eleanor's cooking hasn't changed a bit. Smells like heaven.

The sliding glass doors onto the ground floor's back veranda were wide open, the sheer curtains pulled aside. Cheyenne had always thought her mom left those curtains hanging like that to create the billowy effect when the breeze rolled in from the north. It added to the perception of heading toward some huge expanse beyond the curtains, like a theatrical gateway one must pass to get to Bianca Summerlin on the other side.

Cheyenne brushed past the billowing fabric and slipped out onto the veranda. She pulled her backpack off her shoulder and set it on the stone outside the sliding doors.

Bianca stood at the edge of the veranda, her forearms resting on the banister railing as she stared over the open valley and the acres of arable land that hadn't been farmed for decades. The woman's dark, wavy hair fluttered away from her face in the breeze, which was just strong enough to intensify her expression of deep consideration.

Cheyenne stopped a few feet away. "George still does a great job with the lawn."

Her mom stiffened, which was as close as Bianca got to being startled, then turned. A soft smile bloomed on her face. "Doesn't he? You know, I heard somewhere it was impossible for children to sneak up on their mothers."

"I think we outgrew that a long time ago." Cheyenne joined her mom at the railing and stepped into Bianca's arms.

Her mom smelled like vanilla and sandalwood, which was a masculine scent on its own but more powerful and feminine than any floral perfume. *Just when she wears it.*

When Bianca released her daughter, she ran her hands down Cheyenne's arms, then tucked a bit of black hair behind Cheyenne's ear. "I'm glad you stopped by. I still wish you'd come visit more often. Or at least come spend a few weeks out here during the summer."

"Maybe when I'm done with school." Cheyenne squeezed her mom's hand and released it.

"For the year or when you finish your Masters?"

"I don't know." Looking out over the valley lined by the thick West Virginian woods, Cheyenne leaned against the banister and echoed her mom's stance. "I've been thinking about all this out here a lot more. How quiet it is."

How it gets me to not be a crazed drow who can't pick up her normal human form without it.

"Hmm. I can't imagine what it would be like to leave this now and head back into the city. I remember it being...hectic."

Cheyenne's little stint at the gas station the night before ran through her head, and she snorted. "That's putting it mildly."

"I'm sure things have changed since I stopped being a *city girl*." Bianca chuckled and turned around to face the sliding doors. "Eleanor should be up with our—oh. I swear, it's like you can read my mind."

Grinning, Eleanor stepped out onto the veranda with a tray in one hand. "I should be able to after twenty-five years, don't you think?" She'd arrived with empty glasses, a corkscrew, an empty decanter, an artisan *charcuterie* plate, and a bottle of red wine. She set these down on the patio table to the left and nodded. "I'll leave you to it. There's salmon and braised asparagus for dinner. Should be ready soon."

"Thank you." Bianca wiggled her eyebrows at her daughter and headed toward the table. "Bring an extra glass and come sit with us when you're finished."

Eleanor paused at the sliding glass doors and turned halfway around with a coy smile.

"And another bottle of wine," Cheyenne added.

"I'll plan on it." Grinning, the housekeeper hurried back inside, her shadow passing across the long wall of windows onto the veranda before she disappeared into the kitchen.

"Eleanor's become my secret weapon." Bianca sat in the chair facing the gorgeous view and picked up both the wine and the corkscrew.

"I'd love to hear how." Cheyenne stared at her mom, who focused on opening the bottle with a little *pop*.

She's stalling. Great.

"Any time I have a face-to-face meeting that's leaning toward the stagnant side, I have Eleanor sit with me for a minute or two. She's skilled at loosening up the conversation in the most unexpected ways."

Cheyenne sat beside her mom and leaned her forearms onto the patio table, interlacing her fingers. "Like the time she asked Senator Carradine about his sex life?"

Bianca snorted. "You heard that one, huh?"

When she turned to look at her daughter, Bianca's gaze dropped to Cheyenne's elbows and forearms on the table. That was all it took—one look with no change of expression or verbal reminder—and Cheyenne drew her hands into her lap.

Wow. Even moving away didn't change how much she groomed me with etiquette. "Yeah. I stopped right inside the door behind you and listened to the whole thing."

"That was..." Bianca closed her eyes in thought before pouring the wine into the decanter. "Six? Seven years ago?"

"I think I was thirteen."

"Right. The first of the teenage years. You heard everything back then."

"Not on purpose. Most of the time."

When they exchanged glances, both Summerlin women broke out into light, silent chuckles. Cheyenne glanced down at her folded hands in her lap, interlaced with the shadow of the patio table's iron mesh.

It's funny to laugh about now. My super-human hearing. Or non-human. She wouldn't be smiling about that if we hadn't started this conversation with small talk.

"Mom, I know we haven't—"

"I'm sorry." Bianca lifted a hand to stop her daughter, then pointed at the charcuterie plate and the wine. "I know we set this up to talk about one thing in particular, and we will. Let's at least wait until the wine's breathed, and we both have a glass of it in our hands, hmm?"

That's not good. Cheyenne plastered a smile across her face and nodded. "Sure. We can wait for the wine. No problem."

"Excellent." Her mom shot her a knowing glance, then pulled the charcuterie plate closer and got to work stacking bites of brie and summer sausage on a cracker that looked more like birdseed dried into a square.

Cheyenne sighed and helped herself to the same. *She'll be a lot easier to have this conversation with if she's wined and at least a little dined first. I'm not the first person to think this.*

She ate the first stacked snack and built another, spreading stoneground mustard all over it. "How're things going up here?"

Bianca dabbed the corner of her mouth with a finger, still chewing. "Smoothly. A lot more activity, oddly enough. Much higher demand for consultations in the last month or so with the elections coming up so soon. Honestly, I expected a few…individuals to have come to me sooner when I saw the debates. Everyone's a procrastinator these days."

Including you, Mom. Cheyenne tilted her head in feigned interest, just like her mother had taught her. *'Doesn't matter if you care about what's being said, Cheyenne. The important thing is that you* look *like you care. Very much.'*

Cheyenne had found that advice was unnecessary outside of politics and social engagements of the caliber Bianca Summerlin attended or hosted. It worked very well here.

I wonder if she can even tell?

After listening to her mom talk vague circles around the various political figures who'd sought her opinion on this or that *sensitive subject,* Bianca delivered a courteous sigh and grabbed the decanter. "Thank you for at least pretending to be interested in all that. I know it's hard to focus on anything else."

"Pour the wine, Mom."

Bianca dipped her head, her eyes widening in preparation for the conversation they both knew was coming. "Don't have to tell me twice."

CHAPTER TWENTY-NINE

Bianca lowered the wineglass and closed her eyes in appreciation. "Did you see what year this is?"

Cheyenne licked her lips and reached for the empty bottle, turning it until the label faced her. "Mom."

"I have a crate of half a dozen, and this is the first one I've opened. Excellent aging."

"This bottle's as old as I am." Cheyenne picked up her glass and tried not to gulp it down.

"The occasion called for it." Her mother gave a dismissive wave, then lifted her wine glass and took a long sip.

"If you say so."

"Come on, Cheyenne. I've been putting this off for twenty-one years, and you've found something that makes it impossible to do so any longer." Bianca smirked into her glass, her voice echoing through the fine crystal when she added, "At least let me endure the experience with as much dignity and refinement as possible."

The half-drow clicked her tongue. "You're so dramatic."

"I've earned that right." The wine glass clinked onto the

table, and Bianca twirled it by the stem as she turned to meet her daughter's gaze. "So, what did you find?"

"Something I wasn't supposed to, I'm guessing."

"Hmm, you don't say?"

Cheyenne took another drink. "How much do you know about the other…races of people out here?"

"Very little, Cheyenne."

"But more than you're saying, right?" Cheyenne stared at the well-aged wine streaking the inside of her glass. "Because you'd have to know something if your name's in a document about a maximum-security prison for magicals."

Her mom's eyes widened. "I haven't seen that document."

"Obviously. There was an addendum about Operation FRoE and initiating some kind of new system."

"What did it say about me?"

"The addendum? Nothing." Cheyenne shook her head. "But the original report mentioned an escaped convict. D-class? And suspected interaction between B. Summerlin and Inmate 4872."

Bianca's gaze fell to the iron tabletop and stayed there as she took another long sip of wine. "Did this report have a date?"

"January third—"

"Two thousand. Of course." Bianca's mouth twitched in recognition and memory at the same time. "Then, yes. That would be about me."

"About you and Inmate 4872." Cheyenne leaned back in her chair and studied the lack of emotion on her mom's face. So many years spent hiding her emotional responses from the rest of the world had made Bianca Summerlin a difficult woman to read. Even for her daughter.

Come on, Mom. Don't make me ask the question.

"That's what they called him, I assume. In that prison you mentioned."

"Is it really called Chateau D'rahl?"

Bianca snorted. "I doubt it. Those people are very fond of their codenames."

"Like Inmate 4872."

"When I met him, Cheyenne, he told me his name was Leon."

Cheyenne swallowed, drank more wine, and couldn't look at her mom anymore. *No wonder she didn't want to talk about this. It's like she lobotomized herself to anything related to the man.* "Is that his name?"

For a few seconds, her mom didn't respond. Then, the woman blinked and tipped her head back to look at the rolling hillside behind the lodge that used to be home to both of them. Maybe it still was, but Cheyenne couldn't let herself go there right now.

"Mom?"

"I don't know. That's the full truth." Bianca turned toward her daughter and lifted her shoulders in a weak shrug as if she'd lost all her energy and couldn't move more than that. "I have no idea if what that man told me was real. I don't know where he came from or who he was before that night. I'm not sure I want to know."

"But you know *something*." The halfling set both hands in her lap and stared at her mom. *Just say it. For once, don't make me lance the truth out of you.*

"Yes. I know he's your father, Cheyenne. Leon Verdys or Inmate 4872 or whatever other name he might have used or might still use today."

Cheyenne folded her arms, then unfolded them and ended up pressing both hands to her mouth. *Now we're getting somewhere. For real this time.*

"Okay." She nodded and stared at the empty wine bottle. "So, you slept with a convicted drow felon doing time in a max-security prison for non-human criminals. And then you had me."

"And then I had you." Bianca closed her eyes. "You didn't learn that from me."

"What?"

"The art of simplifying the most complicated things. I haven't mastered that skill, Cheyenne." When the woman opened her eyes, she reached for the wineglass and raised it to her lips. "I *will* say there's a certain satisfaction in just saying it like it is."

Instead of taking a sip, Bianca laughed and raised her glass in a toast to an invisible someone across the table. She chuckled and kept drinking.

"I know it's not that simple, Mom. And I know it made things a lot more complicated for you."

"And we did our best with what we had, didn't we?" Bianca smiled at her daughter and seemed to return to herself. "I'd say our best was pretty damn good."

Cheyenne gave a wry chuckle. "Not gonna argue with you on that one."

They sat there on the veranda, sipping the wine as old as Bianca Summerlin's half-drow daughter and watching the sky morph into shades of orange and pink as the sun set.

"Okay, so that brings up another question."

"Of course, it does."

"Did you..." Cheyenne cocked her head, trying to imagine how in the world this scenario had played out twenty-one years ago. "Did you have any idea he wasn't...I mean—"

"That he wasn't human?" Bianca's laughter didn't lack in bitterness or cynicism, yet there was some fondness in it too. "Cheyenne, I met your father at a New Year's Eve party with some of Washington's highest-ranking officials. He was handsome, don't get me wrong. Mysterious. Calm and somehow gravely intense and...well, he caught my attention.

I hadn't let my guard down like that since my freshman year of college."

"You were drunk." Cheyenne pressed her lips together, fighting not to laugh.

It's not funny. Except because the one time in a million Mom gets drunk enough to have fun, she gets into bed with a drow and gets knocked up just like that.

"Yes. I was drunk. Have a good laugh about it, my love. This might be the only time you'll get away with it."

"I'm not laughing." Bianca's daughter hid her smile in another sip of wine.

"For the record, I hadn't had so much to drink I wasn't completely aware of what I was doing. Lowered inhibitions don't equal heightened ignorance or a complete lack of clarity and judgment."

"See, that's the mother-daughter speech not everyone gets." Cheyenne smirked and watched for her mom's reaction, which had eased out of the already low levels of amusement and now looked much more like regret. "I'm not judging you if that's what you're worried about."

"I'm not worried about that, Cheyenne. If you were to judge me for anything, a few too many glasses of champagne would be the least of it, and we both know that."

They fell silent, and that silence inched its way under the half-drow's skin until she couldn't help but break it. "But did you *know?*"

"Some part of me did, I'm sure. I buried that for so long until the day I—well, when he approached me at that party, I knew there was something different about him. He shook my hand, and there was this..." Bianca glanced down at her hand and blinked. "It felt like destiny."

"Probably magic," Cheyenne muttered into her wine.

"Really, though, you can't blame me for not having picked up on that right away, can you?" Her mom tittered and shook her head. "Even after I found out what he was, it took me years to come to terms with the fact that *magic* is a real thing. Inaccessible to me, of course, but for you?"

"Pretty hard to hide."

"Quite." Tossing her head back, Bianca smoothed the hair away from her face and gazed at the sunset again. "I couldn't deny what was right in front of me when you experienced your...what do they call it? Manifestation? Awakening?"

Okay, now she lost me. Cheyenne stared at her mom, waiting for the woman to continue the rest of that thought.

"Whatever they told me it was, you proved time and again you were different too." A short, high-pitched laugh burst from Bianca's mouth, then she raised her glass again and dipped her head. "I'm sure you can imagine my surprise when I was told in one visit magic exists, elves are running around D.C., and my daughter has the blood of one running through her veins."

The woman drained the rest of her glass, set it on the table, and reached for the decanter to pour another.

Cheyenne waited as long as she could, hoping her mom would expand upon that last bit. But Bianca's embittered smile didn't fade, and she was too far gone in her hidden memories to notice her daughter staring at her.

"Mom."

"Hmm?"

"Who told you?"

"A man who worked in HR."

"Was he from that prison? Chateau D'rahl?" Cheyenne let her mom refill her own glass of wine too, but she didn't move to touch it.

"I don't remember."

"You remember everything, Mom."

Bianca finished pouring, then set the decanter down and froze. "We're having this conversation, Cheyenne. We opened the only Pandora's Box I've had to deal with personally. The insinuation I'd keep more from you after going down this road is frankly insulting."

"I'm sorry." *You're walking a fine line now, Cheyenne. Just keep her talking.* "I didn't mean to insult you."

"I know." After a few more seconds of contemplative silence, Bianca reached out and settled her hand on her daughter's thigh.

Cheyenne opened her hand, and her mom laced their fingers together for a brief and rare moment of taking comfort from her daughter instead of the other way around. "I can't tell you the name of the man who came to explain it to me or who he worked for or how they found us, but what he showed me was enough proof to change the course of every decision I made after that."

"What did he show you?" It came out as a strained half-whisper.

Bianca released her daughter's hand, patted Cheyenne's thigh one more time, and scooted the patio chair away from the table to stand. "The same thing I'm about to show you."

CHAPTER THIRTY

"Maybe I waited too long. Maybe I hoped you'd forget about the whole thing and let sleeping dogs lie." Bianca picked up her refilled wine glass and drained half of it in one gulp. "There's a fine line between confident surety and dreaming."

"I've heard." Cheyenne stood slowly as her mom cast her an unamused glance. "From you."

"Yes, well, if you ever have your own children, Cheyenne, you'll find there's nothing as effective at revealing all the flaws you worked so hard to cover up. Maybe even the ones you thought you'd eradicated." Bianca stepped toward the sliding doors into the house. She pointed inside. "It's in my study."

"Okay." Forgetting her wineglass, Cheyenne turned to follow her mom.

Bianca stopped when Eleanor came bustling through the back room toward the veranda, touting another bottle of wine and her own wineglass and bubbling with excitement.

"Oh." The housekeeper frowned at her employer before glancing at Cheyenne. "I thought I still had plenty of time."

"We're not finished yet, Eleanor." Bianca nodded and stepped past the other woman. "You're welcome to join us if you like. *If* you never mention a thing you see or hear to anyone else for the rest of your life. Including me."

Eleanor blinked as Bianca stepped toward the north wing of the lodge. The housekeeper shrugged and endowed Cheyenne with a conspiratorial grin. "Sounds delightful."

The halfling snorted. "You haven't changed at all."

"Why, thank you very much. We're heading into the study, then?"

"I guess so."

Eleanor nodded at the patio table. "You can't forget your glass *now*, Cheyenne. She had that look in her eye."

There wasn't any point in trying to downplay the type of mood Bianca Summerlin was in and would probably still be in for a day or two after Cheyenne went back home. "Yeah, I saw the look."

Just as she reached for her glass on the table, her phone dinged in her pocket. Cheyenne stopped to pull it out and check the notification. "Whoa."

"Everything okay?"

"Uh, yeah." Cheyenne read the message from Todd.

Looks like your hounds pulled up enough info to flag my system for a possible threat. So thanks for giving me a reason to double-check my security. I'm totally ready to hand them back.

Her programs had gone through every round, which meant she now had GPS coordinates for all four secret IP addresses—hopefully—and if nobody was lying in their own encrypted messages, a location for this giant underground meeting later tonight. "Eleanor, has the wi-fi password changed?"

"Not that I'm aware of, no. You have some extra schoolwork to take care of?"

"Something like that." Cheyenne stuck her phone back into her pocket and headed for the door and her backpack lying on the stone slab of the veranda. *I can't open this stuff here. If anyone finds that connection between the person digging around in their trash and Bianca Summerlin, they'll know exactly who I am.*

She slung her backpack over her shoulder and wrapped Eleanor in another tight hug. The housekeeper chuckled. "Don't tell me you're this excited about being able to do your homework at home."

"Is it still called homework in grad school?" Cheyenne gave the woman a thin smile. "Look, I have to go."

"Oh." Eleanor gazed longingly at the unopened bottle of wine and shrugged. "I'm sure your mother won't have any reservations about sharing this with me, then. At least it was good timing."

"Yeah, there's that. I'll, uh, I'll come back later, and we can sit down, all three of us, okay? Sorry. This wasn't planned." Cheyenne stepped through the sliding door with an apologetic shrug. "I promise."

"Well, then, we'll hold you to it. You'll go tell her goodbye?"

"What kind of daughter would I be if I didn't?" Cheyenne turned and hurried through the living room toward the far end of the house and her mom's study. Neither she nor Eleanor felt the need to mention that Cheyenne had left plenty of times without saying goodbye, and most of those times, they'd been on much pricklier terms with each other.

She stopped in front of the ornately carved French doors into her mom's study. The room beyond looked like it belonged in an eighteenth-century manor with a lord sitting behind the cherrywood desk instead of Cheyenne's mom. "Hey!"

"Now, before you say anything else, I want you to know I haven't thought about this in a *very* long time." Bianca looked up from her computer screen and raised her eyebrows. "Not that I was *trying* to remember, but...what is it?"

"I'm sorry." Cheyenne readjusted the straps of her backpack. "Something came up."

"Did it?" Her mom's face showed surprise mixed with relief, and somehow, a little bit of disappointment thrown in, just to make things interesting.

"Yeah. I have to go take care of it. Kind of a time-sensitive… thing." *Like I can't drop in with the element of surprise if I'm late to the magical crime-ring party.*

Bianca pursed her lips and flicked her gaze toward her computer. "I understand."

"Can we reschedule, maybe? Whenever you have time, Mom. I know you're busy. I still want to—"

"I know. Trust me, I'm just as ready to put this out in the open as you are." After she turned off the monitor, Bianca stepped around her desk and approached her daughter in the doorway. "Go do what you have to do. I'll be here when you're ready."

"Okay. Thanks." Cheyenne let her mom hug her a little longer than she wanted, but she managed not to fidget.

When her mom released her, the woman seemed to have regained most of her composure. "Be safe. And careful."

She has no idea. "I will. Love you."

"I love you."

Cheyenne turned away and hurried back through the house toward the foyer. The door opened without a sound on well-oiled hinges and clicked gently shut behind her before she skipped down the steps to her car.

Whatever she was about to show me, it can wait. It waited twenty-one years. And I have to nail these guys tonight.

Just outside Bianca Summerlin's office, Eleanor stopped in front of the open French doors with that second bottle of wine and her empty glass. With tightly pressed lips and wide eyes,

Bianca regarded her housekeeper and friend of over two decades. Eleanor lifted the bottle and opened her mouth.

"Oh, you know you don't even have to ask." Bianca turned away from the woman, snatched her wineglass off the desk, and settled herself on the divan beside the massive fireplace against the west wall. "Open it."

Despite her employer's well-contained but still obvious stress, Eleanor grinned and brought the bottle with her to the low table in front of the hearth. She wasn't about to pass up the opportunity for a night of drinking with Bianca, and she was fairly certain the woman had more than enough to get off her chest.

CHAPTER THIRTY-ONE

Cheyenne couldn't get to her apartment fast enough. When she did, she made sure every program on her computer was closed and switched her monitor connection to the second tower she used as a backup, just in case. Whoever wanted her to back off would have to wait a little longer to see her next move. *They're watching.*

She logged into the GRND0 app she had built and Todd had perfected, the only one they used for sharing information that needed to stay between them, and clicked on the links to her program results.

Todd's message popped up on her screen before she'd read through anything.

T-rexifus088L: What the hell did you send me?

"Oh, come on. It couldn't have been that bad."

ShyHand71: Pet project. Thanks for renting out the space.

T-rexifus088L: Yeah, I should charge you for that one. Do you know what you're getting into?

ShyHand71: Don't I always?

T-rexifus088L: Well, I thought so. Until your little coded

buddies started sending out alarm signals. I had to shut everything down just to keep the entire world from seeing the smoke.

ShyHand71: Sorry. I won't ask again.

Cheyenne wrinkled her nose and waited for his reply. Todd enjoyed pretending he was a hardass, but he had a soft spot for anyone who could help him tighten the security encryption on the Y2Kickass server. So far, Cheyenne was the only person who fit that description.

T-rexifus088L: Don't be like that. I'm not mad. Just threw me for a second.

ShyHand71: But you took care of it, 'cause that's what you do. I owe you one.

T-rexifus088L: You do.

Smiling, Cheyenne closed out of the chat and dove into what her programs had put together while nesting in Todd's private space on their group's server. She read it twice before she let herself believe what she was seeing.

These idiots had put together a roster of everyone who was planning to show up tonight. She didn't see Durg's name, but that didn't mean she wouldn't find someone who could tell her where to find the scumbag. And Durg didn't need to be there for an anonymous drow halfling to do what no one expected.

No one had asked for her help this time, and this wasn't a case of being in the right place at the right time, like at the gas station. Victims couldn't ask for help before they knew they needed it.

If these gangs are trying to toss other magicals across the Border with no one's consent, that's a problem that applies to me. Not the kinda thing I can refuse to help with, either.

And now, Cheyenne had everything she needed to find these guys before they got their hands on anyone else. Her programs had pulled up a location for their meeting tonight, which was at 11:00 p.m. in the back room of an old event center on the southeast end of Richmond. It was far enough away from most of the population that nobody would walk in on them, but it wasn't in the middle of nowhere.

Lights and lots of cars and a big group of people out in the middle of nowhere is always suspicious, and a lot to take on.

She wrote down the address, then sent the rest of the files—the roster and the other snippets of conversation and check-ins, plus the four separate IP addresses her program had traced back to the originals—into storage on the server she'd encrypted and built a few hardcore firewalls around. *Now to use it.*

The second she filed everything, both monitors went black.

"What the hell?"

This time, the message came across in white, the cursor blinking as the words typed out across the screen.

You're getting sloppy. Remember when I said you only have one warning?

"Who *is* this guy?" Cheyenne lurched up from her chair and slammed her hands on the desk. Then she remembered she still had her old handle tied to the server, which this anonymous stalker had found the minute she'd sent everything into safe-keeping.

Gritting her teeth, she loomed over the keyboard to type a response.

ShyHand71: I'm not into superstitions. Or threats. So unless you can give me proof of something other than hijacking my desktop, I'm gonna keep doing what I'm doing.

The cursor on her blacked-out screen blinked for a few seconds, which seemed to take forever, then the next message appeared.

Stay home tonight. As long as you don't get involved, we can help you find what you're looking for.

Cheyenne snorted. "No deal. *This* is what I'm looking for. If they haven't picked up on that already, they're dumber than I thought."

ShyHand71: That's not a very convincing promise. How do I know you have anything I want?

You'll know when we give it to you. Don't show up at the location you decrypted. You'll regret it.

"Ooh. Very intimidating." Cheyenne glared at the screen. "Makes me even more excited to show up and kick some magical-trafficking ass. So, sorry, not sorry."

She leaned over the keyboard and got ready to tell whoever this was to take his threats and his warnings and shove 'em, but the black screen flashed into white. Then her desktop background returned, and the anonymous message went away.

Cheyenne pushed out an aggravated sigh. "Didn't even let me respond. Not cool. And I'm not buying it."

Turning off both monitors just to keep from seeing anything else that might pop up, she tapped the piece of paper with the meeting's address written in pen and huffed out a laugh. "Good old-fashioned paper. Can't trace that. And I can burn it."

It was only 9:15 p.m., though, which meant she had a little over an hour to kill if she timed this right. The first thing that came to mind was dinner since she'd skipped out on that at her mom's. *Man. And that salmon smelled good.*

Her stomach gurgled. "Try to find me a drow berserker who doesn't need to eat before busting in somebody's party."

She grabbed her wallet and keys and left her apartment for the gas station at the end of the block. The closer she got to the convenience store, the more Cheyenne wondered if that was such a good idea. *Those idiots with guns smashed in the security cameras, but there would still be footage of me in there as myself and then me in there as drow halfling.*

It would be even more suspicious for the twenty-one-year-old Goth chick to *not* stop by her regular haunt for cheap and easy-to-make pre-packaged meals after the place got shot to pieces and torn apart by a couple of bodies flying everywhere.

If I'm trying to be two different people, the human Cheyenne left before any of the exciting stuff started.

She decided it was a safer bet to show her face and look like nothing was different from last time she'd come in for a six-pack and Funyuns. And maybe part of her wanted to check in on Katie and see how her part-time friend was handling everything.

Before she crossed the last turnoff into the convenience store parking lot, that feeling of being watched came back full force. Cheyenne wanted to stop and look around, to find the face around the eyes she knew had been on her all day. *And that's just gonna make me look even more suspicious. Just keep walking.*

The hair on the back of her neck prickled, the paranoia intensified, and her drow magic ignited at the base of her spine.

Deer. Keeping thinking about deer.

By the time she reached the door to the convenience store, she'd pulled herself under control. No gray skin or hints of white in her hair. It was only a temporary relief, though, because she turned toward the checkout counter to smile at Katie and shoot off some witty remark that would at least make her sound more relaxed. Then she stopped, and the ghost of her unformed smile disappeared.

"Where's Katie?"

"Yeah, hello. I'm having a great night, thanks." The man behind the counter in the gray polo with a red collar and the gas station's logo on the left breast nodded vigorously. His smile was just as real as Cheyenne's patience. "How 'bout you?"

She stared at him and shifted her weight onto one hip.

"What? You don't get many polite greetings?" He looked her

up and down and wrinkled his nose. "Maybe if you cleaned up a little, you know. And smiled more."

Cheyenne's eye twitched, and she sent the guy an unflinching glare. *Deer, deer, deer. Even Bambi. Now is not the time for the drow happy place.* "Where's Katie?"

"Jeez, relax. She took the night off." The guy behind the counter ran a hand through his hair, then placed both hands on the counter and shrugged. "Working nights isn't my thing, but I'm making the most of it. I tell you what, there's a whole different kinda people come in after eight p.m."

Without a word, Cheyenne turned away from him and walked down the second-to-last aisle. She liked the instant pad-Thai—just add water and a microwave—but she seemed to have lost her craving for anything. She would have turned and walked back out if it weren't for her growling stomach. *Last thing I need is passing out from hunger in the middle of a fight.*

The chime behind the counter dinged when the door opened, and a new customer walked in.

"How's it goin'?" the clerk muttered.

"Hey."

Cheyenne almost froze when she heard that voice. Then she pulled herself together and picked two packs of instant Pad Thai off the shelf. *I've heard that voice before. Where?*

She turned and headed toward the drink coolers. The customer looked harmless enough, wearing jeans and a dark-green t-shirt that bordered on too tight. He was lean but muscular and had to be at least ten years older than her, if not more. Cheyenne had half-expected to see one of the burglars with guns she'd had a little powwow with, but this guy wasn't one of them. The only thing about him that stood out at all was the small, almost indiscernible tattoo of a gnarled tree on the left side of his neck a few inches above his collarbone. It might have gone on beneath the collar of his shirt, but it wasn't like Cheyenne was about to ask to see the rest of it.

The guy smiled at her before turning his attention to the assorted variety of beef jerky hanging on the shelf. Cheyenne reached into the cooler and grabbed some kind of iced tea without bothering to look at the flavor. She went to the counter to pay for her dinner, trying not to turn around again to look at the guy with the neck tattoo. *I know I've heard his voice somewhere.*

A crash came from behind her. She turned to observe the guy with the tattoo fumbling with half of the hooks on the shelf as they came free from the backing. Beef jerky and bags of Cheez-Its scattered across the floor.

"Sorry. I was just trying to get one bag—"

"Oh, yeah. Forgot to mention that." The clerk chuckled and nodded at the mess at the end of the aisle. "I'll take care of it. The owner placed an order for a new one this morning, but those always take longer than they should to come in. It's the last thing that needs fixing after last night."

The other customer stepped away from the fallen snacks and headed toward the counter to get in line behind Cheyenne. "What happened last night?"

"You didn't hear? Cool. I've only told the story about twenty times tonight, and it still doesn't get old." The clerk glanced at Cheyenne as she set her purchases down on the counter and winked before grinning at the customer behind her.

Seriously? I should—nope. Think about the deer, Cheyenne. She opened her clenched fist and drummed her fingers on the counter while the clerk took his sweet time telling his awesome story instead of ringing her up.

"Place got robbed last night. Well, almost. Nothing was stolen, but a dude walked in with a gun and tried to get the girl who normally works this shift to open the register. Probably why she thought she couldn't come in tonight, so I have her to thank for an extra shift." He hissed out a judgmental laugh and picked up Cheyenne's tea to ring it up. "Nothing happened to *her*, so I don't get why she couldn't come back to work. Women and their drama, right?"

Cheyenne gritted her teeth and glared at him when he looked at her. *I'll show you drama.*

The clerk's smile faltered, then he shrugged and nodded at the guy behind Cheyenne. "Some crazy in a mask walked in at the perfect time. Some kinda superhero wannabe, maybe. Dunno. I didn't get to see the camera footage, but the owner told me this weirdo dodged a freaking bullet. Had some kind of, I dunno, electric whip or something."

"That's...unbelievable." The guy behind Cheyenne didn't sound like he was buying any of it, which she couldn't blame him for. It almost made her smile.

"Right? Then I guess the guy ran away screaming and sent a couple buddies in here to get the job done for him. More guns. Lots of shooting. Bullet holes everywhere." The clerk pointed to the corner beside the end of the beer cooler. The security camera had been taped back into place and reinforced with a couple of pieces of cardboard. "Oh, yeah. Guess we're getting a new camera, too."

"Hmm." The guy standing behind Cheyenne sounded unimpressed. "Maybe you should let your coworker tell the story, seeing as she was there, right?"

"Hey, I heard it straight from the owner. He *watched* the camera footage. So, I can tell the story." The clerk grabbed Cheyenne's first package of Pad Thai and waved it around as he spoke. "I'm sure Katie—she was the one working last night —isn't gonna want to talk about this. It's a cool story, but she's..." He sucked his teeth and made a poor attempt at a sympathetic grimace. "She's one of those real insecure girls, you know? Sits here alone all night six days out of the week and—"

"Dude." Cheyenne pointed at her dinner and cocked her head. "Just ring me up."

The clerk blinked at her with wide eyes and wrinkled his nose. "I'm getting to it, okay? Who crapped in your cornflakes?"

Cheyenne cocked her head the same way, her nostrils flaring. "The guy who thinks this gas station is a hair salon."

The customer behind her snorted, but the clerk just clicked his tongue at her and frowned in disappointment. "Hey, if you don't wanna hear about it, don't ask."

"I didn't." *Is this guy for real?*

The clerk's dismissive smile looked way too painful on his face, and he finished ringing her up before muttering, "Twelve eighty-seven," and tossing a hand toward the card reader.

"Awesome." Cheyenne ran her card, snatched her Pad Thai and tea, and turned to leave.

"Want your— Yeah, she doesn't want her receipt." The clerk crumpled up the bit of paper and tossed it into the trash behind the counter.

As Cheyenne turned around to press her back against the door, she found the guy with the neck tattoo smiling at her. It wasn't just a polite smile coming from a stranger, either. The way he looked at her felt way too much like he knew who she was and where she was going. It was like he was trying to tell her something.

She stepped out into the parking lot and let the door close behind her. *If he had something to say, he should've said it. And now I'm talking about a complete stranger like we have a history. A familiar voice isn't enough to go on. Focus.*

For the entire walk back to her apartment, she repeated a ridiculous mantra about Bambi and the woods and keeping it together.

CHAPTER THIRTY-TWO

The Pad Thai tasted like soggy cardboard with peanuts thrown in. Turned out she'd bought the only flavor of iced tea she didn't like, but she drank it anyway. "I hate mint."

Cheyenne drained the tea and wiped her mouth with the back of a hand. She slumped into the chair behind her computer. She wanted to pull up all the info Todd had returned to double-check that she was heading to the right place.

"Nope. I saw it the first time, and I'd be stupid to open that door. Anonymous creeper's still on my trail."

Cheyenne had a moment of inspiration. She pulled up YouTube and went for the most obnoxious laser-cat video she could find—terrible CG, loud, fake laser blasts, and obnoxious background music that mixed house music and reggae and death metal. She muted her speakers but set the videos to keep pulling the next best match for however long she left the window open. "That's what he gets for tailing me."

Rolling back in her chair, Cheyenne stretched her legs all the way out and spun from side to side, trying not to check her phone every two minutes. *Half an hour. Then I can get the hell out of here and do something useful.*

For half an hour, she practiced slipping in and out of her drow form on command. She tried to repeat using a quick spell between forms, but the third burst of sparks from her fingertips brought up interference on her monitor. The screen fizzled with a line of static. It cleared the moment she dropped the spell.

"Magical sparks and computers don't play well. Huh. Should've expected that."

She thought about trying Ember's cell. She realized how unlikely it was that Ember would have a phone charger, anyway. Besides, Cheyenne didn't have a bunch of time to talk. *I'll check in tomorrow.*

For the last fifteen minutes, she went through her cabinets and tossed everything past its expiration date. Which was most of the mac 'n cheese and a few cans of garbanzo beans.

The alarm she'd set for 10:20 p.m. played an irksome tune called *Harp*. Cheyenne snatched her phone and rushed out of her apartment.

Party time.

It took twenty-five minutes to get to the event center and another five to find a place to park that wasn't along the side street and visible from the building. She ended up parking on a turnoff beside a landfill a mile and a half away, and now it was 10:52 p.m.

Cheyenne headed toward the event center on foot until she was far enough from her car that anyone who'd seen her get out of it couldn't see her anymore—that is if anyone was hanging around a landfill for some strange reason. She brought up an image of Durg's crooked tusks. Heat slid up her spine, and she took on her drow form. She nodded. Durg's face was as effective as thinking about guns, which made sense, she supposed, since the two were associated in her mind.

After a glance up and down the street, the drow halfling took off running faster than anyone would have been able to see clearly. The tall weeds growing on the side of the road whipped after her as she streaked past in a blur of gray and black and white. She only had to stop once to catch her breath. By 10:58 p.m., she slowed outside the entry gates to the event center parking lot.

A sharp crack split the air when she slowed, and the open gate creaked behind her. She stuck out a hand to stop it from moving and hurried out of the lamplight, opting to take the long way around through the dirt and grass. She counted over a dozen cars parked in the lot, so there were plenty of people inside.

There's gotta be someone in there who thinks fashionably late is still cool.

Cheyenne reached the side of the event center in the dark and looked for a door. She didn't find one until she'd skirted the wall all the way near the back, and someone had set the handle so it didn't lock behind anyone passing through it.

You'd think these guys would be a little better at security. Or common sense.

Before she opened the door, she pressed her hand against the wall and let her mind expand through the metal and into the back of the event center. The shapes of glowing bodies lighting up in her mind's eye were blurry and a little muted, which meant a few walls and rooms were between the back-door and the clandestine hangout for magical crime lords. As far as she could tell, this little trick of hers hadn't steered her wrong yet—there wasn't anyone watching the back of the building.

Not sure it's supposed to be this easy, but I'll take it.

The drow halfling slipped inside and guided the door into

place to keep things quiet. Muffled voices came from farther down the hall. In drow form, her hearing was heightened enough that they could be on the opposite side of the building. Cheyenne crept down the hall and crouched behind a trashcan first, then behind boxes of paper cups and plastic lids. She didn't hear anyone following her, and the tone of the conversation hadn't changed since she'd stepped inside.

So far, so good.

When she came to the closest entrance into the center arena, broken down to the bare floors and a few tables and chairs pushed to the sides of the room, she pressed against the wall beside the doorway. Glaring light spilled toward her from the arena, and the voices echoed beneath the high ceiling and the bare walls.

"We said eleven!" That voice was pissed.

I guess fashionably late doesn't fly with magical criminals.

"He'll be here." The second voice, nasal and thick with saliva, made Cheyenne think of a slobbery chihuahua. "Mardok's the one who set this whole thing up. He's got more riding on this than anybody."

"*Where is he?*" The third voice thundered through the arena and echoed much longer than the others.

Cheyenne crouched against the wall and waited until the ringing in her ears faded. She stayed still.

"You want me to call him?" Chihuahua barked. "I'll call him."

"Don't. If he's making a statement, let him make it. I'll talk to him about how we handle things."

"Listen to him." The whisper came from right behind Cheyenne on the other side of the wall, and her drow hearing picked it up as if the wall didn't exist. "Thinks he's already sitting on a throne with a crown on his head. I ain't going down on one knee for any asshole, especially on this side."

Someone beside the whisperer grunted. "Shut it, Rezen. We do what he wants and wait for our day. It'll come."

"Better be soon."

The tension was so thick in the arena, Cheyenne was surprised they hadn't torn each other to shreds already. *Which is why they're all here at the same time. Get one massive deal over and done with so they don't have to do it again soon.*

"I'm thirsty," the giant voice muttered. "Go."

"Yep." Someone with light footsteps strode across the arena and headed for the archway leading into the hall where Cheyenne was hiding.

She crouched lower behind the propped-open door and waited.

Yeah. Let's get in a little one-on-one time.

The lanky magical skittered into the hall and passed right by her without noticing a thing. His bald head was an inflamed shade of red with deep black lines scored through it. Cheyenne wasn't looking forward to seeing his face after a peek at his scalp, but she stood from her crouch and stalked behind him.

Redhead turned the corner into the other hall surrounding the arena and opened a door on the left. He switched on the light and stepped inside, oblivious to the drow halfling following him. She heard the sound of a fridge being jerked open and glass bottles clinking against each other, accompanied by the guy's low muttering about always getting sent to fetch the drinks.

Cheyenne slipped through the door and pressed it almost all the way closed behind her, leaving it open a crack so she could hear whatever else was happening in the arena. So far, it was just a bunch of impatient whining.

"Got time for a little chat?"

The red-skinned magical with his head stuck in the fridge jumped and banged his head on the top, almost knocking himself unconscious. He grunted, drew his head out and up, and rubbed it with a scowl. His eyes widened at the drow standing in the break room with him, and he stumbled back against the open fridge door. The bottles rattled. "Fellfire and—"

"Good one. Now, take a seat." Cheyenne nodded at the round table on the other side of the break room and the six chairs around it.

Redhead's nose wrinkled, and his beady black eyes narrowed. "Who the hell are you?"

"You can sit for a talk, or I can make you do both." Cheyenne spread her arms, opened both hands, and let off a few intimidating bursts of purple and black sparks. "Your choice."

"We don't have no drow on the list. How the hell'd you—"

Cheyenne lashed her hand toward him. The jingling of her wrist chains was covered by the sharp hiss and crack of the black tendrils shooting from her palm. Two lashed around the man's neck, cutting off his sentence and his breath, and the drow yanked him toward her. His sneakers squeaked on the linoleum floor as her fist connected with the side of his face.

The black tendrils disappeared as he dropped, but Cheyenne jerked him back up by the shirt collar before he had the chance to hit the floor. "I'm sure you'll make better choices after this."

She dragged him toward the table, kicked out a chair, and tossed him into it. The guy's blazing-red bald head wobbled on his shoulders, and although it was hard to tell with his all-black eyes, Cheyenne was confident they were rolling around in his head.

"Hey!" She slapped one hand on the table and snapped her fingers in the guy's face with the other. "Come on. We're just getting started."

The guy puffed out a thick breath and tried to lift his head to look at her. A crooked grin split his face. His lips had veiny black lines running across them. "You got no idea who you're messing with."

"Yeah, that's what people keep telling me." Cheyenne buried her fist in his shirt collar again, jerked him toward her, and summoned more sparks that, for his sake, would hopefully be just a warning. "I'm looking for a piece of orc shit named Durg. Ring any bells?"

The guy laughed. She shook him, and he choked when her fist hit his throat.

Maybe bring it down a notch, Cheyenne.

She took a deep breath. "I'm not playing around, asshole. Help yourself out and give me something."

"You came to a—" The guy coughed and sucked a bunch of spit back from the sides of his mouth. "A meeting like this, outnumbered over your head, looking for one nobody orc?"

Half-choked laughter spilled from his open mouth. The guy's black tongue flicked around in there, and Cheyenne turned up the notch on the sparks. They glistened in his all-black eyes, and he stopped laughing. "After I deal with you, I'll be breaking up that little party. You have one more chance before I knock you out for the next month. Wanna try again?"

"You haven't done this before, have you?" This time, the guy ran his tongue between his teeth until it stuck out at her, his wrinkled nose squashed even more by the disgusting grin.

"Ew. I think we're both about to learn a lot."

Cheyenne drew her fist back, jerked up on the guy's shirt, and let her punch fly. She landed a good one. The magical issued a low grunt and a groan of pain as he slumped sideways in the chair.

A new sound made its way through the hallway outside the breakroom. The drow halfling paused and cocked her head. There were a lot of footsteps out there—dozens, all of them moving silently toward the arena.

"Losin' your nerve?" Redhead muttered, black blood on his lips.

"Shut up."

"Aw, come on. You gotta finish what you—"

Cheyenne released his shirt, and with the strength of a drow, swung a hard right hook into his jaw. The guy toppled out of the chair and thumped on the floor, the chair making a metallic screech as it came out from under him.

It's like nobody can stop talking before I have to get serious about it.

The footsteps continued outside the door, and she drifted toward the hallway to peer through the thin opening. She caught sight of black pants, black boots, and what looked like the butt of a rifle before it disappeared around the corner.

What the hell is going on?

She opened the door and slipped into the hall.

"*There* he is!" The loud, thunderous voice boomed in the arena. "Thought you'd play around and keep us on our toes, huh? Not a smart move, Mardok. Even for you."

"I had to take care of some things." The new voice was as low as the apparent big boss' but with an impression of restrained power quivering below the surface rather than a bunch of bluster. "But now I'm here, so there's nothing keeping us from getting right down to it, huh?"

"Looks like it." There was a sneer in the thunderous voice, then everyone inside the arena moved toward the center.

Cheyenne frowned and pressed against the wall again, side-stepping toward the arena entrance. She saw them in her mind —maybe two dozen bodies bending over a large table with whatever plans they had laid out on it. She tried to listen to the much quieter conversation on the other side of the wall, but the whispering footsteps came from all around her, although she didn't see anyone. From both sides of the hallway around her, *and* the second floor where the balcony overlooked the arena.

Somebody's gonna get screwed over.

She sidled close to the entrance right before the big boss roared, "Gryus, where the hell's my drink?"

Another magical came storming out of the arena as Cheyenne stepped away from the wall. She hadn't thought to keep using her little body-count trick and never saw him coming. A troll with neon-green splotches all over his skin almost collided with her.

Two swirling bolts of purple and black magic blazed from the drow halfling's hands and crashed into the troll's chest. He launched back into the arena, narrowly missing two other criminals gathered around the table. The inert troll slid across the floor with a prolonged squeak and came to a stop, the front of his black jacket smoking.

Magical mobsters in every color of the rainbow turned toward the drow.

Cheyenne faced them, her dark magic hissing and crackling around her hands.

The seven-foot-tall boss with a boulder-shaped head of stone—a race she hadn't seen before—yelled, "Who invited the drow?"

Cheyenne grinned. "I did."

Two goblins and a short, fat creature with a protruding forehead shot blasts of green and gold light at her, and the arena erupted in gunfire. Lots of gunfire.

CHAPTER THIRTY-THREE

It was almost too fast for her to follow. Weapons fired from every entrance to the arena on the first and second floors except for the doorway where she stood. For the magical thugs caught by surprise, the shots fired were startling and disorienting. For the drow halfling, they were deafening.

Cheyenne crouched where she was for all of two seconds while the room exploded with bright-yellow staccato bursts from the newcomers and their guns, some of which flashed green from the erupting barrels. Those weren't regular bullets; she could think enough to be sure of that much. The magicals in the center of the arena returned fire with blasts of magic—yellow, sickly green, electric blue, blazing orange—and scattered across the room to fight back to back or take cover behind the tables and chairs pushed against the walls. Guns and magic wreaked havoc on a scale Cheyenne couldn't wrap her head around.

In the chaos of the fray, the short creature with the huge forehead barreled toward her, its mouth open in terror or rage or both. Bursts of dark sludge spurted from its outstretched hand.

Cheyenne raised her hands toward the oncoming creature, and although her throat vibrated and scratched itself raw, she couldn't hear herself screaming over the constant gunshots and the shouts of other magicals and the hissing, crackling, clashing bursts of magic flying all over the place.

Two whirling disks of black fire spun away from her and hit the short creature square in the chest. Cheyenne didn't stop to see what happened to him, but lurched from her place in the hallway and entered the fray. Her blood boiled with a battle rage even stronger than that night at the skatepark, which felt like it had been so much longer than seventy-two hours before.

Two trolls darted toward her, shouting something and pointing either at her or at something behind her. Cheyenne didn't care. The black tendrils of her magic shot from both hands and whipped across the arena, lashing at the trolls and tossing them aside like empty boxes. A blast of red energy zipped past her head, and she ducked before seeing the orc who'd unleashed it at her.

Spit flew from his open mouth as he roared and fired more magical attacks at anything that moved toward him. Cheyenne's own devastating attack spells were purple and black streaks through the air. One of them hit a different orc in the shoulder and spun him aside as he darted in front of the big one throwing red blasts. Her other spell hit the bigger orc in the center of his gut and sent him stumbling backward into the table.

The ground shook beneath the enraged stomping of the seven-foot-tall creature Cheyenne had seen in her mind's eye, that thing with a head like a boulder who considered himself the big boss among these thugs. The guy was built like a tree and bellowed in rage. Everywhere he turned, thick columns of smaller stones burst from his hands and laid waste to everything in their path.

"Bring that ogre down!" The shout came from behind her and to the left.

Cheyenne didn't dare turn her back to the fight when a crazed goblin with spit flying from his snarling jaws ran full speed at her. A gun went off from the same place as that shout, and the goblin jerked beneath the pelting of automatic rounds in his chest.

That was when Cheyenne lost all sense of control and reason. The metallic sting of gunpowder and hot steel barrels and so much blood was the only thing she acknowledged. She heard herself scream, and somewhere in the back of her mind, she terrified herself.

Black tendrils whipped through the air and struck any moving thing in her path. Her hands shot in every direction, sending magical thugs flying and crashing into each other and sliding into walls. She didn't remember when she switched between blazing bolts of black energy sparking with purple and snaking black tendrils that moved like part of her body.

The seven-foot-tall stone ogre bellowed and stormed toward her, his glare burning with red flame in his gray-streaked face. A man garbed in black, wearing body armor and a helmet and firing an automatic rifle, stepped up beside her and took aim at the ogre.

The bullets pinged off the magical's stone-hard skin like spit wads shot from a straw. More weapons from the team in black fired at the ogre, and nothing made a dent.

"Goddamnit, O'Malley! If there was ever a time to use the fell launcher, that would be right goddamn now!"

"Can anyone cover me on the west end of the first floor?"

"On your nine!"

Cheyenne heard the entire conversation through the crackle of radio static and the double echo of the chaos their headsets broadcast. She tried to focus on separating the magicals from the large team in black with automatic weapons who'd stormed the event center right behind her, but everyone appeared the same.

"A-1, I'm about to—" A scream erupted from the operative, wherever he was.

Another man beside her cursed and stepped forward as a snarling troll flung a burst of electric blue energy toward them. Cheyenne raised her arm reflexively, as if she were raising a shield, and a black wall of magic burst to life in front of her in time to keep the searing blue attack from hitting home. The guy in black who'd rushed past her staggered back beneath the dark shadow of her shield, training his weapon straight ahead.

The shield dropped, and Cheyenne blasted the troll through the opposite wall of the arena, which then boasted a troll-shaped hole.

"Shit." The man turned to look Cheyenne up and down.

She stormed forward, consumed by her battle rage, the heat searing through her skin, and the chaos of screams and spells and gunfire.

Two figures rushed toward her with blazing trails of orange and red churning through the air seconds behind their hands. She ducked beneath one of their attacks and slid forward on her knees. When she raised her hand, it wasn't to unleash an attacking sphere of crackling sparks or the black tendrils from her fingertips. Instead, a spell of some unseen force she hadn't known she could cast—hadn't even considered—sent the green-skinned magical straight up into the ceiling. Gunfire rattled from his flailing hand before he crashed into the plaster and brought a rain of it down around them.

Someone dropped from the second-floor balcony. Cheyenne whirled and shot out her snaking tendrils before the falling operative in black gear hit the floor. She wasn't trying to save him, but she slowed his descent enough to preserve his life before she released the coiled black vines from his arms and whipped them toward a tall, thin magical with pale-violet skin.

"Any day with that launcher!" someone shouted.

"Shut up and cover me."

"You cannot stop F'rulz Asharig!" the ogre bellowed. "That regime is already a pile of rotting corpses." The giant magical mobster stormed toward Cheyenne, his fiery eyes blazing bright. "You have betrayed the call of—"

A burst of searing heat flared in Cheyenne's hip, and she staggered sideways in shock and rage. She turned to blast the troll still training his pistol on her and saw the gun flying away from his flopping body with his finger still on the trigger, and his hand and half an arm attached.

The ogre raged across the arena. "Drow! You will perish in flames like the rest of us!"

He talking to me? The pain seemed to have brought her mind back to itself, or at least her ability to reason. Her damaged hip wouldn't hold the weight of her body. She fired a few more shots at the ogre, who kept coming. Cheyenne fell to her knees with a shout of frustration and pain. *Get up!*

An operative in black stepped in front of her and fired one automatic burst after the other, tearing the ogre down as he tried to dodge his attackers to get to the fallen drow.

Cheyenne tried pushing to her feet.

"Stay there," the man in black shouted. "We'll call it even."

"What?"

As soon as she asked the question, a thunderous explosion ripped through the arena, followed by a thick, muted crack. Green light whizzed across the room, heading down from a launch point on the second-story balcony. It wobbled a little, then straightened with a trail of green-gray smoke before it hit its target in the space where the ogre's head connected with his shoulder. The floor beneath them shook, a blinding green light encompassed everything, and the screams and raging bellows and gunfire picked up again.

Cheyenne blinked against the glare of that green burst, the

ringing in her ears drowning out all sound. She let off another burst of crackling black energy at the goblin scrambling toward her, and it swept the magical's feet out from under him as someone else's automatic fire peppered the creature from chest to head.

The operative who'd told her to stay down stepped in front of her and bent toward her to say something she couldn't catch. His voice was a muffled garble within all the chaos, impossible to make out.

She tried to shake her head, and the room spun.

Her hip screamed in agony.

Bright white flashes of light sprayed across the arena and grew until she made out figures moving in front of her.

The next thing she knew, her cheek became acquainted with the linoleum floor and the plaster fragments scattered all around her. The pulsing green lights and ringing in her ears were the only things in the entire world…

Before there was nothing at all.

CHAPTER THIRTY-FOUR

The torment of her body returned before she knew anything else. With far too much effort, Cheyenne opened her eyes.

The bright white lights were still there, but the glare was coming from two blinding orbs. Voices floated down a long tunnel, but they weren't as loud as the harsh, grating breath she drew into her lungs. Her hearing returned.

"...have to run it again."

"I can't run her through anything until she stops that reactionary shifting. It's the shock to her system, most likely. She won't pick one and stick with it long enough to run any more diagnostics than that."

"Then wait until she picks one. Anyone know where this changeling came from?"

"Sir, I wouldn't call that an accurate assessment of what she is."

"Oh, yeah? Fine. Halfling. Whatever. Any ideas?"

"Never seen her before, sir. We didn't have any intel on a drow halfling. She came out of nowhere."

"She's obstructing FRoE operations and needs to be taken care of. Get her out of the way."

"Sir? If I may?"

"What is it, Rhynehart?"

"I was next to her for half the raid, sir. I can't say why or what she was trying to get out of it, but she fought *with* us, not against us. Kept two of my men from hitting the deck, and she kept the ogre occupied long enough for O'Malley to grow a pair with the fell launcher."

"Huh. Didn't go after a single one of our guys?"

"No, sir. If we can figure out what she wants and how we can give it to her, we might have a drow ally. If she can pull herself together enough to understand what's on the table."

"That's a big 'if.' And it'd make asses of all of us if she turns out to be anything other than what you're saying, Rhynehart."

"Yes, sir. Templeton and Payone are writing up their reports now."

Cheyenne blinked. It was as if a bolt of lightning had struck her right between the eyes. A groan escaped her lips.

"Somebody please tell me what's going on?"

Those were the words she formed in her brain. The sound that came out of her mouth was best compared to a braying donkey.

"Well, shit. Sounds like someone's awake."

Footsteps resounded across the floor toward her. The first face she saw was a woman's blonde hair tied back in a severe bun and delicate silver-framed glasses placed down a little on the bridge of her nose. The woman gave the drow a perfunctory glance over the top of her glasses and a flicker of acknowledgment, then reached past Cheyenne's head to grab something.

"Just kill it halfway, Doc." A man in military fatigues loomed in the halfling's vision. Graying hair at the temples. A mustache that couldn't decide if it was light or dark brown. Dark, squinty eyes.

Cheyenne tried to sit up. She moved an inch and dropped her head back onto the pillow. She was about to hurl.

Military Mustache gave her a strained, almost mocking smile. "Hurts, doesn't it?"

"Who are you?" This time, her mouth produced actual words.

"I'll ask you the same question. Wanna go first?"

Cheyenne closed her eyes and swallowed, her throat dry.

Not giving my name today. Not here.

"Yeah, I thought so. For now, you can call me 'Sir.'"

The halfling tried to snort, but it backed up in her throat and made her choke before she coughed enough to bring another round of blind agony stabbing through her head.

"What you're experiencing right now is your body's innate ability to heal itself, aided by our magical-healing formula." Mustache looked her over, his mustache twitching as his lips twisted sideways. "But you don't get the full dose yet. Consider this your first lesson. No pain, no gain. I'm sure you get the point."

"I didn't sign up for lessons or any of your other bullsh—" Cheyenne's sentence morphed into a groan. All she wanted to do was curl up on her side and vomit all over the guy's shoes, but she couldn't move.

"Well, you gave up that choice when you crashed my guys' sting operation. We don't know if that was your intention or if my team of top guys are just lucky bastards, but you need us. We're still figuring out whether we need you."

Cheyenne swallowed her nausea, which made her throat rawer. "I don't know what you—"

"Save it for when you have your head screwed on straight, halfling." Mustache sniffed and nodded at the doctor, who was still checking the monitors and fiddling with IV fluid bags. "We can use skills like yours, however crude they are. We'll talk more when you don't look like a chameleon with a bad case of chronic indecision. When you can conceive what the right answers are, you'll give us those answers."

"This should stabilize her for the next twenty-four hours," the blonde woman said with a curt nod.

"Good."

Cheyenne groaned, tried not to heave. She gagged instead.

"All right, Doc. Better make sure that puke pan's close by."

"Sir."

Without another word, Mustache turned on his heel and disappeared from Cheyenne's view. She blinked against the floodlights in the ceiling that seemed like they were shining inches from her face. "Can you turn off those lights?" she croaked.

"You'll get used to it," said a male voice.

The doctor looked up at the new arrival, nodded, and left Cheyenne alone with another stranger. This guy wore black combat pants and a black undershirt, and his hands were clasped behind his back. Something about his eyes seemed familiar, but Cheyenne didn't trust anything her body or mind was telling her right now.

"You have a real chance here," the man said. "Whoever you are." He was much younger than Mustache, his biceps dancing under the sleeves of his shirt.

Great. Now I'm hallucinating. Cheyenne blinked at him. "Chance at what?"

The man bowed his head. He leaned over her until he was a few inches away from her face. "You better accept I'm gonna be watching you from here on out. You know, just to make sure you don't screw up."

Cheyenne took a deep breath. She couldn't come up with anything that felt worth the effort.

Her last visitor straightened, nodded, and turned away from the bed. "Get some sleep."

Like that's possible. Cheyenne wanted to laugh, but doing

even that made her dizzy and nauseated all over again. As if the guy's final command were a tranquilizer injected into the IV, all-consuming exhaustion overwhelmed her. She slipped away again, the heavy warmth of sleep punctured by wave after receding wave.

This is how Ember slept through the last three days. I get it.

The drow halfling's eyes closed against her will, but when the brightness of the overhead lights faded, she welcomed it.

What have I gotten into?

Inside Cheyenne Summerlin's apartment, the grad student's open backpack sat propped up against the half wall of the kitchen counter. Inside, nestled between her laptop and the uneaten half of a lamb gyro, the copper puzzle box covered in hair-thin etchings of drow runes gave off a soft silver glow. A series of clicks rose from the mechanism at its heart, and two segments of the box detached from the latches holding the thing together and spun in opposite directions to form a new message for its intended witness. A new cycle had begun.

Get sneak peeks, exclusive giveaways, behind the scenes content, and more.
PLUS you'll be notified of special **one day only fan pricing** on new releases.

Sign up today to get free stories.

CLICK HERE

or visit: https://marthacarr.com/read-free-stories/

AUTHOR NOTES - MARTHA CARR

This is the year of the hobbies. First, let me define what makes a hobby. It's anything that doesn't earn money, or is of service, or is necessary – like exercise. A hobby's only purpose is fun. I have mentored a lot of young women over the years and this is one of the first things we tackle. To a person, everyone has been bright, ambitious, talented, caring, and didn't have a single hobby. I fall in and out of that category myself. Life gets busy, work takes off, children or friends need help and boom – no hobbies.

It's tough to even get the brain to think of one. Mostly because we're trying to figure out what we'd like ahead of even trying. That's called contempt ahead of information. Ultimately, what's worked best for me is to ask for a list of five ideas numbered according to willingness to try. That's it. And I set a deadline for when it has to be turned in. Then we chat about each one.

Next step – go gather information on each idea. Where can a person learn more about it? How much will it cost to do it? Do I need any special skills or equipment? Do we know anyone who's already into this? The more information the better. It solves two things. It usually helps decide which one to start first, if at all, and it lowers resistance because now, it's not so foreign. We know a lot more about it. The enthusiasm can build.

Then, you go sign up. The action part that takes a little bit of courage. I set a deadline for this one too. You can hate it and you can quit, but you have to at least try. Willingness will get you really, really far in this life and lack of it can shut a life down.

What has been road tested over and over again is that once a person starts trying different fun stuff, they get hooked. Stress levels drop, obsessing over a job or a relationship drops, loneliness drops. There's something about fun for fun's sake that soothes the soul.

Last year, I noticed I had fallen off the hobby bandwagon. I had been dabbling in some glass work and drawing cartoons and running but it all stopped somewhere along the way. My stress level was high, my work hours were high. Not good. This year, work is more in alignment and I've taken up embroidery so far and I'm back into painting and looking at doing a mural down the lower part of my hallway. I'm also dabbling in baking. Thank goodness there's that amenity center near me where I can drop off leftovers so I don't eat them. Running 5ks is another one because of the way I see them. More socializing than exercise. You run for about a half hour with friends and then you go to brunch. Perfect. The other one I want to do is start a neighborhood D&D game. Next on the list.

Making time for something that only benefits me is a great way to teach myself that I matter and that everything holds together even if I'm not there, but that I'm still welcomed back when I show up again. All necessary reminders. It's like we reclaim that kid part of ourselves every time we do it. What's your latest hobbies? More adventures to follow.

AUTHOR NOTES - MICHAEL ANDERLE

THANK YOU for reading our story! We have a few of these planned, but we don't know if we should continue writing and publishing without your input. Options include leaving a review, reaching out on Facebook to let us know, and smoke signals.

Frankly, smoke signals might get misconstrued as low hanging clouds, so you might want to nix that idea.

If this is the first book by me you have read, know that there are dozens of rabbit holes (series) you can go down after you finish this series!

Goth Drow the character was an effort to merge a slightly darker protagonist (well, as dark as we can get) while making her something we don't see too often in a story.

Who would think to create a Goth-looking human as a way to hide a Drow lineage?

(If you know of some stories which have already done this, please don't tell me. Allow me to enjoy my blissful state of ignorance.)

Inside the team working on this series we named the

project "the Goth Draw" story. Which, of course, got shortened to Goth Drow.

By the time we needed to come up with a series name, we were all so accustomed to that name we (and by "we," I mean I) couldn't think of anything I liked more than Goth Drow Unleashed. The rest of the team agreed, and there you go.

The story of how Goth Drow became the series name is revealed.

The title naming credit goes to Jake Caleb, the artist for the cover. He will often put in placeholder titles to see how book covers will look with the typography. Then, he gives the cover preview to Martha, who (almost every time) loves his title and runs with it.

I think she is getting a little too happy with just getting Jake to come up with titles, but let's not mention that to her. The fact they ARE good has nothing to do with anything. At least, not with me giving Martha grief about title laziness. I feel certain she will explain how it is an efficient use of resource talent.

That's how I would argue the case, anyway. Since I don't think she will read these *Author Notes,* (please see comment above about not telling her) I should be good.

Ad Aeternitatem,

Michael

CONNECT WITH THE AUTHORS

Martha Carr Social

Website: http://www.marthacarr.com

Facebook: https://www.facebook.com/groups/MarthaCarrFans/

Michael Anderle Social

Website: http://lmbpn.com

Email List: http://lmbpn.com/email/

Social Media:

https://www.facebook.com/LMBPNPublishing

https://twitter.com/MichaelAnderle

https://www.instagram.com/lmbpn_publishing/

https://www.bookbub.com/authors/michael-anderle

OTHER BOOKS BY MARTHA CARR

JOIN THE ORICERAN UNIVERSE FAN GROUP ON FACEBOOK!

BOOKS BY MICHAEL ANDERLE

Sign up for the LMBPN email list to be notified of new releases and special deals!

https://lmbpn.com/email/

For a complete list of books by Michael Anderle, please visit:

www.lmbpn.com/ma-books/

Made in the USA
Middletown, DE
02 November 2023

41822076R00156